Bother at the Barbican

Bother at the Barbican

Guy Cullingford

PIATKUS

Copyright © 1991 by Guy Cullingford

First published in Great Britain in 1991 by
Judy Piatkus (Publishers) Ltd of
5 Windmill Street, London W1

*The author asserts his moral rights to be
identified as author of this work*

British Library Cataloguing in Publication Data
Cullingford, Guy
  Bother at the Barbican.
  I. Title
  823[F]

ISBN 0-7499-0089-X

Phototype in 11/12pt Times by
Phoenix Photosetting, Chatham
Printed and bound in Great Britain by
Billing & Sons Ltd, Worcester

Chapter 1

"Do you know . . ." began Mrs Harris and stopped aghast, her hand over her mouth. She had been going to say, "Do you know that this is the first funeral I've seen leaving here since we came."

It was the sort of remark, light-hearted intimate comment, that had often passed between herself and her husband. It was his funeral.

It was true that the Barbican was at its most discreet in the disposal of bodies. A fall from a tower block, a collapse at a concert, a mummified corpse in a luggage locker; any such minor irregularities were tidied away promptly; the sole obsequies being, as far as one knew, only the muted whispers of porters.

And, indeed, why should the well-heeled residents be constantly reminded by a benign management that life was fleeting? They had enough of that in the newspapers and on their television screens.

Mr Harris was different. He had been a tenant of long standing. He had lived here, paying his rent and rates on the day they came when the theatre was still a hole in the ground. Though he had been a person of repute in his day, since his retirement he had felt no further desire to shine in public. He cheerfully paid subscriptions to societies with good motives, but accepted no duties. He bought tickets for functions he had no intention of attending. He gave no offence to his neighbours and never complained of their little idiosyncrasies. He might not be known by name to most of them but he was recognised as a pleasant and unassuming man. When he died,

1

with the valid excuse of old age, the Barbican was ready to do him justice.

The funeral cortège gathered and left from the forecourt. At first his widow, reading from the undertaker's brochure that all coffins would be collected from the deceased's place of residence, had a moment's fanciful vision of a hearse rising to the fourth floor. A wild notion. The funeral party went down in the lift, along the podium and descended the steps where the coffin, bedecked and in position, awaited them. It was a dull and draughty day at eleven o'clock in the morning. The funnelled wind blew its customers into Crispin's and there were few onlookers. The Director – and surely this was too important a description of one looking so shabby? – shepherded the company into the rather antique limousines and off they went, through the mouth of the tunnel and into Aldersgate.

In the first of the cars rode Mrs Harris as chief mourner accompanied by her two brothers and only sister. Mrs Harris had made up her mind not to weep if she could help it, so she concentrated her attention on the route to the crematorium. As a drive it was dismal. They wound their way through the back streets, passing terrace after terrace of hard-wearing but hideous houses, whose ground floor view of their neighbours' look-alikes across the road was blocked by the coloured lozenges of parked cars.

"Exorbitant," muttered Rupert to his brother Fred, after a hasty glance to see how thick was the glass separating him from the driver. He had arranged the funeral himself and he knew that the cost would come out of Hugh's estate. All the same the amount, London-weighted, nagged at him. Fred nodded but hoped that his widowed sister had not heard the grumble. His other sister made a warning face at him. But Mrs Harris continued to gaze steadfastly through the side window. She would rather listen to the racket of concrete mixers and power drills than anything that any of her relations might say. She would rather see hoardings and scaffoldings; obsolete monstrosities being torn down, office buildings, equally monstrous, being built up. She would rather see diggers with ugly square mouths cramming rubble into their maws, giant cranes teetering crazily into the sky; anything,

anything, rather than see the back of what they were following.

Still the sad procession crawled on at its decorous pace, sometimes blocked by some cumbersome vehicle going even more slowly.

Out of the side of her eye, Mrs Harris caught Rupert consulting his watch.

Oh, dear, we shall be late, she thought. How vexed Hugh would be! It was a phobia of his which had often brought them to the railway station in time to catch the train before the one on which they intended to travel.

At last they arrived. They went through the iron gates and between clusters of small, dirty crosses, relics of the old cemetery. They came to a halt by a low wall against which leant a dispirited group of plastic-shrouded flowers. And lo and behold, they were too early, not too late.

The Director eased open the door gingerly as though afraid that one of the occupants of the tip-up seats might fall out, and remarked, sotto voce, to the Chief Mourner: "I'm sorry, Madam. We shall have to wait a few minutes. The chapel has not yet been vacated."

At these words a heavy load slipped from the heart of Mrs Harris.

This was simply business, a recognised ritual in the interest of hygiene; no more than Corporation dust carts queueing up at the rubbish disposal tip. What did it matter now? What was the significance of the undertaker's delicate probing? Would she like the curtain drawn at the finale? Would she like the ashes scattered in the Garden of Remembrance or would she prefer them in a neat little urn, carefully numbered and stored? Which did she favour, piped music or the harmonium?

This was absurd and nothing to do with her long marriage to Hugh. The sweet and the sour of it, the hopes and the fears. The gradual acceptance of each other's faults and virtues, the welding together of two individuals into something stronger than either, and so subtly that an outsider could not even detect the join.

She watched with sublime indifference through the open chapel door as the outgoing party made its exit from the other

3

side of the building. She was prepared to do whatever was expected of her.

In due course, perhaps sooner than was generally supposed, the same charade would be enacted over her own discarded flesh and bones. She was content.

But she did hope that when it was all over, one of the family would give the representatives of the undertakers a good tip. They looked as if they could do with it. Whoever it was, it wouldn't be Rupert.

"It's just like the inside of an American prison as seen on TV," said Malcolm, standing a little aloof and staring out from his aunt's plate-glass window at the flats opposite. It was in reality two windows, one fixed and one sliding, which ran the whole breadth of the room.

"No. It reminds me much more of a building set I had as a child. Wooden, of course. Miniature planks of all sizes, including some stubby ones to be used as uprights and on which one balanced dear little half moon arches to give the effect you observe over there."

"I like my idea best," insisted Malcolm. Indeed he did, always. That was his misfortune. And perhaps in this instance "best" was the proper word and not "better".

"Look, you must admit," he continued indulging in a new flight of fancy, "neat, identical cells, row upon row. Just to prove my point, here come two warders to take a snoop over the rails."

"Silly boy," said his aunt, moving up to him, "they are staff from the penthouses, watering the window boxes."

"Who lives there?" asked Malcolm idly.

"How should I know? Someone once told me that they belong to the architects who designed the whole place."

"I shouldn't think that they would want to dwell on their misdeeds."

He turned sideways so that he could better examine the residents' garden far below, with its very green grass and the horse-chestnut trees still a long way off from producing their candles. Meanwhile his aunt examined him. Though he was Rupert's son he was nothing like Rupert. There's nothing really wrong with his profile, she admitted to herself. He might be quite passable if he would get his hair cut and shampooed.

He was ill-groomed and slovenly clad, looking like an immature, grant-aided art student which was just what he claimed to be, as it happened.

"What is that ominous building which rears up behind, Aunt Bert?"

She was disconcerted for a moment. "Bert" was her name, short for Bertha, an abbreviation used by her brothers and sister for as long as she could remember. His aunt she certainly was too. It was the combination that she had never before encountered.

"They call it 'The Bastion', I believe."

"Good for them. Who guards it?"

"Some say that it belongs to Japanese bankers. It's very mysterious. Often the lights are left on all night."

"A common practice in offices. It's as cheap as turning them on and off. Safer too."

"Yes, but now and again they *are* turned off. All but one window."

"Curious race, the Japanese. No accounting for them."

"Sometimes two men stand right on top of the building. Those can't be Japanese. They're giants."

"It's only perspective."

"Yes, but I don't honestly think . . . your uncle and I thought that more likely it was a plant generating electricity for the whole complex. Occasionally it belches forth thick black smoke."

"Like *Under the Volcano*, eh?"

"I didn't know you read Lowry."

"Oh, I see films. And we share the first name."

He swivelled to look in the other direction, remarking: "And then there's the church."

"St Giles, yes."

He locked his fingers together in nursery fashion and then turned his wrist, showing the fingers criss-crossed.

"And there are the people."

She laughed. "One man and a dog."

"Aunt Bert, you are a funny one. You haven't the slightest urge to find out what actually goes on behind those façades. A neighbour spins you a yarn. You half-believe, half-reject."

"It doesn't worry me. I suppose I'm not inquisitive."

"What did I say! Now, if I were in your shoes, I should be out and about all over the place, spying out the land."

"You wouldn't be exactly popular," she remarked dryly. "Most people in the Barbican like to keep their affairs private."

"Ah, but what power I should have! It would be far more exciting than life classes at Chelsea."

He paused, then posed the question.

"Are you going to stay on here?"

"I don't see why not."

"Well, the rents . . ."

"Hugh didn't take his money with him."

Or leave any legacies, the meany, thought Malcolm.

But he said, biting back any criticism of his uncle which he guessed would not be welcomed: "Won't you be lonely?"

"People are so kind. You'd be astonished how sympathetic they are. Even the porters."

"Yes, – now. It may wear off. Never mind, I shall keep you cheered up."

She wasn't sure that she felt properly grateful for this reassurance. His visit had come as a complete surprise.

Her legs began to ache as they did nowadays after standing.

"Let's sit down, shall we?"

They sat down side by side on the sofa, still looking out upon the apparently deserted rows of flats which Malcolm evidently believed held many delirious secrets.

Mrs Harris might not be inquisitive but she was perceptive. And sitting there in a blessed hiatus of silence she decided that it would not be wise to let Malcolm come to the conclusion that she was rolling in money and all alone in the world.

To this effect, she began to speak in a quiet, meditative voice, rather different from their previously animated bantering.

"There are those who are convinced that the Barbican is inhabited only by the wealthy. Once I heard one of the guides with a tour proclaiming to his group that 'this is where the rich live'."

As Malcolm declined to comment, she continued: "It may

6

be so in the tower blocks. I don't know about them, but these are only the old council flats."

Malcolm came to life suddenly.

"If all council flats were like these, there'd be no riots."

He surprised her. She would not have thought that moral indignation was his forte.

"Cement is a ghastly material," he went on. "Fit for nothing but sticking bricks together. From outside these flats are an abomination. Inside they are ideal."

"You're not serious?"

"Oh yes, I am. This room, for instance. Just the right size."

"The right size for what?"

"For a party, of course. You'd need to move some of the furniture into the corridor. You could serve drinks from the kitchen counter. It would make a splendid small bar."

By "you" did he mean her or "one"? she wondered.

"Then there's the separate loo and the bathroom. So convenient if you have to throw up."

"Malcolm!" she protested.

"And that super bedroom. Naturally you and Uncle Hugh had twin beds but I'd go for a big double, exotic and fabulous, straight out of Harrods."

He had gone too far. His prattle ceased to amuse her.

She said slowly, as if seeking the right words, "Some things are better not mocked. Hugh and I loved living here. It was just the place for us. We could be absolutely private yet we never felt shut off from the world."

She turned away from him and, using the arm of the sofa to help herself up, stumbled off in the direction of the fitted kitchen which adjoined the living room. Immediately he was on his feet, all concern.

"Is there anything I can do, Aunt Bert? What do you want?"

She stood quite still.

"I want Hugh back," she said.

The compression of great grief into a single sentence unnerved him as nothing else would have done. He was prepared for a few facile tears. It was an acknowledged fact that the old have parted with their deeper emotions. He was shocked into stuttering, "I'm sorry . . . really, I n-never

7

meant. . . . Look here, what about a nice cup of t-tea?"

It was all he could think of at the moment. Women had hot cups of tea in times of stress and then they felt better.

There was a pause while she struggled to regain her composure. After which she remarked in a steady voice: "Do you know, I'd much prefer a glass of red wine."

"Well, that's easy. There must have been plenty left over after the fu—" Here he came to a halt.

"It was all done by caterers. When they cleared up they took away what was left over."

She went on into the kitchen and gazed up vaguely at the glass-fronted cupboard. Truly, all that it now contained was a bottle of dry sherry and another of soda water.

He came round and joined her, slipping a scarecrow arm about her shoulders. She could feel the boniness of it through her cardigan and strangely enough it was comforting.

"I've an idea," he said. "The wine bar is just about opening. Let's trot across there and have a snack and a glass of their plonk. Do us both good." He gave her a quizzing glance. "That's unless you're too proud?"

"Oh, no. Hugh and I often went there before he became too ill."

"Right. You go and make ready and I'll pull the curtains. Make it more cosy for when you come back."

But when she disappeared in the direction of the bedroom, and he had done what he had himself suggested, he made a swift return to the kitchen for a quick, silent scrutiny. He opened drawers, looked in cupboards and even managed a peep into the fridge. There was very little food besides nothing to drink. All it felt safe to acquire were two silver teaspoons which he slipped into the pocket of his lamentable jeans. Not till he heard the flush of the loo did he drag on his own outer raiment which had come to him from Lillywhite's, via Oxfam.

His aunt was wearing an expensive tweed coat and carried her handbag. He held the door open for her and remarked: "Shall I leave on the light? It scares away burglars."

When they emerged from the lift on to the podium, it was already dusk and the lights were on in the Barbican Centre as they would be all night. But the steps down to it as yet carried

8

no pedestrian traffic. It was too early for theatre and concert-goers. They were the first in at the wine bar moreover, though later on some nights it would be packed. He had his hand lightly under her elbow as they crossed the slippery tiles and then settled her at a table for two at the end furthest away from the bar. As he started off to go to it, she slipped into his hand a ten pound note which she had tucked up her sleeve.

He gave her a grateful look but a few steps away he returned to whisper that wine was cheaper by the bottle than by the glass. At any other time she might have questioned this logic. Now she simply opened her purse and added another ten to the first. Off he went.

Although the curtains were drawn, the place was still chilly, lacking the warmth contributed by a crowd. She shivered a little and it seemed an age before he returned with a bottle and two glasses. He poured for them both and touched her glass with his before drinking thirstily.

"Ah, that's better," he said. "I ordered quiche for us both, hot. It looked the best bet. The girl will bring it."

"I don't feel hungry."

"Never mind, you can toy with it. Drink up, you look as if you need it."

Meekly she obeyed.

"I thought we might run into Jilly. But Rosie says she won't be in tonight."

Jilly was the daughter of Bertha's sister Alice, and her niece. Mrs Harris had a misty recollection of being told that Jilly was attending the Guildhall School of Music and Drama and of meeting her at the funeral party. But somehow, after returning to the flat on that day, events had ceased to register. She knew that someone had relieved her of her wrappings and put her into a chair. She supposed that she had replied automatically to whatever was said to her. She knew that her relations were being catered for by previous arrangement. The bill had been paid. It was purely a family gathering – *her* family for Hugh had none living. She had been conscious of one thought only that was perfectly clear; the burning wish to see them all depart, and as quickly as possible.

"Is this a haunt of Jilly's?" she asked, the wine reviving her. "If so Hugh and I never saw her."

9

"But you would have come at lunch time, I expect, along with the Yuppies and their PAs. Jilly doesn't show up until evening. She only comes here for the bread."

"Really? Is there something special about it?"

"You are an old duck," he said, giving her a grin usually associated with gargoyles. "Bread stands for money. In your day it was dough. Tomorrow they may be calling it pasta. It's all the same thing. The stuff you need to sustain life."

"Is Jilly hard-up, then?" she asked. "I should have thought . . ." But she didn't say what she thought which was that Jilly's parents were prosperous enough to give their daughter a decent allowance.

"All the young are hard-up. Didn't you know that, Aunt Bert?"

At this moment Rosie arrived with their portions; two large slices for Malcolm and one small slice for his aunt. This did not trouble Bertha who had little regard for the English version of the quiche. To accompany this was a good slice from a French loaf – real bread, not silly slang – with a metal knife and fork done up in a serviette, a nasty word for a nasty object.

Malcolm began to devour his snack with great gusto but Bertha crumbled her bread and mediated upon Jilly. After which she took a swig of her red wine, which mysteriously never grew less, and demanded: "What does Jilly do here?"

Little maggots of worry crawled in her brain for what did young girls do in wine bars?

"She waits at table."

"Oh!"

Mrs Harris, democrat though she was, blenched at this occupation. Malcolm, glancing up with a piece of mushroom speared on his fork, observed, "We all of us wait . . . for Godot . . . or the big bomb. Besides, she likes to escape from her pad – her digs, I mean. She shares with two other females, both dreadful bores."

Actually, they were Lesbians which was not Jilly's style.

"Well, it's nothing to do with me, of course. I don't suppose I shall ever see her again."

"Oh, but you will. Both she and Donald have made up their minds."

10

"Was Donald the other boy at the funeral?"

"No, that was Gus in his civvies. He's a novice at a place called St Joe's not more than two stations away from you. Donald said he couldn't get the time off. He works at a bank and is a great one for duty. My belief is that he wanted to dodge his old man. They are too much alike and quarrel like cats."

"And you and your father?"

"We're so different that already I can feel your heart warming towards me."

At this they looked each other full in the face, his eyes stony and impenetrable, hers blurred and bewildered.

"I don't understand this sudden interest in me," she said. "You none of you came to call when Hugh was alive."

"He wouldn't have stood for it."

That was true enough. Hugh would have been perfectly polite but he would soon have shown them the door. She supposed she could do the same even if at the moment she felt like a hermit crab without its shell.

He put the last morsel of quiche into his mouth and straightened his knife and fork.

"Don't fret about it, Aunt Bert. You haven't even taken a bite out of yours. Let me take it away and bring you a slice of gooey chocolate cake with a dollop of cream on the top."

A prolonged shudder was sufficient answer.

"Well, I'll fetch one for me and a cup of coffee for you to put steel in your legs."

With this delicacy consumed, the wine bottle emptied and her coffee drunk, he rose suddenly from his chair and came over to hers, ready to pull it back for her as she followed his example.

"Time I got back to my cardboard box on the Embankment before some other feller takes a fancy to it."

"Oh, Malcolm, don't be so silly."

"Well, what I do have isn't much better, you can take my word for it. I'll see you back home."

This he proceeded to do, opening both doors for her, the one from the podium and the one giving entry to her own flat as the same key did for both. The only trouble was that she couldn't personally seem able to get it into the hole.

11

"See you soon," he promised, and stepped back into the lift which he had put on hold.

Unwashed, uncombed and without cleaning her teeth, she collapsed into bed in her petticoat and pulled up the duvet. But doped by alcohol and stimulated by caffeine, before she fell into the heavy, dreamless sleep of exhaustion, she thought to herself: Surely there should have been some change from twenty pounds?

The maimed person, whose state would have been described by a hospital as "critical", had turned the corner and was now on the perilous road to stability.

Chapter 2

Bertha's siblings were all living at a safe distance from London, for which she was thankful. Nothing less than a funeral would have induced them to come there. On the other hand their offspring were drawn to the great city as if by a magnet.

Bertha was the eldest. Her mother had died when she was eighteen, leaving an eight-year gap between her and Rupert. Her father could never understand how his wife had become fertile again after so long a lapse and pretended that she had a lover. A cruel joke this, as each unwanted pregnancy left the poor woman frailer and frailer and unlikely to attract anyone but himself. In the end Alice killed her; such a beautiful blue-eyed baby to be an innocent murderer.

Who was to care for this orphaned trio? Bertha, of course, ready but far from willing. Her father, though prepared to provide for his family, declined further responsibilities, particularly those of a domestic nature. At that time, like everyone middle-class, they had a servant who was called a cook general. She cooked and she cleaned from morning to night whilst Bertha, relieved only by the boys' attendance at day school, was in constant conflict with her brothers and sister.

Eighteen was just the age for hungering after romance. There she was, superintending Rupert's homework, patching Fred's trousers and helping Alice perform functions too indelicate to mention, when she should have been out dancing with some gorgeous boy. Actually, any boy would have done provided that he didn't have acne.

She knew them, oh, she knew them too well.

If Wordsworth was the one who said "The child is father to

13

the man" he would have had her complete agreement.

Pity the person who had to prise a penny out of Rupert's pocket money for somebody's birthday!

Fred had turned into the farmer he was destined to be, even if it was only sheep on a hill farm instead of the rich arable acres he had dreamed of possessing. Probably his pants were still patched, they were a part of his nature.

As for Alice, she had used her blue eyes to obtain what she wanted, a husband to keep her and a pigeon pair to do her credit. And no doubt she kept them all waiting on her hand and foot if not for the same purpose. From past experience, Bertha recognised that, with her winning ways and her good looks, Alice could also be pretty demanding.

"Don't you fret, Miss Bertha," the cook general had said. "Some fine day Mr Right will come riding along."

She was a good prophet for finally he did, in a secondhand AC, very sporty, which hurtled him over a hedge and into a meadow from which he was rescued little the worse by Bertha out walking the dog. In return he rescued her from her kith and kin, bearing her off to London after a whirlwind courtship, without parental consent, where he made an honest woman of her.

Her father, though dismayed, did not bother to pursue her. He prudently married the cook general, thus saving her wages and avoiding any great change in his household arrangements.

When the first rhapsodies of their union had subsided without the result which might have been expected, Hugh had asked Bertha, "Do you want children?" to which she had replied emphatically, "No."

"Neither do I," he said, "so that's settled."

Whether this was from an aversion to infants, or anticipated jealousy of a son, or a fear that she might go the way of her mother, Bertha never knew. Or cared. They were complete as they were.

She had no wish to become ugly and cumbersome as she remembered poor Mama. Or to start by heaving over a basin with morning sickness only to end with misgivings about getting to the hospital in time. Would there be complications? Would the child be born perfect in brain, heart and limb?

14

She would never again submit herself to the inescapable routine of a baby or its demands as it grew.

All the same she had to be fair in this instance. She might claim to understand and dislike Rupert, Tom and Alice, but as there had been no inter-visiting while they were young, she knew nothing about their children or how they were likely to develop when grown. Malcolm was not Rupert although he was his son. He had a sense of humour which Rupert never had. Did he resemble him in feature? A little perhaps. They were both abnormally skinny with the same healthy appetite. Did Malcolm's tendency to sponge in the wine bar show an inheritance of Rupert's parsimony, or was it simply real need? She had once heard that the genes of aunt and niece were closer than those of mother and daughter. Presumably that also applied to aunt and nephew. Malcolm should be given his chance.

And if the others came along too, as he predicted, weren't they also entitled to be considered as individuals rather than replicas of their parents? There was always the possibility that this sudden enthusiasm for her company was a wily dodge of their seniors to keep an eye on a cranky old lady. There is always hanky-panky where there is money about. Did they think that, freed from Hugh's restraint, she would go crazy with credit cards, sell off the furniture or even take a cruise with the over-sixties with the idea of finding a new mate? Or were they after a peek at her will? If so, they would be surprised to discover that whatever she left was to be divided between Rupert, Fred and Alice. For that they could thank Hugh. He had the old-fashioned belief that money should remain in the family.

But Hugh had gone and he had left her a problem along with big money. What was she to do with herself in the few years remaining? She was a different person. She was Mrs B. Harris, not Mrs H. Harris, as every envelope reminded her. She was a widow. Since her bereavement she had read much about the plight of widows. The attraction of like to like, she supposed. If one has a stye in the eye, one reads about nothing but styes. Widows were second-class citizens, never asked to a party, avoided by men.

The odd thing was that the porters, the barometers of the

15

Barbican, had never been more considerate. But, of course, she had never been asked to a porters' party, not even when Hugh was alive. To be truthful she could not remember the last time that she and Hugh had gone to a party. Had they become recluses then? No, they had simply grown older and preferred to be by themselves.

Earlier on, they had often visited the theatre and the concert hall but latterly Hugh was reluctant to tempt fate. She supposed that even a widow might attend a matinee unaccompanied – or a lunch-time concert. But no one could call that a solution; it was only a reassurance that her new status need not cut her off completely from the rest of humanity.

At first, soon after Hugh's death, she thought that the problem had solved itself neatly. She found herself fully occupied with answering letters of condolence and informing those others who obviously never read obituary columns. She had sessions with her solicitor, her accountant. At least she concluded that they were hers as they could no longer be said to be Hugh's. She had to contact the Estate Office about retaining her flat. That was all right as Hugh had made them joint tenants. She had to go through his files, most meticulously kept, to see what they contained. She had to pay off a few outstanding accounts, resign on his behalf from a number of societies. She was always busy. Yes, busy was the word for it, like a tiny insect scurrying about in a small radius. She was tidying up the remnants of Hugh's life, she wasn't striking out on her own.

Gradually all this activity dwindled away. Apart from an occasional letter from her solicitor asking for some scrap of information or describing how he was dealing with probate, her mail-box now proferred little more than high class begging letters, there were plenty of those, also proposals on how she might best invest or re-invest her money. Occasionally there was also a terse note from the management asking her if she was pleased with the way her windows were cleaned or telling her when the lift or anything else pertaining to the establishment would be off.

Well, what to do now? Because of her age she rejected any idea of devoting herself to good works. She hadn't the stamina. In fact, she *was* a good work. Already many kind

16

folk were offering to do her shopping and, as she felt that it would be ungracious to refuse, her cupboards were packed tight with assorted soups, the only thing she could think of on the spur of the moment. Fruit was what she wished to eat, nothing else, especially oranges; their sharp, tangy juice seemed to slake her thirsty sorrow. But this general concern over her fate astonished her. The Barbican, en masse, was behaving like a village; perhaps that was what it was, a London village. Bertha had not mentioned her immediate neighbours to Malcolm, one of whom she knew well. But Malcolm had admitted himself that he was nosey; it wouldn't do to encourage him. He amused her, though, and was something entirely new to her.

There was a rich assortment of youth to be seen in the Barbican; mostly visiting rather than inhabiting it. There were the silent and absorbed following their miniature scores in the Concert Hall; those who listened to Shakespeare in the theatre as if every word was as fresh as the day it was minted and the play itself dramatic reality, as against her own acceptance of it as a stringing together of admired quotations.

There were those who streamed past their bedroom window late at night, let out from the cinema and making a horrible racket much to Hugh's vexation. There were those young hooligans who kicked in windows, rolled flower tubs into the basements and in many another unpleasant way asserted their personalities. None of these had she ever spoken to, certainly never for a moment imagined entertaining in her home.

But suppose. . . .

Would it do? she wondered. Since these four youngsters were apparently determined on visiting their ageing relative as Malcolm affirmed, why should she seek to prevent them? Whatever their motives, and these would probably reveal themselves in due course, they were of the same blood. Commonsense nudged her – so were Rupert, Tom and Alice. But now enthusiasm was overcoming discretion, heart was gaining the lead over head.

If she could like them and take an interest in their aims and ambitions, perhaps give them a helping hand, wouldn't that make a purpose for her and fill in the gap between Hugh's death and her own? Their lives as a married couple had been sheltered and happy but had they discharged their debt to humanity? Hugh would have scoffed at this notion, but Hugh was no longer by her side.

The very few facts she knew about her nephews and niece were largely derived from Malcolm. Donald was a clerk in a City bank; he must have decided that he would sooner look into the mouth of a till than into that of a patient. Sensible fellow. Gus was a theological student. She didn't even know whether Roman or Anglican. He must have preferred parishoners to sheep, or did he sense some resemblance? She did have a vague impression of Jilly from the funeral party. A blonde girl dressed in actressy black contrasting strongly with the black worn by her mother. Alice was sure to be in black for a funeral. Yet she remembered an Alice in white at her marriage to the dentist, a most enchanting bride, and Jilly was like her in looks though it was to be hoped not in character.

Yes, she would let them come and make their impressions upon her. She would soon sort out the wheat from the chaff; and if it was all chaff she would know what to do. Yet she recognised that she hadn't Hugh's ability to deliver the coup de grâce. Once they had their feet over her threshold she would find it almost beyond her power to dislodge them. She was still wavering. At the very back of her mind was this preposterous notion that if, on further acquaintance, they proved worth it, she might change her will in their favour. Or even choose one of them as the sole beneficiary. How that would shock Hugh – or would have done, she reminded herself. But, after all, the money would still be left in the family, only skipping one generation.

No, on reflection this was all silly nonsense. Better write them all short notes saying that she wished to be left alone and enclosing a ten pound note in each to soften the decision. If only she knew where they lived!

Two nights after Malcolm's visit, she had her first attack of nerves.

"You must be terribly lonely," sympathised Mrs Sprite that same morning. Mrs Sprite was the neighbour whose flat adjoined hers and she came bringing an offering of spring water. She knew that Bertha would not drink anything that came out of the tap unless it was boiled and the bottles were heavy.

"No, I am not, truly," said Bertha, though she was sure that Mrs Sprite did not believe her.

"Well, knock on the wall any time," advised Mrs Sprite kindly as she went back through the window opening which took her back home via the balcony.

It was true, however. She and Hugh had lived in the flat for so long that his imprint was everywhere. He had sat in the chairs, eaten his meals at the table, even stood at the sink washing up. Sometimes, three weeks after his death, she still found his handwriting on the pad diary where he had entered appointments ahead. It was impossible to think that he had departed for ever; it was easier to believe that he had just slipped down to Crispin's for the paper, even when she realised that she now had to fetch it for herself. She didn't envisage him as anything as absurd as a ghost. He existed so vividly in her memory that he could not be gone.

Yet that night, after she had finished her meagre supper and done the chores that followed it, when she came to sit down on the sofa, it dawned on her suddenly that there was no one beside her.

She picked up the paper and folded it to display the crossword which they had always worked at together. She found her ballpoint and studied the clues. They made no sense at all. She had always been the one to start it off; Hugh's brain worked more slowly and he needed a letter or two to inspire him.

She took off her glasses and cleaned them and when she put them on again she found that her fingers were shaking. She lowered her hands to her sides to control them and the paper slipped off her lap and on to the carpet. She had drawn the curtains to make things, as Malcolm described it, "more cosy" and now it wasn't cosy at all. As she stared at them she imagined that they were moving, billowing out sneakily at the folds. Perhaps one of the communicating doors was open? The one between here and the corridor, letting in a whiff of east wind from the bedroom. She dared not look over her shoulder to see.

In the daytime the Barbican was full of noises; the cries of

19

children at break, the tools of workmen making repairs, the rushing of artificially controlled water. But at night those flats facing the inside were as quiet as the grave; it took a festival of fireworks to disturb their decorum. The high ceilings, the cement floors stuffed with electric wiring, the wall to wall carpet, kept them inviolate. In the winter and spring months often only the beat of pop music somewhere adjacent disturbed the silence.

But tonight the silence unshared seemed terrible and she listened in vain for a break in it. Any tiny reassuring murmur would have done; the drip of a tap, the hum of a convector, the rattle of the refrigerator starting up. If there were any such, her increasing fear paralysing the tiny blood vessels in her ears stopped her from hearing them.

The cage of her apartment which kept her as safe as any elderly woman could be began to feel like a cage must to a wild animal, straight from the jungle. The bars closed in on her – no, how silly, there were no bars – it must be the walls. Her throat seemed to close too; it was difficult to breathe. There was not enough air but if there was insufficient air why did the curtains continue to move? The room was too hot – no, it was too cold. She was chilled to the marrow – she was stifling with heat. She felt as if she was sweating from every pore, yet when she wiped her forehead with her handkerchief it remained as dry as a bone. Her hand was still shaking but now the palsy seemed to come from the wrist.

She moved her head a fraction, slowly, to see if she could. What a sad, dismal shade was avocado! How could she ever have thought that her furniture went well with it. Back again came the head on stiff neck muscles. Only her pride and the conviction that she couldn't get there, stopped her from thumping on the connecting wall as Mrs Sprite had advised.

But, after all, there in the corner was succour: the box. Prising herself up from where she sat, she half-walked, half-crawled towards the skirting and, fumbling, pushed down the switch on the plug. It must have been already tuned in because at once there sprang into colour and full cry the usual cops and robbers, of infinite variety but always the same. She didn't even tune it down but returning and flopping down on the sofa, stared at it with glued eyes as if she were watching the answer to the riddle of the universe. Thank heavens, there they were at the police station, everyone talking at once. There was the ubiquitous telephone on the desk and it began to ring in its imperious television way. "Brrr . . . brrr, brrr . . . brrr."

And suddenly she realised that her own telephone was accompanying it. Released, she struggled up to get to it before it stopped ringing.

"Yes, yes, who is it?" she demanded.

"Aunt, this is Donald."

Blessed sanity returned. This was Donald, male and matter-of-fact if sounding a trifle injured.

"Oh yes, how nice."

"Aunt, I came round to see you but your entryphone was out of order. There was a notice that advised callers to make a telephone call instead. They said the call would be free."

"I'm sorry, Donald. A free call, that's fine."

"But when I got there the telephone was out of order as well."

"Oh, but then where . . ."

"I'm back at the YMCA."

"Oh, but Donald, how exasperating for you. If you're not too exhausted come round again and I'll be at the podium to let you in."

She had often passed the YMCA on her way to the Aldersgate shops and she knew that it was no distance to walk up the ramp and across to her flat.

But his response was unenthusiastic.

"Really, I think it's too late. And there's a nature film I rather wanted to catch."

"I quite understand. But how disappointing for me."

"Look, aunt . . ."

Just like Thatcher who always said "look" when she meant "listen".

"How about tomorrow evening at seven-thirty?"

"That would be wonderful. Do you need to be fed?"

Perhaps that was too baldly put but she remembered Malcolm.

"No thanks, Aunt. I wouldn't dream of putting you to the trouble. We have a very good canteen here."

21

"Well, coffee or sherry, whichever suits you best."

"Sherry would be very acceptable."

Good. So he was human after all.

"Splendid, then I shall expect you at seven-thirty, I think you said."

"Yes. Make a note of it in your diary if you're likely to forget."

"Oh, I shan't forget. You need not ring. I'll be there at the door to greet you as it's too much to hope that the entryphone will be working by then. Oh, Donald, I'm so looking forward to seeing you."

It was the absolute literal truth.

Chapter 3

Instead of a cook general, Bertha had Concetta. Concetta was short and swart with strong features. Her skin was so sallow that sometimes she looked as if she could do with a wash. She had come from Northern Italy; not the roseate lakes but a region prone to earthquakes. Bertha had visited the great art centres with Hugh; Rome, Florence, Sienna and others. They had never been anywhere near the poverty-stricken village which had spawned Concetta. The land was rocky and the soil grudging. There were far too few natural resources to provide a living for its natives who, having little else to do, bred profusely. For this reason Concetta left it as soon as she could to go into service in London. She had learned the hard lesson that it is better to eat in another country than starve in one's own. She married an East Ender and with that forswore all things Italian except her religion and pasta. She spoke a kind of basic English, heavily accented, which never improved however much she listened to television. This she helped out with mime which, because of her nationality, came to her easily. Though once, when they were new to each other, when she tried to convince Bertha of their privations at home by the simulated eating of berries even to the spitting out the pips, Bertha misinterpreted, thought she wanted to be sick and sent her off promptly.

When their marriage became as rocky as Concetta's birthplace, she and her husband parted by mutual consent, and she drifted into the Barbican as an office cleaner. But this meant working in the small hours so, bye and bye, on the word of mouth recommendations of various porters, she started to hire herself out to any flat owner who needed help and was willing to pay the going rate for it. She was a good worker and was soon fully booked. Through the years, as the population of the Barbican was forever coming and going, she became au fait with every make of flat from those in the tower blocks to those of lower status.

Bertha was delighted to be selected by Concetta who was known to be choosy and, at first, she was under the impression that her newly acquired help worked only for the titled as Concetta frequently referred to "my lady". It was only when "my gentleman" cropped up as a substitute that Bertha realised that this was Concetta's generic term for her employers. Concetta worked two hours on Tuesday and two on Friday; the only problem was when those hours were supposed to start. Once begun they went on relentlessly for two hours. Concetta liked Bertha but, being Italian, she preferred Hugh. She much admired the old world courtesy with which he held open the door for her departure. She never heard his words as he closed it. "Drat that woman! She has ruined my whole morning!"

She wept openly on hearing of his death.

"Was good man," she observed, wiping the tears from her eyes. "Religious, no?"

"No," assented Bertha. She was sorry to disappoint.

"Our Lady will look after him," said Concetta confidently.

A red rubber-gloved hand touched Bertha's arm lightly and compassionately. Concetta did not intend to abandon Hugh's widow for both sympathetic and practical reasons. Whilst truly grieving she was scheming on how to prevent Hugh's clothes, which her lady was sure to wish to discard, from getting into the hands of the porters or the Salvation Army, none of whom would know man-made fibres from pure wool. She liked her job here, it was almost her best. Really rich people in very expensive flats always expected full value for the money they paid out and that was what made her late for her other appointments. They often gave parties where the perks did not keep pace with the penalties; wine-stained carpets and unpleasant bathrooms. But this small flat she was able to keep in perfect order by a not too rigorous routine,

24

which allowed for stopping for coffee and biscuits. She had learned the do's and the don'ts of it. Madam liked wax polish on the furniture; she could not abide sprays. Madam preferred disinfectants to smell of disinfectants rather than honeysuckle; she would not have bleach. Well, we all have our little whims and fancies.

On the spur of the moment Concetta determined to take her lady under her wing and see her through the first dangerous weeks of her widowhood. Not only would it be a charitable act but it would please that poor dear polite soul who had passed away. Here Concetta hurriedly crossed herself, much to Bertha's surprise. And later on, thought Concetta – God forbid it be soon – she might reap a reward, a legacy for lifelong devotion. How good that would be! She could take a rest from her labours, how long would depend on the size of the legacy, and make jaunts to the West End to the big Marks and Spencer's and even Selfridge's.

As the days went by it seemed that the most pressing problem was to persuade her protégé to eat. Bertha had lost interest in food since she had no one to share it with. With Hugh there had been set meal times; now she only ate when she felt hungry which was seldom. Concetta did not approve of an all fruit diet.

She discovered the tins of soup when she was wiping down the doors of the kitchen cupboards. It would have been all right if she had brought it herself, but having appointed herself Guardian Angel she disliked competition.

"Who bringa da rubbish?" she demanded.

"Kind friends," retorted Bertha, stung.

"Ha! They should be enemies. Better a nice lamb chop, fat and juicy."

Bertha shuddered. "I can't eat meat, not yet anyway."

Evidence of that was plain to be seen. The oven remained spotless, never used.

"Then I shall bring you pasta," said Concetta firmly. "Very good, very make strong."

"I don't much like pasta," protested Bertha feebly.

"We see, we see," said Concetta, going through a mime of dangling spaghetti into her mouth and then licking her lips. They did see, indeed they did. To Concetta, the deprived

25

child still, in woman's disguise, supermarkets were bliss. Just to wander up and down those aisles and feast her eyes on the packed shelves was perfect entertainment. She could not read English. What matter? She could read figures. And figures were prices which were there to be compared with one another. She had a keen eye for a bargain. Who needed to read when every product had its picture upon it? And if the product didn't quite live up to the picture, why make a fuss? Life itself never did live up to expectations. The pasta of which Concetta approved needed no picture; it was packed for all to see in a neat plastic box.

Each time she came to the flat she brought pasta. Sometimes green, sometimes white; sometimes stuffed with different substances into big postage stamps or cunning little pouches. Sometimes masquerading as sea-shells or flattened into bunches of tape. Bertha became convinced that pasta, like a creature of fable, could assume any shape that it liked. Bertha did some stuffing herself. After she had paid for it and Concetta had departed, she stuffed it straightaway into her Garchey. It gave her great pleasure, all the more for being slightly tinged with guilt, to run the tap over this disgusting stuff until the right level had been reached and she could pull up the tube.

"But that's a wicked waste," exclaimed Mrs Sprite, who popped in by way of the balcony every so often to see if Bertha survived.

"I don't care," she said, unrepentant at being caught in the act. "Now it can live up to its name. It's a waste disposal unit, isn't it?"

She thought that this was rather smart for one in her state of depression.

"The only thing that worries me," she added, "is that I wonder if it might swell and start coming back."

"You could give it away." Her neighbour was still reproachful.

"You're welcome."

"Now, Bertha, you know that we're both on a diet. I must lose weight before we go on our holiday."

"Who should I give it to then?"

"Maybe one of the maintenance men."

"You know they live on steak. If I gave it to anyone in the Barbican, Concetta would be sure to hear of it."

"She's got eyes like gimlets. She must be suspicious when it all disappears."

"Ah, I'm not as dumb as you think. I boil up a few pieces, drain the water off and leave the saucepan for her to clean."

"And what did she say to that?"

"She hoicked out a bit with her finger and said it was mushy. You know that all Italians like their pasta *al dente*, in other words, tough."

"You're afraid of that woman."

"Don't be absurd, Patsy."

"Yes, you are. Otherwise it would be the simplest thing in the world to tell her not to bring any more pasta."

"Then she would bring something worse. Fish, I expect."

"Just tell her you intend to eat out in the future."

"Now, that *is* an idea."

"And do it, Bertha. You must have lost a stone since Hugh . . . went."

"That should please my doctor. It's no fun going to eat out alone, Patsy. It makes one feel self-conscious."

"Then take one of your nephews."

"I might."

Patsy took a long look at her neighbour. Then she asked: "Have you got rid of Hugh's clothes yet?"

"Yes."

"Good. It's the only thing to do."

And how does she know, wondered Bertha, when her Sam is as healthy as any man can be who has to spend half the year in the air on behalf of his firm. Soon he was due to fly off again with his wife for his annual vacation. Bertha thought that he might have preferred to stay at home with a book.

Acting on Patsy's advice and Concetta's broad hints, Bertha had parcelled up all Hugh's belongings – his tailor-made suits, his Jermyn Street shirts, even his underwear – and donated half to Concetta and half to the porters. Neither recipient appeared to be pleased. Had each got the wrong half or did each think that they should have had the whole? Left to herself, Bertha began to brood over what had been said and to admit that what she had so strenuously denied might be the

27

truth. She recognised that her attitude to the Italian woman had been gradually changing; how much was this due to a change in Concetta? With Hugh around, she had just been a joke – a bad joke sometimes – but a joke nevertheless. They were amused by her mimes and if Hugh was kept waiting too long for his twelve o'clock drink by her prolonged activities, behind her back he would mime opening the sherry bottle and pouring out the wine into two glasses, after which he would raise one to his wife. In a flat of that size it was impossible to escape from the noise of her hoovering or the small thuds which accompany the conscientious shifting of furniture. When it got too much even for Hugh's patience, he would beckon to Bertha and toddle off to the bedroom to retrieve his coat, while she paid Concetta for the morning's work session. Then they would both slink out to have that drink down in the Barbican Centre, leaving Concetta to finish and close the door behind her when she departed.

Why couldn't she do exactly the same thing now? Bertha asked herself. Anyone who had worked in the Barbican for a long number of years would never endanger her job by being light-fingered. Indeed Concetta was irritatingly circumspect, putting infinitesimal remains in saucepans into saucers and bringing back small coins discovered under the sofa cushions with all the self-righteous satisfaction of a retriever. Then why did Bertha on the one occasion that she slipped out for a cup of coffee in the Terrace Restaurant (a more suitable drink for a widow) feel fidgety and wish that she'd moved her diamond brooch to a more secure place than in the toe of one of her stockings?

Am I one of those women who become suspicious and cranky when they lose their partner? thought Bertha in a panic as she scrabbled away at the thin plastic packet which contained her brown sugar. For she had heard of such cases though she had never heard of a man being affected in the same way. Widowers at their worst only grew morose. Was a good marriage just a balance guaranteed to keep its practitioners sane and clear of obsessions? Could one say that Concetta's manner was less respectful; more on the cajoling and bullying side? Yes, one could. Anyway her work hadn't suffered, the flat was cleaner than ever. But whereas Patsy was delighted that Bertha was to be visited by her young relations – "Just what you want!" she had exclaimed. "A new view-point . . . take you out of yourself," – Concetta had frowned and turned surly.

"Nevvew . . . what is that?"

"My sister's son," explained Bertha.

Concetta sniffed. "Why he not visit before when husband alive?"

It was too complicated to explain to her Hugh's aversion to family contacts.

"Is after your money. I say it. Beware!"

She turned both thumbs down.

Perhaps that is better than suggesting that I should make him a nice lasagne, thought Bertha. She was more glad than ever that Donald was coming. Perhaps she could tell Donald about this particular problem. And seek his advice.

Chapter 4

At seven-thirty precisely Bertha went down in the lift to meet and greet Donald. Intuition informed her that he would be there on the dot and intuition was right. Probably he had been hiding behind the nearest ventilation shaft with his eye on his watch. She let him in and he shook her warmly by the hand.

Short back and sides, she thought as they ascended, and a mackintosh as near to a Burberry as his salary permits. What a pity! He might have had Hugh's if they had been nearer the same size. As she inserted her key into the flat lock, a scared-looking female put her head out of the opposite door and as swiftly withdrew it.

She took his raincoat and seated him in the wing chair facing the sofa where she herself intended to sit. She wanted to observe him. At first sight he hadn't appealed to her as his cousin Malcolm had. But she wanted to be fair to him and not to make a hasty pre-judgment. She forgot that he too had feelings even if expediency advised him to conceal them. Donald despised anyone old not holding a position of authority. He shrank from flabby skin, weak ankles and false teeth. When he looked into the long strip mirror of the communal bathroom he used, he saw a young, fresh-complexioned face with a pleasant expression he falsely mistook for charm. He leaned back in the chair, crossed his legs and prepared to use it.

"What about that sherry, Donald?"

"Thanks, Aunt. That would be quite a treat for me. I'm usually a beer man."

"Something to eat? A few biscuits perhaps?"

31

"No, thank you. I had a whacking great helping of macaroni cheese before I set out. Jolly good it was too."

Shades of Concetta!

She poured them both a glass from the one bottle remaining in the cupboard. It was Croft's Original, too sweet for her taste but she didn't suppose that he would object to anything so long as the colour was brown. Nor did he.

"You've made it very cosy in here," he remarked as he sipped away gratefully.

Remembering how uncosy she had been only the evening before, she did not immediately answer him but, after placing her glass on the coffee table separating them, also sat down, smoothing her skirt.

"I was very annoyed at not being able to make contact with you last night," said Donald. "Doesn't say much for their maintenance though I'd give them top marks for security."

"As safe as a bank, eh? Though I don't think that banks are particularly safe nowadays."

"Oh, they're all right if you're not in the firing line."

"But I thought that's just where you were bound to be, Donald. I pictured you ensconced behind your bullet-proof glass with a neat little card in front inscribed 'Donald Potts'."

Bitch! She must know that he was only Grade 1, that he hated his name above all else and was as determined as his sister Jilly to change it pretty damn' quick though that seemed easier to do on the stage than in a bank.

But all he said was, "I'm afraid I haven't risen to that eminence yet, Aunt."

Indeed what he did at the moment was to carry out the simplest straightforward duties with a superior breathing down his neck all the time. But wait, he intended to rise, grade by grade till eventually it came to dealing with major accounts, taking major decisions, until finally about fifteen years later they made him a bank manager. Then he would know how to reply to spiteful old females. Though, of course, she would be dead long before that. In the meanwhile he would continue to bone up on the Stock Market until opportunity knocked.

Bertha was already sorry for baiting him – but he did look so like her brother-in-law without his horn rims that she

32

hadn't been able to resist trying to take him down a peg or two. She understood that he was just a callow youth in a really horrid blue suit (the sales?) with his foot on the first rung of a ladder that might take an interminable time to climb. But his will to succeed, his fake, ingratiating manner, the very tone of his voice, reminded her so forcibly of his father's admonition to "Open a little wider, please" that she found it difficult to carry on a sensible conversation with him. She reprimanded herself, he is *not* his father. As a consequence of that she found herself asking: "How are your parents?"

"Oh, Pa is working flat out. He's in love with his job, always has been. He used to make Jilly and me clean our teeth after every meal. We grumbled no end, but we're glad of it now."

He disclosed the most perfect row of teeth in what to her was an unctuous grin.

"And your mother?"

"Oh, she's fine!"

"Yes, but what does she do?"

"Has coffee mornings, goes shopping, gets her hair set and nails manicured – that sort of thing."

"I see . . . another of those women's libbers."

"Well . . . oh, I see. That's a joke."

"A bad one, I'm afraid."

"Most afternoons she plays bridge."

"Bridge? Alice?"

"Nothing serious. She likes the bridge rolls and the little pink cakes."

"Who looks after her?" Even at this distance of time, Bertha couldn't imagine Alice looking after herself.

"Why, she isn't mental or anything like that."

"No, no, I mean . . . is there still help to be had where you live?"

"She has various women who clean and cook. And then there's a French girl au pair. What about you?"

"I have an Italian."

"Is she any good?"

For an instant Bertha was tempted to confide in him about Concetta, then quickly changed her mind. How would he take it? Who could tell? It might start all sorts of hares; reports to the old folks at home for instance. He entirely lacked humour and anyone who lacked that was a menace. "Such men are dangerous". Shakespeare at it again, but he was referring to leanness, if she remembered correctly. Any accusation that might be brought against Concetta would sound absurd to anyone who didn't know both parties well and might even boomerang on the person who made it.

"She's not perfect. Who is? But I couldn't manage without her. For one thing, I couldn't get up there to clean the inside of the windows."

"They're high, aren't they? Especially the ventilator bit."

"Yes. I tried it once and fell off the steps."

"Oh, I say. I hope you didn't hurt yourself."

"I broke a leg. Not off me, off a small table, Oriental Chippendale. It taught me a lesson. I didn't venture again."

She didn't bother to enlarge on the incident. It was ages ago, before the coming of Concetta. In cleaning one window she had forgotten to lock the other. It wasn't quite shut; she had leaned on it for support and it had closed, upsetting her balance.

"Concetta leaps on to the top of those small metal steps like a mountain goat. That's the sort of country she hails from, so perhaps that's where she got the idea."

"How much do you pay her, if you don't mind my asking?"

"Four pounds an hour."

"Whew!"

"That's the going rate here."

The subject exhausted, conversation languished.

But Bertha thought that behind that broad, pinkish fore-head some cerebration was taking place. She guessed right. Donald was thinking that he was getting nowhere fast. The old lady seemed grumpy. He couldn't exactly put his finger on what was wrong but she acted as though she bore him a grudge.

He leaned forward and regarded her earnestly.

"Look, Aunt, I'm sorry that I couldn't make it to the funeral."

"Oh, we managed without you, Donald. We managed."

"I want to say that if you're in need of any financial help, you've only to ask."

She was amused and touched at the same time.

34

"Well, it hasn't come to that yet, dear boy. I'm still solvent."

He coloured. The red rose from his neck to his cheeks showing through his fair skin. She had never seen a man blush before.

"I didn't mean it that way. I meant if you were in need of financial advice. I'm used to looking through statements and that sort of thing – I can easily spot errors. And I'm good at planning a budget. I have to do it for myself. And it wouldn't cost you a penny because I'd do it for free."

She was more amused than ever but now alerted as well. The bare-faced cheek of it! He was trying to worm his way into her private affairs. After a short pause she said calmly: "That's very kind of you, Donald. I appreciate your offer. But really I don't have any trouble with my accounts. You see, I know what I can afford to spend and I spend it. As to the rest, I have a very good accountant and he unravels my income tax and advises me on investments."

"Are you sure you can trust him?"

"We've been trusting him for two decades! I don't suppose he'll turn crooked because I'm left a widow."

"I've noticed that elderly people are apt to keep too much cash in their chequeing accounts. It pays better to hive it off into Higher Deposit Rate."

"Really? How interesting. Let me top up your sherry."

"Well, thanks. I hope I'm not being pushy, Aunt. But I'm on your side. And, after all, what are we sent into the world for if not to help others?"

"You can't have been watching much television news lately."

There was a break whilst he sipped away thoughtfully. Then he asked: "Have you been able to get Uncle Hugh's probate settled yet?"

Goodness, was this inquisition never going to stop? Probe and drill, drill and probe; never did a lad take (as they say) more after his father.

"These things never hurry themselves," she parried.

"It must be a great worry."

"Not at all," she replied smartly. "You see, I'm lucky there too. I have an excellent lawyer."

And the more of these staunch and impeccable servitors I can summon up, the better for my protection.

"Are the neighbours all right?"

"Why do you ask?"

"Because the one who popped out and popped back again looked a bit dotty."

"Oh, she's just timid. She heard the lift coming up and thought it was her husband. When she saw that I was ushering in a young man she immediately vanished."

"She's married then?"

"Yes. Did you think she was living in sin? His name is Jaffa and he's an eminent psychiatrist practising in Harley Street."

"That explains it. She's probably one of his ex-patients. She looks half there."

"They're both there until the week-end," said Bertha, wilfully misunderstanding him. "Then they go off to Epping where he has a nursing home."

"Ah," he said as if that explained all. "Do many of the residents go away at the week-end?"

"Well, most of them escape to the country."

"Don't they like the Barbican?"

"They like it all right, but I expect that they are glad of a change."

What a fool thing to admit, Bertha, she thought, if he's up to no good. I bring in the lawyer and accountant and let go of all the Barbican residents! It was true enough, and at public holidays especially she and Hugh had rather enjoyed the feeling of being in sole possession of their part of the huge complex. It was different when one was alone, no doubt – she did not look forward to that.

"What did you say his name was . . . Jaffa? Sounds foreign."

"Oh, Donald, don't run on about the Jaffas."

"Being in that profession doesn't put him in the clear, you know. I've heard that most of those chaps go ga-ga themselves in the end."

With those convictions how lucky it was that her nephew had not met up with him face to face. For poor Dr Jaffa was the cinematic conception of a mad professor, with staring eyes over which hung eyebrows more fearsome than Denis

Healey's. Although she knew very little about him, Bertha felt bound to defend him.

"Nonsense. He always goes to the Royal Garden Party. As for his wife, she's as sane as . . . as I am."

She imagined that he gave her a curious glance at that but he only said: "That's fine, Aunt. I know that my parents would be very upset if they learnt that you were sleeping by yourself in a flat next to somebody cuckoo. Are you intending to stay on at the Barbican?"

"Why not?" She gave him the same answer that she had given Malcolm. But he did not mention the rent. He had decided to steer clear of anything to do with money.

"I think you're sensible. It's an amazing place, isn't it?"

"Yes. Full of surprises."

"I live on the doorstep so to speak and as yet I haven't seen anything like the whole of it."

"I don't expect you feel much like beating the bounds after a tiring day at the bank."

"No, though I don't have a long train journey like most of the chaps. I walk it from Moorgate. Up the escalator, over the bridge, through the Centre and down the ramp and I'm home."

"It sounds easy put like that but it would be too far for me. What do you find to do in the evenings when you're not visiting a bereaved aunt?"

"I'm always busy. Studying the Stock Market in the *Financial Times*; listening to the news; keeping an eye on Jilly."

So Jilly had to have an eye kept on her, did she?

"All the same I mean to get round to it. I shall mark it out in sections with the aid of the plan."

"Very business-like."

"Didn't you find it bewildering when you first arrived?"

Bertha was so relieved by this move from the particular to the general that she felt that she must do all she could to encourage it.

"Indeed we did. We thought that we had to go round by the road to get to the other side of the bridge. And the first Saturday we toured the City in a taxicab seeking a bottle of dry sherry, not even knowing that there was Crispin's, open every day of the year except Christmas."

"It's appallingly sign-posted. I'm always being stopped by foreigners who want to be told where to go. What do they think the words 'Follow the yellow line' mean to a Chink or a Jap?"

"That they are being hotly pursued by the security men," suggested his aunt flippantly.

This sally passed right over his head.

"Now if they translated it into several languages, it might make a bit of sense. I could give the management a lot of useful tips if they asked me."

But they won't, thought Bertha, with some satisfaction.

"There should be a lift to the podium instead of those steps. Some visitors don't even know how to get to the Barbican Centre."

"I once met a Frenchwoman who was threatening to shoot the person responsible for the directions."

"Really!"

"She got lost in the tunnel."

"Pa told me that there was an entrance to your underground car park from there."

"Yes, but you couldn't get to me that way unless the porter rang up from the Box."

They might have gone on forever swapping tales, true and apocryphal, about the mysteries of the Barbican but the mention of the car park had brought back to his widow the memory of Hugh's funeral. Suddenly she tired of the game and all that she wanted was to be rid of Donald as quickly as possible. But her wits had deserted her temporarily and all she could think of was the reproach suggested to her by Concetta.

"You never bothered to come to see us when Hugh was alive."

He blushed again.

"But, Aunt, Pa always said that Uncle Hugh wouldn't stand for it."

"Yes, yes, he was quite right. I'm sorry, Donald, I'm not making sense. You must go . . . another time . . ."

She was clearly what Donald would himself have described as "in a state".

She went off to collect his mackintosh and push it into his

keeping. Even Donald could see that he was being dismissed.

"But, Aunt, I don't like to leave you like this."

"Just go."

So he went, after scribbling down his telephone number for her and urging her to contact him if she needed further assistance.

How lovely it was to find herself alone in the flat! She sank down on the sofa, too exhausted to make the strong cup of tea for which she longed. But in less than five minutes she was deciding that she had made a fool of herself. Donald was no hero, yet he was no arch-villain either. He was just a raw provincial of unpromising parentage with too good an opinion of his own abilities. He was nosy certainly but he did not see beyond the end of his nose. His vetting of her financial position sprang from his occupation and possibly was prompted by the family. His offer of help might even be genuine. And she, what was she but an elderly female exhibiting the first signs of the persecution complex? What did they call it? Paranoia? She must guard against it.

But what a bore he was, so different from Malcolm.

She wondered however he had obtained a position in a City bank. But his father had probably capped the teeth of somebody with influence who knew somebody who knew somebody . . . that was how it went nowadays. Perhaps, in spite of his gaucheries Donald was a mathematical genius!

Now, Malcolm . . .

This was the very first occasion on which she heard Hugh's voice.

It said in her ear, "One is as bad as the other." At this stage she knew perfectly well that it was not really Hugh. It was her own sub-conscious, imitating him. But the intonation was so exactly the same and the remark so like the ones they were in the habit of exchanging with each other over the years which required no answer because of their long intimacy and because, au fond, their thoughts were alike.

She gave a profound sigh.

The last time she had uttered these seven particular words was in reference to the Tory and Labour Parties.

Chapter 5

Donald and Jilly were sitting side by side on a brown pseudo-leather banquette in the foyer of the Barbican Centre. They had made a beeline for their usual spot, chosen for its seclusion, although at the moment the crowd hadn't even begun to populate that vast area. The bar had just opened and they each nursed a half pint of lager which was all that their means would allow. Jilly disliked the foyer which she described as tasteless and especially the huge hanging light which she dismissed as utterly bogus, a word she used frequently. When left to itself and not hyped up by reflected colours, this creation was in some white metal resembling tinfoil.

"It was designed by Michael Gantry, an Australian," Malcolm had once explained to her patiently. He was a mine of information on such matters.

"I don't care if it was designed by Picasso," Jilly had retorted. "It would still be horribly vulgar."

The truth was that Jilly didn't like chandeliers even in cut glass and thought that the only fate suitable for them was to fall from a height like the one in the *Phantom of the Opera*.

"It's your turn to see the old cow next," said Donald.

"I've thought about it and I'm not going. I'll break it to Malcolm when he arrives."

"I can't say I'd blame you. She's got a tongue like a spike. But Malcolm will be properly wild. He's set his heart on this project. And you know Malcolm . . ."

She should do, she thought. They had been buddies since childhood. But sometimes she wondered. One of the things she did know for certain was what he was like when opposed.

41

"He's gone into action already. He's seen the Will, so he says."

"I don't believe it. How could he?"

"It was on the day of the funeral. When you were all at the flat."

"That proves he's a liar. I was *there*, don't forget."

"However besotted you are about Malcolm, you can't keep your eye on him one hundred per cent of the time. He says Uncle Rupe tipped him off where to find it. His pa had been shown a copy of Hugh's which left everything to Aunt but he couldn't very well ask to see hers."

"What refinement on his part," muttered Jilly. "And what a damned nerve on the part of them both!"

"Oh, there wasn't any real risk. He says that Aunt was in a daze and Uncle Rupe chatted up the rest, including you, my dear sis. If Malcolm went missing it would be taken for granted that he'd gone to the loo."

"And where was this famous Will then?"

"It wasn't exactly hidden. It was in the shallow top drawer of the bureau when you lift back the flap. The bureau was in the bedroom. I suppose there wasn't room for it anywhere else."

"Not even locked?"

"It wasn't the crown jewels, Jilly. It was just the copy of an ordinary Will. And Aunt must have been there with Uncle Rupe earlier on. Her Will was kept with Uncle Hugh's. That only makes sense."

"So Master Spy found it and scanned it, and what did it say?"

"It was all to be divided between the three of them in equal shares."

"What's the fuss about then? They're home and dry unless some outsider nips in and pips them at the post."

Donald scrutinised his sister in much the same way he might have done a cheque over which he had some misgivings. She was two years his senior but as he was a male he had been deputed by his father to monitor her behaviour in London. So he arranged to meet her once a week at a place which suited them both as a venue for approximately an hour. This was fine for Jilly; there were plenty of other hours left for her to follow her own inclinations. Besides she was reasonably fond of her brother, though not as fond as she was of her cousin Malcolm, a fact accepted by Donald who pretended to be jealous.

Sometimes Malcolm joined them, sometimes he didn't. Anyway he knew where they were to be found. And suddenly there he was, having arrived soundlessly through the magic door and over the thick carpet, commanding at once: "Fetch me a pint, there's a good guy, Donald. You're the wage earner or I'd offer to pay."

"And me a curranty biscuit," joined in Jilly as the willing vassal moved off and Malcolm slid over into his place.

"I don't know where they get those biscuits," she continued. "I've never seen them anywhere else."

"They have them specially made because of their keeping qualities. You could take one of those biscuits to the top of Mount Everest and I guarantee that not one currant would fall off. You're looking stunning, Jilly."

"Am I? That's nice."

He was right. She had cast off a very old sheepskin jacket bequeathed by one of the lesbians and was revealed in a sort of shift in scarlet that she had run up for herself on a sewing machine that might have come out of the Ark. It only did chain stitch. However outlandish her clothes, culled from street market stalls or cobbled up by herself from remnant material, Jilly always looked good. She had a yen for dramatic effect and the bright red set off her blondness. She was an ash blonde, while Donald's hair was mousy and Malcolm's dark brown. Today for a whim she had left off her make-up and, under a platoon of small light bulbs, her naked face seemed even more fragile and flower-like.

She would have been shocked at the idea of sleeping with a cousin though she was not the pure virgin hoped for by her father.

Her bond with Malcolm, or rather his hold over her, might be explained by a stronger will, a superior intellect, but it was really the submission of love. Jilly had loved Malcolm since he had come to stay with them as a small boy and showed her how exciting it was to be disobedient.

"I can't say the same for you," she said sourly after surveying him. "You look a mess."

43

He shrugged and wagged his head sideways at her. Though he was not sporting a beard no one could say that he was clean-shaven.

Donald arrived back with a pint of beer and the biscuit, which he gave one to each. Grudgingly they made room for him on the seat.

"I can't get into it," complained Jilly as she struggled to tear the plastic bag with her left hand, still holding the half of lager in her right.

"Give it to me," said Malcolm, setting his pint on the carpet. Tackled in the right way the packet surrendered at once. He broke the biscuit in half, gave Jilly one piece and kept the other for himself. He took a large bite out of it.

"Well?" enquired Donald, with a glance at his sister.

"Of course," said Malcolm, "she's agreed to come in with us."

"I haven't," said Jilly, nibbling delicately between the currants. "I don't even know what he's after."

"I'm after Aunt Bert's money," said Malcolm. He took another bite.

Jilly stopped nibbling. "That's futile as well as being criminal. If it's going to the parents it will filter down to us in the end."

"Ah, but when?"

"It's a matter of simple arithmetic," said Donald, his face serious and earnest as if imparting the facts of life to a child. "For that money to come to us it needs seven people to die. This only needs one."

"If there's to be any rough stuff," retorted his sister vehemently, "you can count me out."

"Oh, Jilly," mourned Malcolm, brushing the crumbs off his chest. "how you misjudge us! I wouldn't harm a hair of that old lady's head. I'm as devoted to her as you are."

"*I'm* not devoted," countered Jilly indignantly. "From what I saw of her at the funeral she's a miserable old beldame."

"What do you expect from people at funerals? Given the right setting she's not at all a bad old stick."

"Donald doesn't think so."

"Well, I expect she slapped him down when he wanted to be her financial adviser."

A flush from Donald assured him that he had homed in on the target.

"And," added Malcolm, "it would be a downright shame to deny Aunt Bert the pleasure of a visit from her talented niece."

"Don't call her by that absurd name. A visit wouldn't give either of us pleasure. I won't pretend what I don't feel."

"And you an actress! I did think you were serious about your profession."

"Perhaps I'm as dumb as you always maintain."

"Not dumb by any means. Thick is the appropriate word."

"Put her wise, why don't you? You can't expect her to co-operate if she isn't given the facts."

"You do it," said Malcolm, as if happy to be relieved of a boring chore. He leaned over, recovered his beer and drank a deep draught.

"You see, Jilly," explained Donald, "it isn't as if Aunt liked any of those to whom she feels compelled to leave her money for family reasons. You must know that from what they say at home."

"Oh, I do. I was brought up on it. How Bertha deserted that motherless brood as soon as opportunity knocked. Ma never forgot being left in the lurch as a baby."

"Right. There's no love lost on either side. That's why they only meet up for special occasions – weddings and funerals."

"I seem to remember that they came to Ma's wedding. She and Pa got a canteen of cutlery. I guess that was routine."

"Silver plate. And you can't remember it, Jilly. You weren't even born. Sorry, Donald."

"Shut up, then," said Donald, quite crossly. "Are you listening, Jilly?"

"Yes, but you're pretty long-winded."

"You must have the gist of the past if you want to make sense of the present," intoned Donald at his most pompous. "That's why they have flashbacks in films."

"I can never catch on to those damn' things."

"Well, this is clear enough. Uncle Hugh did what he considered his duty. He was a great one for that and that's why the money is left as it is. But he didn't see why he should fraternise and he made his views plain. That's why we never

45

went to them on visits when we were youngsters, like we used to exchange with the others."

"I used to think that it was because they were always travelling about."

"That's what was said at the time. But whatever hard feelings Aunt has about the rest of the gang, they can't apply to us. She doesn't even *know* us."

"Lucky old her," remarked Jilly dispassionately.

"I may not have made a good impression at a first approach but I can always try again. I was invited. Given the chance, she'll come to realise that she's glad to have young relatives close at hand, ready to help in any emergency."

"Now I dig it. She begins to think we're so lovely that she dashes out and changes her will. Really!"

"All right, scoff. It's not my idea, it's Malcolm's. But it's not as silly as you seem to think. Most old ladies are susceptible. They *enjoy* changing their wills and it's generally in favour of the first person who happens along. Why shouldn't we take advantage of what is recognised as a common phenomenon?"

"A little sympathy wouldn't come amiss surely, whatever the result," suggested Malcolm, rolling his eyes.

"Exactly. Aunt is lonely and in a state of shock. The Barbican is an impersonal place and she's not likely to have many friends. She can do with cheering up."

"You make me sick, both of you."

"It's Malcolm's idea."

"Then let him go it alone."

"Have a heart, Jilly. I can't. It would look too blatant. Besides, I shouldn't like to collar the lot at the expense of you three."

"You're not dragging Gus into this?"

"He wants to come. He intends to visit Aunt Bert whatever you decide to do, my sweet coz."

"Then he doesn't know what you have in mind."

"He doesn't know every jot and tittle of it, granted."

"What the heck is that?"

"I dunno. But it sounds good. He knows that it's to do with money anyway."

"Money? Gus? What would Gus want with money?"

"Not for himself. It's for his precious Order. They are nearly on the rocks, no fooling."

"Well, let him share in it but don't let him take part in any monkey business. It's simply not fair."

"I must have him, Jilly. I need him. He's the only one who can never be suspect. Everyone trusts him. Aunt Bert may have more to her than appears on the surface. But she could never doubt Gus."

"She may not be as rich as you think. But everyone who lives in the Barbican is stinking."

"It's not the life style, it's the attitude. I'd bet my shirt on it if I had one. And would my honoured father be interested in peanuts?"

"Pity she doesn't bank with us," said Donald. "Then I could give you the exact figure."

"You mind how you go. You've made one boob already."

"I've taken Aunt's measure now. She's pretty cute in some ways, but healthwise she's shaky. Has giddy turns; told me she fell off a pair of steps. And to lose a partner at her time of life doesn't help. I doubt if she'll last very long."

"You make yourself sound like a vulture," said Jilly, shuddering.

"And you sound like an unfledged student of drama," said Malcolm, quick to hit back. "Aunt Bert is good for a few years yet, I daresay. After all, she has to survive long enough to make a new Will."

"It would serve you right if she started to like one more than the others and left that one the lot."

"It's a risk," he admitted. "But psychologically improbable. I'd guarantee that of those three she prefers brother Fred. Yet as things now stand they all get the same hand-out."

"Yes. And has it ever occurred to you, Mr Smarty-pants, that what you are trying to do is to rob your own parents?"

"And who cares a toss about that?" exclaimed Malcolm, aroused. "They aren't exactly starving, not one of them. If they weren't so bloody mean we shouldn't have to resort to such ploys. My father is a miser and I don't mind who hears me say it. I hate him."

You're afraid of him too, thought Jilly, then moved on to

examine the shortcomings of her own mother and father, hers and Donald's.

"When I was a kid," she mused, "they used to give me anything I asked for. Made a fool of me, really. Huge teddy bears, trikes, musical instruments, party dresses. But now I have to wear the cast-offs of my affluent friends."

"You can count yourself lucky that you have affluent friends. I don't know anyone prepared to pass over a tee-shirt."

"They were glad when I opted for the bank instead of the university," said Donald.

"Your exam results weren't good enough," interrupted Jilly with sisterly candour.

Donald flushed but he carried on regardless. "I don't say I don't enjoy a reasonable salary but when I've paid my lodging dues and the laundry there's not a lot left over. I never have steak, only minced meat and macaroni cheese."

"I've eaten more hot dogs than there are pet ones," said Malcolm.

"It's all part of this theory on Pa's part that having money removes the incentive to work."

"I don't like work and I don't intend to do any."

Jilly turned startled blue eyes upon him. "But Malc . . . creative work, that's different. Your painting? – "

"Why should I have to paint pictures for people to buy? It's just sordid. I don't even want to paint for my own amusement. Oh, I admit that sometimes I start off enthusiastic, but long before I've finished I'm bored with it. No, I won't work."

"If I want to be famous I know that I have to slave away at it."

"Why should you want to be famous? Far better be infamous. It requires less effort and it's far more fun."

"You don't feel that you want a settled existence . . . a routine?" demanded Donald who, in spite of his grouch over the loss of three pleasant years at a university, secretly found the daily grind satisfactory enough.

"Going to work, coming back from work; all to fill the belly and turn on television. Donald, you're an idiot. Bar the dole, inherited wealth is the only way to escape working. That's why I want it."

"Why I want it," said Jilly, "is to buy nice clothes, designer clothes preferably. And not to have to rely on sex to get me out to a decent restaurant with good food and wine. And I want to be young enough to enjoy it."

"And why I want it is to be able to buy shares and to invest in any company showing the right sort of profit. Money breeds money. But you must have some capital to begin."

"It's like not having an Equity card because you haven't had the roles, and not having the roles because you haven't an equity card. All right, Malcolm. I promise to visit her once, then I'll see."

"Good girl. Donald will go anyway. And Gus will ask permission to call on his recently widowed aunt out of sheer piety. We'll meet again as I believe someone says in *Macbeth*."

"*Macbeth*! But that's a bad omen."

"Oh, you actors!"

But the old superstition had made Jilly uneasy. She sensed that Malcolm's feeling for his father was what she would have called a love-hate thing. For one wild moment she thought that Uncle Rupert might have had a hand in all this in the same way that he had engineered the peek at the Will. But no, she decided. He may have believed that a steady flow of relatives would keep sharks off his sister but he would never have done anything to put his own inheritance at risk.

Donald was not altogether happy either.

"What happens after we've put in our visits?" he asked Malcolm.

"That rather depends on Aunt Bert's reaction. We shall just have to play it by ear."

"I don't like the idea of Aunt being there in the flat by herself. She has some very odd neighbours."

"Why doesn't Jilly move in?"

"Exactly. Why doesn't she? She'd be a comfort to Aunt and save her board at the same time."

"The flat has only one bedroom."

"I know, but . . ."

"If you think I'd share a bedroom with an old woman you must be off your dot. I loathe age. It makes me feel sick. If ever I get to be thirty I shall kill myself."

49

"You won't, you know," said Malcolm. "You'll go on to be forty, then fifty, then sixty, then seventy. Just like Aunt Bert."

The three young conspirators were no longer the nearly sole occupants of the foyer. Gradually a big crowd numbering hundreds had been assembling. They stood chatting in groups, queueing up for programmes or snatching at snacks washed down by beer or glasses of wine. It might have been that each and every one had his or her problem. It might have been that some of them had solutions as drastic as Malcolm's waiting to be put into effect.

But whatever anxiety gnawed or disaster loomed, it was all shelved for the moment at the prospect of an evening's entertainment of music or drama. Nobody in that foyer appeared to have a care in the world.

Malcolm was the first to make a move. Donald followed his lead, recollecting that he had a date with a fellow resident to play snooker.

"Christ!" Jilly sprang up, clutching the sheepskin jacket. "I've just remembered that I've got lines to learn."

"A part?" enquired Malcolm, truly interested.

"You must be joking! The only part I'll ever get to play is in your damned plot."

"That's a horrid word, Jilly."

"Plan then, if you like that better."

"Just call it an idea," said Malcolm. "That's all it is at the present."

Chapter 6

On the morning of the day when Jilly was destined to visit her, Bertha sallied forth to post a necessary letter. It was one of the few things in which the Barbican failed her. Either one had to face the hazardous crossing of Aldersgate which, with the exception of Saturday and Sunday, zoomed with traffic coming from all directions, in order to reach a big-bellied pillar box, or one went across the bridge to two flat ones let into the wall in which for some reason she reposed less confidence. Or, of course, one could entrust the posting to Concetta who, as she couldn't read, was likely to put into the country box anything addressed to London.

Bertha chose the bridge. It was further to walk but entailed less nervous strain even if as a route it depressed her. It was a sort of flat-roofed tunnel bearing the weight of the conference rooms along which hurried maintenance men pushing trolleys over the tiled floor. They weren't the only users of course. On the right hand were offices where staff tapped away at typewriters, studied files and moved from desk to desk with an air of earnest endeavour. On the left hand was a series of work shops, half hidden from the public by venetian blinds in which engineers, plumbers and carpenters (she supposed) screwed and welded and hammered away at mysterious tasks to which they alone held the key. She liked to think of these contrasted activities as the brains and guts of the huge conglomeration. But in reality it was a very dull walk only enlivened by an opening which invited VIPs to step in.

After that she came to the booking hall with its queues, its posters, its information leaflets, and the daily bulletin board

51

citing what was on offer and the possibility or impossibility of obtaining seats for the same. Between the hours of one and two, it would be full of people but now it only held a few stragglers who flopped about on the seats or studied in a desultory way the handbills of forthcoming attractions. On through three sets of doors and she passed the Cut Above Restaurant, as lack lustre as any eating place before business begins. How undemocratic the name, she thought. A few bored security men marooned in their slip of an office brooded over a deck of buttons and switches.

Happily for Bertha her ordeal was nearly over, her objective gained. On her way back over the bridge she had dallied on it, leaning over to look at the falling water which, coursing languidly between cement islets, must yet be the driving force of the whole system. Behind her back many hurried by in both directions. She knew nobody and was known to nobody; suddenly the world was a bleak place.

Soon she was proved wrong. On a level with the library who should emerge from it but her shy neighbour, Mrs Jaffa, weighed down on each side by a plastic container full of books. With a pang of guilt, quite unnecessary as after all it was Donald and not she who had made the derogatory remarks, Bertha hastened to her and took over one of the loads.

"How very kind! Paperbacks are easier to carry but Rolf complains of the print."

They had only taken a few paces together when she made an abrupt stop. "Oh, do you think . . . would you mind if we went into the bookshop together for a few moments? It would be such a treat."

Who would dream of denying a treat to this wistful creature with her head at an angle and a bright pleading eye?

The shop was a comparatively new venture, the books on the shelves being so fresh from the press that they made the newest library fiction appear dingy by comparison. Several people were browsing. Mrs Jaffa apparently had no intention of buying. It was enough for her to move slowly along feasting on the titles. She paused. "Viragos," she murmured ecstatically. She was referring to the publishers and not a bevy of women with arms akimbo.

Progressing in alphabetical order, which was how the books were arranged by the names of their authors, towards A and the exit they passed out of view of the young man at the cash desk. Here the stock changed character, from books to cassettes and on the left hand printed gift wrapping paper and other assorted objects, finally to a bowl of small souvenirs of the Barbican.

Did it actually happen? Could it have happened? No, it just wasn't conceivable. But here they were both outside with Bertha still wondering. She blinked, she had temporarily lost faith in her vision. But Mrs Jaffa, eyes bright as a sparrow's which had swallowed a crumb, tugged at her sleeve.

"Oh, do you think we could go down to the Terrace for a nice cup of coffee? It's so seldom that I have a companion. And I've got a free hand and can take hold of the hand rail. I always feel trapped in the lift."

Without a yea or a nay, she tripped off to the spiral staircase with its glass casing. Bertha had never used this way herself before, the descent made her feel slightly dizzy. Somehow they were safely on terra firma with Mrs Jaffa, cheeks rosy with excitement, still in charge. At the counter they collected their coffee cups but as Mrs Jaffa dug down inside her plastic bag amongst the books for her old-fashioned purse, determined to host the occasion, disaster struck. Out popped an absurd miniature policeman sheathed in plastic who fell downwards as all things must and bounced away under the counter.

Mrs Jaffa was suddenly convulsed with terror. "I *must* find it. I *must*."

She and Bertha bumped heads scrambling for it and finally it was retrieved and handed back by a visibly amused fellow customer.

But Mrs Jaffa was undone. She abandoned her coffee and fled out to the Terrace, leaving her neighbour to pay the bill and to follow her out with two cups on a tray. She was discovered by Bertha on a cast iron chair very near the artificial lake, still trembling.

Bertha sat down on the other side of the table and rested her bag of books on it. So Mrs Jaffa wasn't a sparrow after all; she was a thieving bird, a magpie. How gratified Donald would be at the justification of all his misgivings.

53

"I'm so ashamed," said poor Mrs Jaffa. "*So* ashamed."

It was too difficult to come up with the right answer. To put it plainly there wasn't one.

"Drink your coffee," advised Bertha kindly.

Mrs Jaffa took a small sip. "I can't help it, you know. It would have been all right. Rolf would have taken it back tomorrow. He always does."

"Are you warm enough here?" Bertha asked. Although they were sitting in pale sunlight there was a chill in the air. "When you have finished your coffee, shall we start back for the flats?"

"I would rather be here. Water is therapeutic, you know. Rolf always advises it for his patients."

"I always thought that applied to immersion."

"Immersion relaxes the limbs. To regard water relaxes the mind."

For the first time Bertha detected the existence of another language behind Mrs Jaffa's careful English.

Well, that explained it. Foreigners might be excused anything, even kleptomania. As if reminded telepathetically of her lapse, Mrs Jaffa dived a hand into her pocket to feel for her booty. Yes, there he was, quite safe, that rotund, thumbnail bobby.

"If he had been lost," said its purloiner seriously, "there would have been nothing for Rolf to return."

Bertha shifted her gaze to the lake. Its flat surface shimmered. It was too early in the season for the fountains to play. The ducks were absent but below she knew there were goldfish, small carp, which would rise if tempted by bread.

"See how calm it is," said Mrs Jaffa as if praising it for a serenity she did not herself possess. "It is therapeutic for both of us."

"Do you think that I require it?" asked Bertha, surprised.

"Oh yes, my dear, you are still quite ill. It is a very severe shock to lose one's husband."

Bertha was struck silent, wondering if this extraordinary statement even if coming from such a source might not have a grain of truth in it. Was she repeating again something that her own husband, that noted alienist, had said? Was this why she, Bertha, often walked from one end of the flat to the other

54

to fetch something and found that having got there she had completely forgotten what it was that she had come for? Was it this that caught her at a loss for the next sentence over the telephone? Was this why she couldn't even start the crossword? But Hugh's death was not unexpected. It was not accidental, announced by the police at the door. He had not fallen down in a fit or suddenly expired as he sat in a chair. He had died in his bed and she did not know until morning that he was no longer with her. That was shock, was it? Yet she remembered being perfectly composed as she rang the doctor to tell him. And later the doctor on leaving, after making the necessary arrangements and advising her to get in touch with her relations, had said: "Well, it comes to all of us and he had a long happy life. Will you be all right, or shall I leave you some sleeping tablets?"

For some months she had recognised that he was dying and he recognised it too. He had no wish to eat. It took him a long time to dress and when this was accomplished he would sit reading the paper or simply watching the great expanse of sky that he could see through the window.

Occasionally he would beckon to her to sit down beside him on the sofa and then, saying nothing at all, he would take her wrist between his own fingers and thumb.

Did she delude herself when she still felt his comforting presence around her in the memories he left?

She said at length as if the words were drawn from her by need to believe that somewhere, in some place, he still existed: "Of course I knew that unless we fell from an aeroplane or crashed with a car, one or the other of us had to go first. But we had this habit from living so long together of making small comments on whatever happened in our everyday life. Well," she finished up defiantly, "I still hear him."

Mrs Jaffa nodded her head sagely and continued to nod it in rhythm. "A symptom. There is no need to despair. I, too, suffered a shock, many years ago. And gradually I recovered till all that was left was this small social defect. I never did anything like it before."

A few vague speculations as to the nature of her neighbour's shock chased themselves round Bertha's brain. Was it rape for instance? And did an ultimate recovery predicted for her include a small social defect? Undressing in public perhaps?

"My husband hanged himself," said Mrs Jaffa simply.

A shiver ran down Bertha's spine. Oh Donald, I owe you an apology, really I do.

"I should have said 'my late husband'," amended Mrs Jaffa.

It was dreadful enough to be funny.

Mrs Jaffa must have tired of speaking of sad matters, for she now changed the subject entirely. She said in her usual chirpy voice: "What an improvement you have made in that young man. And in such a short time."

Bertha stared at her, suspecting some new deviation, but then revelation dawned. Mrs Jaffa, having seen Malcolm arrive on the first occasion had later confused him with Donald. At the idea of Malcolm metamorphosed into Donald, short back and sides, their aunt wanted to hoot. However, in the circumstances she thought it wiser to explain the situation.

"You saw two separate persons," she explained with more gravity than she felt. "I can understand how you became confused as their visits followed quickly upon one another and the light isn't good on the landing. They are my nephews and there is another to come so don't be surprised. You are unlikely to mistake him for Malcolm or Donald. He is a Roman Catholic theology student."

It seemed to her more respectable than saying that Gus was a novice.

"I am Roman Catholic too," sighed Mrs Jaffa. "But, of course poor Rolf, being what he is, is nothing. Not even an Agnostic," she added.

By common consent it appeared that they had sat there long enough by the water to be sufficiently tranquillised. Being cold might have had something to do with it. They gathered up the plastic bags and started on the way home by the stairs.

"Did you find anything interesting?" Bertha asked. Too often she returned from the library with unreadable books.

"I cannot answer for the contents but I bring back the usual. Three mysteries for me and three romances for Rolf."

"Surely you have the distribution reversed?"

"Oh no, Rolf uses the romances to send him to sleep and I have a dull life, so I have the mysteries."

They both laughed and were on comparatively friendly terms when after going up in the lift together Bertha passed over the bag containing the romances – or was it the mysteries? – before letting themselves into their respective flats.

Bertha congratulated herself on escaping comparatively unscathed from an embarrassing situation. For her luncheon she made a dish of scrambled eggs; she felt as if she needed something bland to counteract the experience of the morning. That and a strong cup of sweet tea must, like water-watching, have had a calming effect for afterwards she put her feet up on the sofa and drifted off into a dreamless sleep. When she awoke, refreshed, the sun was streaming in at the window. She opened it and went out on the balcony to stand there for a few minutes beside her plants, readjusting her thoughts, before going back into the room. She took up her book but a vague uneasiness still persisted, a sort of fog in the mind.

She had gained a new insight into a neighbour with whom she had previously only a nodding acquaintance. Whilst Hugh was alive she doubted whether she had exchanged more than a few hundred words with Mrs Jaffa. Exchanged? The words came from her and were simply comments on the weather or asking whether the postman had come, to which Mrs Jaffa had assented or replied briefly, smiling. So why assure Donald that this woman was sane? She recalled her own words: "as sane as I am". If Donald ever caught a breath of this! She must guard her tongue, she mustn't speak of this adventure even to amuse Malcolm. For what had to be protected was her own reputation for sanity, not Mrs Jaffa's. As a couple, she and Hugh could have lived on undisturbed even if one of them had developed an oddity or two. But alone . . . let her step but an inch over the border of what is regarded as normal behaviour, and the family would fall upon her, headed by Rupert. She might appoint an attorney to take charge of her money, but the real crux of the matter would be, was she fit to live alone? Did she need protection? What would it profit her to explain that what she needed protection from was her family?

She would have been more worried still if she could have been a fly on the wall of the adjoining flat after Dr Jaffa returned from Harley Street.

Dr Jaffa was not at all discomposed by the shop-lifted policeman. He sat with the manikin cupped in the palm of his hand, brows beetling but a lift to his mouth above the alarming beard.

His wife had edited her story. In her edition Bertha had no knowledge of what had happened. Mrs Harris had just helped her carry some of the library books and they had then had a nice chat by the lake.

"I shall drop by and return him tomorrow. I know them there."

"I'm sure the young man didn't see. His desk is too far away."

"I shall take him back all the same," said the doctor firmly. "It will avoid any misunderstanding later. Unless you wish to keep him as a souvenir, my dear. Then I shall pay."

But idly turning the packet over he saw the price tag stuck on to the plastic. "I shall take him back," he decided.

"Poor Mrs Harris. She is still very distrait. She hears voices."

"Does she indeed?" exclaimed the doctor, professionally interested.

"Only one voice, I think," Mrs Jaffa corrected herself hastily. She had gone too far, and she knew what her husband was like on the war path.

"One is more than enough," he announced grimly.

"But, Rolf, I too . . . I too have my . . . my kink."

He showed his teeth in a smile.

"Yours is just a peccadillo, my dear. Voices are different."

"I am sure that poor Mrs Harris is as sane as I am."

Her husband had ceased to listen to her.

"Joan of Arc heard voices. The Yorkshire Ripper heard a voice. One voice is more dangerous. I shall keep my eye on that lady."

Chapter 7

In the excitement Bertha had forgotten every word about
Jilly. So, when she was buzzed on the entryphone (which had
evidently been repaired) just before the Nine o'clock News
she guessed that someone had pressed the wrong number or
that some half-witted lads were larking about.

"Jilly," announced a perfectly modulated voice from below.
Jilly had managed to rid herself of the flat Midlands accent
which still plagued Donald.

"Oh, Jilly! I'll press the button. You know the way up."

She opened the flat door and stood there to receive her
niece as she stepped out of the lift. This was partly to avoid
any repercussions from Mrs Jaffa. But no one interrupted
their meeting. Jilly was carrying a bunch of flowers with a pink
bow, hurriedly snatched from a restaurant table. The bow
was her own contribution.

"Hullo, Auntie dear," she said with a near kiss on the cheek
as she passed over the threshold.

"Don't call me that," exclaimed Bertha indignantly. "Auntie" in her mind was forever associated with the disreputable
penguin who accompanied Pip, Squeak and Wilfred in the
Daily Mirror of long ago. Jilly, of course, was far too young
ever to have seen this strip cartoon. She was somewhat puzzled. As she handed over her offering she said carelessly,
"Well, they call me 'Potts' and I have to put up with it."

Then, remembering that she was there to charm and not
offend, she added: "As you like, darling. Well, there it is!
'Darling'! That fits anybody."

So it did, in her chosen profession.

Bertha would have helped her off with her coat but she wore none, being attired in bright yellow cotton trousers surmounted by a chunky black sweater decorated with white zigzags, coming down well beneath her neat bottom. Bertha was amused but not amazed that even in this extravaganza the daughter of Alice contrived to look beautiful.

She suggested: "Would you like to take that off? We have under-floor heating as I expect you know and it gets very warm."

"Not unless you wish to see me topless, darling. I'll just pull it out if I want to let the air in."

She strolled over towards the window in high heels which left little pockmarks in the carpet.

"Darling, would you mind very much if I draw the curtains while you put out the light?"

When Bertha had complied, Jilly let out an ecstatic sigh of pure pleasure. "Ah! I have been dying to see this at night ever since the day of poor Uncle Hugh's funeral. I knew it would make a superb backcloth."

Old woman and young girl, they stood watching it. Bertha had left the absurd flowers on the kitchen counter and for the first time she felt at one with her niece.

On the black grape of the sky, for it somehow seemed curved and not flat, was superimposed the stark outline of The Bastion, below which to the left stretched a long line of lesser but substantial buildings, nearly every window a-gleam.

"Too many lights altogether," grumbled Jilly. "Makes it look like a cut-out Christmas card. But then the needle spire and the crane in contrast. God, aren't they fabulous?"

"What about the stars and the moon?"

"The stars are all right because they are only pin-pricks but the moon is utterly bogus. It's a television cliché, that's all. Switch on the lights, darling, and I'll shut out this stunning sight if I can find the right cord to pull."

When Bertha's eyes came into focus again, she took a quick look at Jilly who had, uninvited, settled into the wingchair and lounged there, languid but still graceful, with her legs crossed. Her features were the same as her mother's, her hair the same ash blonde, her eyes the same blue. But backing this prettiness was the quick intelligence denied to Alice.

Bertha wondered if Hugh would have been won over by her. Though he had an aversion to boys he liked young girls in the nicest possible way and would watch fascinated by their antics as they came out of their city school on to the broad platform which overlooked the residents' garden and provided an outlet for their mid-morning break. In their brightly coloured uniforms they formed patterns, grouping and dispersing like the fragments in a kaleidoscope. Then there would come the summons and they would all disappear until they re-emerged in their outdoor clothing to go home through the iron gates. Latterly, when he was unable to leave the flat, their appearance provided a break for him too, making him forget for a few minutes that the end of term was coming for him as well as for them. They were his last contact with youth even if it was through plate-glass. Yes, Hugh wouldn't have been human if he hadn't been attracted to Jilly though he might have applied her own word to her: bogus.

Bertha came to with a start to find her niece regarding her with a blue stare. So she too could sum up. The truth was that Jilly had been stung by Malcolm's reference to her acting ability; she took this part of her life seriously. If she could charm hardboiled casting agents into giving her an audition, she decided that she could make mincemeat of any old lady, and that she was proposing to do.

"Didn't you want me to come, darling?" she asked, a mite wistful.

"I don't know whether I did or I didn't," admitted Bertha. "I don't really know you, you see."

"We must remedy that. Let's settle down for a nice cosy chat and become acquainted."

"What about the flowers? Shouldn't I put them in water first?"

"They've only just come out of it," admitted Jilly candidly.

She was the English Rose tonight; the make-up had gone back on but not heavily. Just to the degree likely to be acceptable to an elderly relative.

"Do you want anything to eat? Something to drink?"

"No, thank you. I've been out to dinner with a . . . a friend. Just a cheap little place."

She did not enlarge upon her escape from any further commitment that might have been expected; the hasty brushing-off, the promise of future enjoyment. She was accustomed to the use of skilful extraction from amorous situations.

"I expect you have plenty of friends."

"Oh yes, of a sort. And I can always fall back on Donald and Malcolm. And Gus, I suppose, at a pinch. Though he isn't a free agent."

"I can understand your reliance on Donald. I didn't know that you had close ties with the others."

"They're my blood kin, darling. And we were often together as brats."

Blood kin! Wasn't that the very claim on her that Bertha had put forward herself? Yet how did it marry with her distaste for Rupert and Alice and even Fred who were undeniably her closest blood kin.

She wondered if she could become genuinely fond of this little poseur. Would she shed her theatrical skin when she felt more at home? Could she eventually be trusted, confided in? After all she is *my* niece, thought Bertha, just as she is Alice's daughter.

"I never met Uncle Hugh," said Jilly, "but I believe that he was a sweetie. Don't you miss him terribly, darling?"

Sympathy undermined Bertha's defences.

"Oh, I do, Jilly. Though sometimes . . ." Here she pulled herself up sharply. Instinct saved her. She had been going to tell Jilly all about hearing Hugh's voice. Instead she finished up lamely: "Sometimes I feel worse than others."

The strange thing was that this exchange had served to remove the constraint between them both and the next hour passed pleasantly enough. Jilly expounded on her ambitions and prospects, the one so over-weening and the other so under-achieving. She enjoyed using her new vowel sounds, the mastery of which gave her renewed confidence; they had once been the despair of her coach.

And Bertha, freed from discussion of her own private affairs, played up to her niece delving into her theatre-going past to produce examples of breath-taking successes. The understudies who given the chance of the leading lady breaking her leg (nothing else would have kept her from performing) had risen in one night from obscurity to stardom. The small parts which by the sheer excellence of their handling had stolen the show. It was only when Bertha followed up these tiny hits of her own by recounting the absolutely true story of the peer of the realm who had taken the bride from the boards, that she found that she had a flop on her hands. To give up her brilliant career for a silly old earl was not in Jilly's repertory at all. Only complete failure could have brought her to that, and in general, the nobility is not interested in failures.

From this impasse they were rescued by Jilly herself branching out into a detailed description of life at the drama school. Unfortunately this was so peppered by names of which Bertha knew nothing and cared less, that she began to fidget and suppress yawns.

Jilly, who was fast developing that sense of timing so indispensable to the art, saw at once that a quick exit was called for and, rising, suggested: "I can take you to the theatre, any matinee you like and nothing to pay. Do you like Shakespeare, darling?"

"Anything except *King Lear* and *Midsummer Night's Dream.*"

"Would you settle for *Macbeth*?"

"Yes, if they don't wear red noses."

"That's simply to stimulate those who have had the Bard rammed down their throats at school."

"All that it stimulates in me is a sense of outrage."

Jilly let out a ripple of silvery laughter which even to her sounded false.

"Darling, I suspect you'd favour a proscenium stage."

"Of course. With a nice red velvet curtain in front."

"But, you know, there is a real reason for doing away with the curtain. The audience is so busy gawping away at the scenery that it misses the first few words of the play."

"Every dramatist knows that. In my day they got over it by using a few throwaway words."

"Or the parlourmaid dusting the mantelpiece."

Suddenly it occurred to Jilly that the conversation had taken an acrimonious turn. This would never pay off.

63

"I'll see what I can do. I expect you like stalls. When I've got it arranged I'll ring up and make a firm date."

She's good-hearted and I'm an undeserving old bitch. She's given me flowers. I've given her nothing.

The mention of velvet reminded her of a long opera cloak she had which, wrapped in tissue, had remained for many years in a drawer. It might please the child.

It did. The cooing delight with which she greeted the unveiling of this sumptuous relic might be extravagant but was obviously sincere.

"Oh, darling, darling Auntie, this is going to make the most miraculous off-the-shoulder full-length evening gown that ever went to the ball."

If she winced at the idea of ruthless scissors hacking their way through that priceless panne velvet, nothing of this showed. Bertha's expression remained calm.

"Let's find a large carrier bag for you to take it away in."

They parted at the doorway on most amicable terms. Bertha deserved her kiss on both cheeks. Each was left thinking that, on the whole, the meeting had been a success.

But as Bertha walked back towards the bedroom to tidy up she distinctly heard Hugh's well-loved voice at her ear.

"A charmer, but what else is she?"

Chapter 8

The next morning at eleven-thirty, Patsy Sprite blew in from the balcony. This was a fair description of Patsy's entrance as she often gave the impression of being accompanied by a stiff breeze.

"Has that woman come?" she demanded, referring to Concetta. "No, I see that she hasn't. Set her going when she does and then leave her to it and have lunch with me. I'm all alone, Sam has just gone off to Japan." She spoke as if he had just gone round the corner.

"It's kind of you to ask me but I don't know . . . I'm a bit reluctant to be out when she's here."

"Oh, pooh! You and Hugh often left her to her own devices when he was alive. She's no more likely to steal the family silver now than she was then."

"I know, Patsy. It's just that I have this feeling . . ."

"Forget it. Lunch is at one and I won't wait a moment longer. It upsets my digestive clock. If you stay with Concetta you won't get a bite until two."

"It's tempting. What are you having . . . if it isn't a rude question?"

"No pasta anyway," said Patsy, grinning like the Cheshire Cat as she vanished by the way she had come.

Concetta's knock came at twelve. No excuse offered, she put down her shopping bag, donned her overall and changed her walking shoes for bedroom slippers without a word said. Then from the vantage point of the kitchen counter she surveyed her kingdom to see if any alteration had taken place in her absence.

At once she spotted the drooping flowers. She nipped her nose at the base to signify that not only were they dead but decomposing. Taking the kitchen scissors she proceeded to decapitate each bloom before cutting the stalk into two-inch pieces to stuff down the Garchey.

"Who brought, eh? The nevvew?"

"As it happens, my niece," remarked Bertha mildly.

"What day she come?"

"Yesterday."

"Dustbin flowers!" exclaimed Concetta. "You should have spat in her face!"

"That's enough, Concetta."

"I speak my mind. My gentleman would have wished it. These nevvews and nieces, they are up to no good. They think you are . . ." Here she tapped her own forehead significantly. "They are out to suck blood."

Afraid that she might be going to give a demonstration of this activity, Bertha intervened.

"Shall we get on with cleaning this room first?"

If she thought to mollify Concetta with the plural, she was mistaken.

Tapping her bosom this time to denote the dwelling place of the heart, Concetta continued: "I, Concetta, am the friend. I bring pasta, bottled water, detergent from Safeways. Nothing is too much trouble. But for what? Nevvews and nieces! You despise me. I am the *tuttifare*, the cleaning woman, the drudge!" she finished passionately.

"Stop talking nonsense and get on with the windows," said Bertha more briskly than she felt.

This was enough to send the cleaning woman (self-designated) into a sulk. It was a noisy sulk, however, consisting of bringing the materials for the operation together with the maximum of violence. But once she had started upon the endeavour she was silent. One cannot say much from the top of kitchen steps with one's back to the room.

Meanwhile, her mistress (if this was the word for her) went into the bathroom to bathe her face in preparation for the visit next door. She had been forced to conclude that she could not exist in this atmosphere until two o'clock. After she had brushed her hair and changed her dress, she heard the

66

Hoover and went back. As she could not hear herself speak above the racket, greatly daring, she removed the plug from the wall socket. Concetta swung round, still attached at cord's length to the handle of the vacuum sweeper. She seemed to have calmed down.

"I am going into Mrs Sprite's to have lunch with her. I will leave your money on the counter and you can close the door behind you when you go."

"You have forgot the window latch. I will put it up and you can use your key and come in again by the door."

"Thanks. You're quite right. The outside window cleaners might come."

"The heavens might fall," commented Concetta. Bertha was counting out her eight pounds.

"Remember you also owe for the goods I have brought. The ticket is there."

"Oh, I'm sorry. Yes, I see."

Relations were still not cordial, but improved.

"It is good for you to have lunch out. You do not eat enough here and that is why you fly at me for no reason. And Mrs Sprite is a nice lady. She will not be after your money either. She has enough of her own."

Whilst Bertha sipped gratefully at her sherry, she re-enacted as much of this performance as she saw fit, knowing Mrs Sprite to be something of a chatterbox. But the relief at being out of her flat was so real that the pitch of her voice rose as it always did when she was over-excited. Patsy was much amused.

"Poor old Conch! She's mad with jealousy. After Hugh died she thought she had you to herself, to bully or cosset just as she pleased. Now, with all these youngsters milling around, she knows she hasn't a chance."

She began to laugh heartily.

"Oh, don't," implored Bertha. "She may be cleaning the lavatory."

The lavatories were back to back and, as their two vents were connected by a central shaft, somehow had the extraordinary capability of transmitting a voice from one flat to the other.

"If she could hear me she could also hear you," said Mrs Sprite.

67

"Whatever would she do to me if she did?"

"Aren't you growing a wee bit paranoid, my pet? Come on, drink up. Let's eat."

Lunch with Patsy in Sam's absence was always chancy. Sometimes it was a dreadful dietary concoction with a side glass of Perrier water, sometimes a plateful of low calorie, vitamin-added biscuits to be accompanied by milk, sometimes fillet steak with green beans and today, praise be, it was smoked salmon. Patsy must have found a new expert.

As she took her seat on an ebony-coloured chair in the Swedish tradition Bertha thought, and not for the first time, how strange it was that a room of exactly the same size and shape as her own, its mirror image, could look so entirely different. It wasn't simply a matter of ancient and modern. It went deeper than that. The Sprites' was expensively trendy. One wall was covered by greenery, each exotic example cared for by Patsy with the same attention that a fond mother might have given a talented child. The carpet was off-white on which squatted four off-white leather armchairs. The dining table and coffee table were both in black glass. The drinks cupboard, also doing duty as a sideboard, was black lacquer with Chinese motifs. The floor-length curtains, buff in Bertha's, were here a splendid turquoise in wild silk. The whole lot looked as if it came from Heal's and probably did.

With the salmon went a delicious white wine, chilled to exactly the right temperature by the hostess and lavishly poured by her into richly engraved glasses.

Bertha raised her glass. "To the nice lady. That's what Concetta calls you."

"I know where she got that. From the porters' box. They call everyone a nice lady. Essence of tact but not strictly true."

She proceeded to give her guest a resumé of the life-style of several ladies in the block who did not, for one reason or another, merit this description. Bertha was only half-listening.

She was having problems with her helping of salmon. The long, pink fleshy slices on which she had started with enthusiasm would not diminish. She persevered but each bite stuck in her throat. She could not hide what she could not eat with only a quarter of lemon. Her head drooped and she put down her fish-knife and fork with a sigh of despair.

Immediately Patsy interrupted her offering of scandal, leaning over the table to cover Bertha's hand with her own, no less sympathetic because it was loaded with rings.

"Poor old girl. It's the shock."

"I didn't even know that I had it until somebody told me."

"It always comes as a shock in the end, however much one realises that a person is failing."

"Hugh never failed at anything in his whole life," said Bertha proudly, wilfully misunderstanding her.

"Oh, pet, for Godsake, it's only a way of putting it like 'passing away' or 'gone home'."

"Hugh's home was with me," said Bertha, then admitting to herself that she was being silly she continued in a more rational tone: "Hugh always used to read the obituary columns and it's surprising how many of the people we knew have died in the past year. Gone, if you prefer it."

"That's your time of life, Bertha. With us it's divorce. All our friends are thinking about it, are getting it or have got it."

"Well, it isn't so final."

"It's a curse all the same. When they both used to come to dinner, how do you know now which one to invite? Do you have the man because you like him better or the woman because you're sorry for her?"

"It's a problem," agreed Bertha.

"And you're another. Not eating, not getting out and about."

"I'm supposed to be going to the theatre with my niece."

"Well, that's a good thing. But what you really need, Bertha, is to get right away. What you want is a long holiday in the sun. Why don't you come with Sam and me when we go?"

The impulse of generosity is apt to out-distance its practicality. Bertha thought that she caught a flash of anxiety in Patsy's blue eyes as she raised her head and looked into them. She could imagine Sam's reaction to such a suggestion!

She hastened to say: "I don't want to leave the flat, Patsy. I'd rather stay there. I feel that once I leave it I shall lose touch with Hugh altogether."

And that isn't healthy, thought Patsy. There is something sick about that.

But she thought that it would be asking for trouble to tackle Bertha on the matter. How would she herself react for instance if Sam . . . passed away? She never minded if he was absent but if he were gone altogether would that be different? Well, God forbid . . . and not a divorce either.

She said: "I don't feel easy at leaving you here with only the Jaffas for company. He's never there and she's . . . well. . . .

"Of course there are the young people but then . . . Bertha, they haven't been trying to touch you for money, have they?"

"No."

For a slice or two of quiche and a bottle of red wine, scarcely came under this title. The cloak she had offered. Even Donald, though no doubt he would dearly have liked to manage her money, had not asked for any of it. Quite otherwise, in fact.

"That's all right then. If they try anything like that on, you tell me and I'll tell Sam. He'll soon sort them out."

Bertha did not tell Patsy that she had any thoughts about changing her Will. That would have meant starting an argument. But, as she sat drinking her after-lunch coffee, she had an idiotic desire to warn Patsy against inviting Mrs Jaffa into her flat. There were so many little items on the coffee table that Mrs Jaffa would have found irresistible.

The last thing that Patsy said to her as she showed her out was, "Now, if there's anything the least bit wrong when we're away, you cable us and we'll be back on the next plane, I promise."

Bertha thought of Sam in his bathing shorts or whatever he wore on the beach, being informed of this crisis.

It was her utter inability to conjure up his possible rejoinder to the summons which was occupying her mind as she re-entered her flat.

The first thing she saw was Concetta's wages still lying on the kitchen counter. She had taken the money for her purchases but abandoned the rest.

Now, what did this mean? Was she coming back for it later, or was it a gesture to signify that she was abandoning her lady for ever? Who could tell?

70

Chapter 9

That evening Gus came. He had trouble with the entryphone. He found the name "Harris" and pressed it. But he did not know that you had to speak into it or above it. Bertha said, "Who is that?" again and again but all she got in return was a series of frenzied buzzes until at last she released the door from sheer exasperation. And now I have done it, she thought, for Patsy had warned her against such behaviour. Now I have let in a gang of desperadoes or a homicidal maniac and for whatever happens I shall be the one to blame. She waited nervously with her door half open and when she saw Gus come out she could have swooned with relief.

The odd man out. For when she had assured Mrs Jaffa that she wouldn't mistake him for either of the other two, she spoke more truth than she knew at the time. For the funeral he had come in a homespun tweed suit but now he wore something rather like a bathrobe in black . . . frieze, would it be? . . . reaching to his ankles and tied in the middle by what had a strong resemblance to rope. She ushered him in hastily, fearful of alerting her neighbour.

"My dear Aunt Bertha, here I am at last," he announced cheerfully, and he kissed her forehead which was at least a change from being pecked on the cheek.

"Then come and sit down. Can you take that thing off?" she asked, cautioned by her experience with Jilly.

"Not very easily unless you don't mind seeing my vest and underpants."

"I don't mind but perhaps you'd better keep what you have on for the present."

"I expect I should have put on a suit. But I had to get special permission from Father Superior to come and was in too much of a hurry. Of course he understood when I explained the position. He sent you his blessing."

Bertha was tempted to reply "That was very civil of him" but restrained herself. Instead she regarded with wonder, tinged with affection, this strange apparition. He had what might be described as a crew cut. He told her that he and another novice operated on each other. Well, it might have been a tonsure. At least that she was spared. He had his father's brown eyes and ruddy skin and if what she imagined was a rent in his garment and not a deep pocket he had other inherited tendencies as well. She wouldn't be the one to offer to mend it but she did offer food and drink.

"If you have a hunk of bread and some cheese," he said, "that would be fine. We only drink water in England. I don't know what they do at the parent house which is in France."

"Oh, is it?" she asked as she busied herself in supplying his wants, half the loaf and all of one week's cheese. "Whereabouts?"

"About thirty miles east of Paris."

"A little bit different from the East End."

"Yes. It's in the country."

"And what is the name of your Order?"

He sounded bashful. "Well, in full it's 'Les pauvres de St Joseph'. The locals call us 'Les Povers'."

"Sounds like a pop star."

She brought his bread and cheese round to him on a plate. She guessed that he would not need a knife, nor did he.

"Doesn't that look good?" he said. "You know, it isn't of Arithamea, it's the pig man who flew."

"Really! Now, isn't that extraordinary. Hugh and I saw him in Assissi."

He did not question this curious statement, contenting himself with muttering the shortest grace in the world, two words, before he began to savour his treat. He did not eat as if famished like Malcolm though he was clearly hungry. He masticated each bite slowly as if to prolong his enjoyment. It was as if each mouthful was manna.

He is a born accepter, thought Bertha, a natural truster, and she envied him.

"It was a stroke of sheer luck," she said, returning to the Saint. "We were just there for two days. And on the first of them they were moving his body from one resting place to another. I don't know where he came from or where he went but his body stayed overnight in the crypt of the Cathedral."

"His actual body," Gus marvelled, stopping to take a drink of water. "Delicious water, it must come straight from a cold spring."

"From my refrigerator. And it was all conducted with great pomp and ceremony. The body was in a glass coffin in a glass hearse, and the crowds were immense."

"What did it look like?"

"I think it was mummified. I am ashamed to say that I don't really remember. Do you think it was true?"

"As true as your account of his pilgrimage. Why should anyone invent such a story about a pig-man? Now if it had been the Father Superior one might have had doubts. Oh, won't he love this yarn when I tell him!"

"Well, you know him better than I do."

"He will enjoy it all the more because I am their goat-boy. Suppose I should soar up to the ceiling in the Chapel?"

"Goats! You keep goats?"

"Yes, and I milk them and make a sort of cheese. Not at all like this cheddar."

"You have grounds then?"

"Quite a large garden. Big enough to grow vegetables for us all."

"How many of you?"

"Just twenty all told. I was the twentieth."

"Gus, how on earth did you get there?"

"Well, it wasn't anything as miraculous as the levitation of our Patron but it was pretty odd all the same."

"Tell me."

He finished the last crumb of bread and placed the empty plate back on the table.

"Ours is a teaching order and, believe it or not, at one time it throve. It had communities of nuns as well as monks and these were run in pairs, so to speak. It was convenient, I suppose. The nuns had a priest at hand and, I won't swear to this, but perhaps the nuns baked them a dish or two. Anyway these particular nuns ran a convent in Stepney to which my mum went."

"I never even knew that."

"But you knew she was an RC and devout? Hence my name. She thought I might want to become Pope."

"Poor Gus."

"Gus it was and never Augustus. But she was right in one thing – I wanted the religious life and no other."

"What about your father?"

"He always gives in to her, with two exceptions: sheep and the Church of England."

"Go on."

"Isn't it boring?"

"No."

"All right then. As Roman Catholics are scarce in our part of the country and a bit thick in the head, my mum wrote to her old Convent to ask for advice."

"I guess it had closed."

"Yes, and all the nuns gone back to France. Her letter got passed to the Father Superior of St Joseph's who was still hanging on by the skin of his teeth and he sent for me by the next post. They needed a goat boy; the old man who tended them had just died . . . and I suppose he imagined that a boy from a sheep farm was an answer to prayer."

"Now you are laughing at me."

"A little, not much. I'm cutting it short."

"And beginning to sweat. No, don't take it off yet. I'll fetch you a silk dressing gown of Hugh's from the bedroom and then you can be decent as well as reasonably cool."

It was a garment so intimate that she hadn't been able to part with it, but never had she dreamed that it would be put to this use. While she was gone he took his plate and washed it under the tap. He was in the kitchen drying it when she returned. He thanked her and disappeared with the robe in the direction of the bathroom. He came back showing it off; it was several inches too long until he had hoisted it by its cord. They stood facing each other between the sink and the cupboards.

74

"I always sweat when I'm nervous," he said. "I've come here to beg."

He might just as well have hit her. Coming so soon after Patsy's probing question this direct request for cash came as a blow. Especially from this particular quarter.

There was a long pause. "So that is what you came for?" She couldn't keep the hurt out of her voice.

His brown eyes burned with sincerity. "I came to comfort you. You must believe me. The other is only secondary."

"You don't beg for yourself obviously."

"It's the electricity bill. We simply can't meet it."

Bertha had the grace to begin to laugh in which he joined her.

"Let's consume another unit or two in order to discuss the situation," she said, filling the kettle.

"What do you want to drink?"

"A nice big mug of cocoa."

"I don't keep it. You'll have to settle for tea."

"Gladly. Anything penitential. It's been such a cold winter, you see, and the house is a barn and some of the Fathers are old. We do try to economise, I assure you."

"Pass me the tea-bags. Is the parent house wealthy?"

"Reasonably so. They still have the château and the vineyard."

"Then why not send the bill in to them? It's their responsibility after all."

"That would be playing into their hands. They are longing for an excuse to sell up. And they would be even more eager if they knew what the Father Superior has been offered for the site. The house is a Victorian white elephant. The developers would pull it down, it's the garden they're after."

"And you're afraid that you'll lose your position as goat-boy?"

"Now it's your turn to pull my leg. Of course they would be willing to absorb us into their establishment. A handful of men and novices . . . we might even be useful. But we can't go. We can't be spared from here."

"No one is irreplaceable."

But she knew that she lied. To her Hugh was irreplaceable.

"No one who lives here can imagine what it is like to live

75

where we live. It's such a short distance, I daresay I could walk it if I tried. It's Lazurus at the gate, you know, full of sores."

"The poor we have always with us."

"Oh, it's much worse than that. We were never rich at the farm. It was always a question of hand to mouth and hopes for the next lambing. Yet comparatively we were millionaires. I shan't attempt to describe the conditions. Multiply what you see on television by ten. Ugly things happen in the streets and uglier in those miserable houses. And don't ask 'What about the dole?' or 'Is there no supplementary benefit?' or I shall be reminded of Scrooge.

"There were what we called really poor in the village, and not all that clean or pure in their morals. But I never knew what it was to be destitute and degraded until I came to St Joe's."

"It must be brewed now. Do you take sugar?"

"Yes, please. Three spoonfuls. Sheer greed."

"There you are then. What do you do exactly that makes you think that your services are indispensable?"

"We can't function as a school. I doubt if the education authorities would allow that. But we teach all the same. We teach people how to read and write, those who want it, the young and the old."

"That should be the job of the State."

"You can't share your troubles with the State."

Nor with some of its bureaucrats, she thought. It came to her suddenly that he was one of those charmed few who could enter the lives of others, however diverse, and belong. Without being at all aware of it he trusted and was trusted instinctively in return.

"Some don't speak any English at all. We try to instruct them in Basic."

"And the Catholic Religion?" she suggested slyly.

"We have a sort of chapel on the whole of the first floor which we use for our own services but which isn't open to the public because there is already a Catholic Church in the neighbourhood. But, Aunt, can't you get it into your head? This is a mixed population, black, white and khaki, and as full of beliefs as there are holes in a colander. So we don't press it.

We visit the sick and the dying. We try to bring hope to the hopeless, justice to the oppressed and comfort to the lonely."

"As I am supposed to be? But in the main I am not. How could I be lonely in a place bursting at the seams with fresh ideas and new life? And with such memories?"

Here was one who given his nature and his professed faith, *must* understand if she confided in him that she sometimes heard Hugh's voice. But when she told him about it she found it more difficult to explain than she had expected.

"They are just comments," she said, bringing it out slowly and painfully. "But I think that they must come from Hugh because often they are different from the conclusions I have reached myself. What do you think?"

"I think that anything that makes you have faith in the resurrection is all to the good."

He did not attempt to dispute it. In his contacts with diverse nationalities and divers races, one thing had become clear to him, to be bereft of some sort of belief, however ludicrous it might appear to the majority, was to be lost indeed.

And suddenly she turned to more practical matters.

"Where is my cheque book and how much is it? Though I can't see why you can't have a talk with the proper authorities and pay it off by instalments."

"Instalments are only possible where there is future income. Oh, my beloved Aunt Bertha, it is three hundred pounds and fifty-six pence. An immense sum. Is it too much?"

"It is too much for a lost cause." She was grappling with her hand-bag where everything wanted first always seemed to come out last. "Here it is. Who shall I make it out to?"

"The Father Superior."

"Yes, but what is his name? That will make more sense to the bank. You'd better write it and I'll sign it. I hope you're not going to follow it up by a rate demand."

"We don't pay rates."

He wrote laboriously, resting the cheque book on the kitchen counter. She guessed from his lack of expertise that he was not used to filling in cheques, but he was by no means stupid and completed the stub for her equally carefully, something she often scamped herself.

"Jerome Duclaux," she remarked. "You didn't tell me that he was French."

"He is of French extraction, if that doesn't make him sound too much like a tooth. But he has lived here all his life."

She signed it, and he examined it, his brown eyes glistening.

"Wait until the Reverend Father sees this!"

A moment's doubt assailed her. "I hope that he didn't put you up to it!"

"He can't beg from people, he can only beg from God. He's been on his knees in the chapel every spare minute this last week."

"And who is to say whose tactics paid off, yours or his?"

"Does it matter? What does matter is the time. I must shed this finery and get back into my habit. I'll read my office in the train." He disappeared and re-appeared with great speed, kissed her hastily on the forehead again and was out of the door and into the passage before one could say a Hail Mary. Or before one could ask after his family or question him on the likelihood of his being able to pay a second visit.

As he stood waiting for the lift to arrive, he asked her: "Any chance of you becoming a convert?"

"Pigs might fly," she answered, as the lift appeared and he got into it.

"Well, one pig-man did," he retorted as the lift door closed on him.

She thought afterwards that it was ironic that the question that Patsy had put to her and which she answered truthfully had so soon been stood on its head. She had been touched to the tune of three hundred pounds odd by one of her young people. What did it matter? If the money had gone to glory in more than one sense, so might many other donations to charity. And knowing what her own electricity bill had been she decided that some of those poor old monks at St Joseph's must have been perished in spite of their robes.

Chapter 10

Elderly ladies do not like to be visited early in the morning. They like to waken of their own accord, slowly, to discover where they are. In Bertha's case that brought with it the idea that she would be all the better for a hot cup of tea, in her pre-widow days brought to her by Hugh. Was she grateful for it at the time? No. It was either too weak or too strong or the milk had gone off. Hugh had taken little notice of these grumblings; he had recognised them for what they were, early morning blues.

When he was dressed and had made himself breakfast, always consisting of two slices of toast accompanied by Tiptree marmalade, he would, while he was able, walk to Crispin's for his *Times* which no one would deliver for him at the Barbican. As he was wont to digest it from cover to cover, including the copy devoted to business, it would last him to shelter behind when he was joined by his wife, in a silence approved by them both. Until it was time for the coffee pot to bring things back to normality.

After the tea had taken hold Bertha, who was not a breakfast-eater, liked to sit up in bed in a dressing jacket, to listen to the eight o'clock news which Hugh had abhorred.

Once she had listened to the news and forgotten most of it, it was her habit to go into the bathroom and there spend a pleasant hour or so, lingering in the bath, dragging herself into her body garment, studying her face in the mirror which gave the most flattering return of any glass in the flat. This was followed by brushing her hair, deciding if it needed a re-perm; in fact doing all those small daily tasks which would enable her in the end to present a calm front to the world.

But the young think only of their own needs and how soon they may be implemented. And Malcolm's most pressing need at the moment was to see his Aunt Bert. When he had judged the time ripe for Gus to be back with his brethren, he had rung the Novice-Master at St Joseph's and asked for permission to speak to his cousin. The Novice-Master's voice, often as sour as a lemon, now dripped honey. "Un moment, s'il vous plaît."

That old sobersides, Gus, was positively rattling with excitement.

"Aunt Bertha wrote a cheque for over three hundred pounds to cover the heat and lighting bill for St Joseph's."

"She must be out of her mind!"

"When I say she wrote it, that's not strictly true – I wrote it and she signed it."

"What! Now I know she's senile."

"Don't you believe it! We had a perfectly sensible conversation. I admit that she thinks that Uncle Hugh still speaks to her but, after so many years living together, I think that's quite understandable. It may even be true. Who are we . . .?"

"Oh, come off it, Gus. What does he do? Offer advice?"

"It comes more in the way of comment, from what I could gather."

"Did Uncle Hugh tell her to give you a cheque?"

"It was for 'Les Pauvres', not me. It may have happened soon after we had been talking about him. Anyway, what does it matter?"

"As you say. Well, that's one problem the less. I'll be in touch."

Malcolm's attitude to Gus was ambiguous. Like Donald and Jilly, he had known him since childhood. He had spent many school holidays at the farm, for though the idea was for an interchange of visits, it transpired that Malcolm was more at the farm than the other way round. Fred was too good-natured to protest. Besides he thought that Malcolm made good company for his son who was growing up a bit solemn and, let's face it, religious. Malcolm never ceased to amaze Gus. What other boy would do so recklessly those things not

80

expressly forbidden on the farm because no one had ever thought them in the realm of possibility? But what fun it was to be with him and how dull when he departed.

At that age loyalties are easy to come by and merit has nothing to do with it. The two went on many expeditions together, on foot or on bicycle. Up the hills and down the valleys, along the lanes and into the village. It irked Malcolm that wherever they went, people said "Gus, look after Malcolm," never the other way round. At first he thought that it was only from Gus's mum who was bound to be prejudiced; then he noticed that it came from all sorts; the hill shepherds, the farmhands, the village shopkeeper, even the vicar and the doctor, both local celebrities. Now, why was this? He was a head taller than Gus, a year older, and a great deal more clever. At last he had the answer, even if it was unflattering to himself. Gus was trustworthy. He didn't need to do anything to prove it; he just was, and all around him acknowledged it. This was why his cousin was necessary to Malcolm's plan as Jilly dubbed it, or "idea" as he preferred to think of it. Already Aunt Bert was one of the converted.

But he certainly didn't intend Gus to go off with the spoils. That three hundred pounds had found its way to Les Povers, when it might have been in his pocket, made him see red. If Aunt Bert was going round the bend at that rate, he must re-jig his procedure, and collect as much as he could whilst the going was good.

Although his conversation with Gus had been short, two other ideas had sprung from it. The cheque signed but not written – he must speak to Donald about that – and the mystic voice which instructed, or commented; where was the difference?

First thing on the agenda was to see Aunt Bert for himself to assess her condition. That was why he was up bright and early. Malcolm came up in the lift with the postman, quite against the rules. Postie was late as always and it may be that he took pity on Malcolm standing there with his cumbersome burden. Anyhow, if security isn't broken now and again, who is to know that it exists?

As soon as the letters had dropped into the box and the postman had disappeared on his upward way, Malcolm did not hear a voice, he discovered one.

As Aunt Bert approached the door to collect her mail, she heard a squeaking plaint: "Let me in, let me in, or I'll huff and puff your house down."

Bertha knew that it wasn't the wolf, so she concluded that it could only be Malcolm. No porter would have dreamed of playing such an asinine trick. She didn't know how he got there and at this hour of the morning she was not disposed to care. She opened the door and there he stood, propping up with one free hand a most remarkable object while with the other he held open the letterbox flap. Long and flat and diamond-shaped, it looked like a kite without its tail. He righted it and she could see now that it was squarish and covered with marbled paper. She was sufficiently acquainted with such things to recognise it as a portfolio.

"You might as well come in," she said rather crossly. "Though I don't know what you're doing here at this time of day."

"School's on strike," he lied glibly. "I thought as I was coming this way you might like to see some of my art-work."

It was fortunate that this wasn't one of Concetta's mornings. What she would have made of Malcolm in the flesh, goodness knows. Or indeed of any of the other three. Donald alone might have escaped downright condemnation but even then she would have been pricing up to the last penny the cost of his clothes. In the tower blocks she was accustomed to seeing Savile Row suits and bespoken shoes. It wouldn't have taken her long to divest Donald of his pretensions.

Yet, as Malcolm, portfolio under his arm, advanced into the room, Bertha's conscience nagged at her. He might be a genuine artist; she had so far no proof otherwise. And Van Gogh must have looked equally remarkable to good Dutch citizens.

"Do I smell coffee?" he enquired hopefully.

"No, you don't. I'm just going to make mine," said his aunt tartly, then added with some grudging, "Help yourself. There's the jar."

Malcolm abandoned his art-work and came round into the kitchen. "Instant coffee! I'm sure Uncle Hugh never settled for that."

"He didn't. But I can't be bothered. . . ."

82

"Aunt Bert, you don't have to be bothered. I'll see to it if you show me the pot and the packet. Unless you want me to grind beans."

"We stopped grinding beans long ago. Well, there you are – and the kettle's just on the boil. I turned it off when you started making that stupid noise."

"There was some post, you know. You collect the congratulations from Littlewoods and I'll get on with this job."

"There's never anything interesting nowadays."

Malcolm was warming the pot and measuring out the coffee. She was pleased to see him display such domestic skills.

"Do you need me to set out the cups and saucers?"

"No, you sit down and relax."

It was nice to be waited upon. She left him to it. He brought it round to the coffee table on a tray.

"Now it just has to settle." He looked at the clock. And what did it matter if he gave her hers in a cup she used to break eggs into, it was cracked, and that the brown sugar came in its bag? It might have been ambrosia she was sipping. They finished the pot between them.

"Who taught you to make such excellent coffee?"

"Oh, I'm a man of many parts. You wouldn't believe the jobs I've had to take to keep alive in the long vac. Did I ever tell you of the stint I did as a meat porter at Smithfield?"

"No, because you knew I wouldn't believe you," his aunt remarked dryly.

"Good for you. Though I did eat one of their breakfasts once. Bacon and egg and all the trimmings, including black pudding. Set me up for a week."

"If you're always hungry, why don't you go home in the vacations?"

"I hate my father." He said it quite coolly.

"Why?"

"Because he's such a mean bugger . . . I'm sorry, Aunt Bert."

As this exactly tallied with Bertha's opinion of him, though she wouldn't have used the same words, she was at a loss for a reply. Did she herself hate Rupert? Such violent feelings subside in old age, yet there was a time . . . yes, there was a time. Misers have always excited the writer's imagination . . .

and who had ever loved a miser except the poor woman, his wife, in *Riceyman Steps*. But wasn't it unseemly to say the least that she and Malcolm, so close to him by the tie of blood, should harbour such animosity? What made Rupert that way, and was there any excuse to offer for it? It certainly didn't stem from early privation. One might fancy that there could be some sensual satisfaction in letting gold run through the fingers, or in fondling precious gems, but today's wealth was mainly in paper and who could find pleasure in handling a bundle of shares?

"You've gone quiet, Aunt Bert."

"I've been thinking. It must be in his genes."

"That's a fine excuse, I must say. All God's chillun got genes."

"What about your mother?"

"I haven't heard a word from her since she left him. I don't know where she is or even if she is dead or alive. And I bloody well don't care."

A change of subject was obviously required. "Perhaps we'd better have a look at those masterpieces," suggested Bertha though it was the last thing she desired.

Immediately he put aside his emotions and became extremely business-like. He took away the coffee tray and brought forward the portfolio.

"You must sit in the wing chair so we can get the light behind you and I'll display them one by one against the back of the sofa. Like this. Exhibit one. The Barbican."

Her heart sank. She had been hoping against hope, though she disliked being put into the position of critic. Let there be something here to compensate for his wretched background. Didn't his quirky conversation lead one to expect some originality? And if this were so, would she be capable of pronouncing on it? All modern art forms were tricky, even Hugh said that. And none more than his own speciality. First, he said, one had to distinguish between the phoney and the unfamiliar. Then one had to examine the unfamiliar closely for technical merit, and more difficult yet for that quality which would give it a right to last. Time will sort it out, he would say. What about the Impressionists? Though he'd scoffed at the price they now fetched. And she remembered how once a middle-aged man had passed them both – at the Tate, was it? – growling into his moustache as he passed the exhibits, 'It's a cod! It's a cod!' And she remembered Hugh's laugh.

She need not have worried. A daub is a daub is a daub, to misquote. Malcolm must have attempted the Barbican for her express benefit. The Barbican had its foundations in a smear of brownish fluid, probably varnish, across which was scrawled the signature of the artist . . . simply "Malcolm" without his surname. One word, like "Picasso". The painting of the Barbican was large, they had that in common.

He was watching her. "What do you think of it?"

She hesitated. "I'm not qualified to judge." The classic escape.

"It's for sale, you know."

"What are you asking?"

"No reasonable offer refused. But I could get a hundred for it from a fellow who is interested in my work."

A hundred! In an instant suspicion arose. Last evening she had parted with a cheque for three. No matter that it was for a cause that she had decided was worthy of support. By so doing she had shown herself as ready for fleecing.

She followed where the thought led her.

"Have you seen Gus?"

"No, I haven't." No need to say that he had spoken to him. "Have you?"

"Yes. He came here last night."

"And what did you make of him?"

Again she hesitated. "I was . . . impressed."

"He's one of the best. Was he in his habit?"

"Yes. I was wondering, does he wear sandals? I didn't notice and in this weather. . . ."

"No problem. Army surplus boots and socks knitted by Mum. A curious bird, isn't he?"

A bird! Mrs Jaffa!

"Not a magpie, I hope."

"What makes you say that? More like a blackbird. He used to sing in the choir. Now he's got quite a good baritone voice."

"Like Hugh's." She sighed.

There was a pause. He jerked his head towards his painting.

85

"So you don't want it?"

"I'm afraid not."

"A bit too avant-garde for you, is it? Pity. I thought it would look rather nice on your avocado wall."

She winced. Never. She would not insult Hugh's memory even to rescue Malcolm from penury. She debated whether she should give him some small sum. Perhaps amongst the rest of the collection there might be a sketch of the size she could buy and hide away. There was nothing. She had never seen a body of work so devoid of appeal. Or talent. She couldn't think how he had managed to get into any reputable college of art in the first place but the insignia of the portfolio was proof enough of that. And on a grant too. They must have had places to fill. Riffling through the lesser offerings despondently as she kept shaking her head, at last he came to a batch of nudes which he hastily turned back to front but not before she had caught a glimpse of the one on top. Pornography. Well, well. . . .

"Don't look so shocked, Aunt Bert. I can always flog those. More market for that sort of thing than for something more ambitious."

Surely the boy could not be in earnest. If he was then he was a fool which she very much doubted; and if he wasn't, then he took her for one which was worse. She determined not to give him a penny. One false step now and he would be on her back until the day of her death. Whatever she decided in the matter of her Will, she had no intention of being eaten alive. She did not deny that he was a needy case but he had contrived to exist before he met her and he must go on contriving. The earlier irritability, assuaged by the coffee, returned. Nor was Malcolm in much better humour.

He tied up his artistic efforts and remarked: "So I'll just ring up 'no sale' and be off. I'm meeting a fellow for lunch. May I leave this encumbrance with you and collect it this afternoon?"

"I'm sorry, you can't, Malcolm. I shall be out at the hairdresser's."

"What about Uncle Hugh's extra key? Let me borrow that and then I can come in and collect my stuff when I'm ready."

"How did you know I had Hugh's keys still? They should have been returned to the office."

"You told me, don't you remember?"

"Did I? Well, you can't have them anyway. They're special. They give entrance to all the houses. I wouldn't let them out of my keeping, not even for the day."

"Okay. Keep your wool on, Aunt Bert. I'll just have to leave this in your bedroom in an inconspicuous place until the next time I come."

So saying, he carried it off to the nether regions whilst she sat there in a fine state of indignation, deciding that wherever he put it, it was going to remain an eyesore for an indefinite period; an object for Concetta's disapproval.

When he came back to take his leave he said, stiffly, "Oh, by the way, Jilly asked me to tell you that she has been able to get tickets for the theatre. She said she'll be 'phoning you."

"Oh, thank you. I'm sure that I shall enjoy that."

The inference was inescapable.

The fellow Malcolm was meeting was Donald and they were meeting at a Pizza Pub on the High Walk. Though Donald admired Malcolm he never arranged to meet him anywhere too near the bank for fear they might encounter some of his colleagues.

Now as they queued up for their pizzas, Donald remarked: "We'll go Dutch today," in case there might otherwise be some misunderstanding.

"But natch," agreed Malcolm and thought that it was lucky for both of them that Aunt Bert kept her handbag in the bedroom. The pub was filling up with its lunchtime customers and when they had taken their spoil to a corner seat, Malcolm left Donald on guard whilst he went after the beer. The din was growing every minute and by his return the racket was so great that any secret was safe in it.

Donald chewed over the cheque idea in the same stolid way he disposed of his pizza, though he swallowed the one while rejecting the other.

"For one thing, the only person she'd trust with a blank cheque is Gus and he wouldn't play ball. Even if there were such a cheque it would have to go through an account. It would be far too risky to cash it in over the counter."

"I haven't got an account any more. But it could go through

yours, couldn't it? After all, it might be a birthday present."

"And what about when the cheque came back to Aunt with her monthly statement? No, take my word for it, Malcolm. That idea's a non-starter."

Malcolm's next suggestion he considered even less feasible, and when it appeared that his own baritone voice was in danger of being used as a persuader, he really took fright.

"No, look here, I say . . . this is quite mad."

He thought that Malcolm really wasn't up to his usual form today. It was as if he had suffered some kind of reverse.

"I don't see that there's any risk entailed at all. We should all be there and it only takes a glass or two of red wine to blur Aunt Bert's perceptions. I know that for a fact. Old Gus wouldn't have anyone on, neither would she. If she told him that she heard Uncle Hugh's voice, that's gospel truth. At least. . . ."

"All right. I don't dispute it. All I say is if you want a baritone voice, you use yours."

"I would but I have this peculiar timbre. She'd spot it at once. Anyway, she's more suspicious of me. I'll talk to Jilly. I daresay she could provide a baritone whisper."

"Don't you drag my sister into anything criminal."

"But it's just a joke, Donald. Even if Aunt Bert caught on it's still just a joke. And it would push things along famously. Put a little momentum into the project."

"Strikes me it's time that project died a natural death."

"No, that's reserved for Aunt Bert. Oh, come on, Donald, be your age. It might not work, I'll admit that. But if it does we're in clover. And you believe what you want to believe. That's the basis of all frau—successes. Look out!"

"What's that? What's up, Malcolm?"

"Just an olive stone shot off my plate."

"You've made me all nervy."

"I don't know why. You'd think we were going to demand money with menaces. All we are trying to do is to suggest to Aunt Bert the most useful place for her fortune when she has no further use for it. Like charities and research programmes. I bet your bank tries to persuade people what to do with their money when they're alive."

Donald temporised. "I shall have to talk it over with Jilly."

"Right. You do that. I don't know how we're going to chisel anything out of that old buzzard otherwise. I've worn myself to a frazzle trying to get her to invest in one of my best pastels. No soap."

"I should think not."

"What do you mean by that insult?"

"Didn't you know that in his heyday Uncle Hugh was one of Christie's European advisers on paintings?"

"Oh, God," said Malcolm.

For some time he digested this news and his pizza in silence. Then he demanded abruptly, "Who told you?"

"Pa or Ma, I forget which. What did you think he did for a living?"

"I dunno. Something in Import and Export like my revered parent."

"Your Pa doesn't go rocketting about all over the globe."

"Not he. He stays in his mangy old office afraid to open the window for fear he lets some heat out. But, I say, the walls in that flat are as bare as a model's bottom. How come with all that pull he didn't collar an Old Master or two to hang up?"

"Pa said that he had this bug about all great works being available to the public."

"Christie's sell to the highest bidder and that means the private collectors."

"Pa said he said that all big private collections find their way sooner or later into art galleries, because of death duties. Though they don't call them that now."

"What do they call them?"

"Inheritance Tax."

Chapter 11

In spite of her proclaimed aversion to the aged, Jilly went up
to the flat to fetch her aunt to the play. She excused herself to
herself by pretending that as it was a full house they might
miss each other in the foyer. Absurd really, for what are
foyers for if not for meeting and the one at the Barbican
however large was not like the ground floor of Harrods at sale
time. The truth was that some of Jilly's fixed ideas were
beginning to crumble a little at the edges; the gift of black
velvet may have had something to do with it. Although jib-
bing at it in the first place, Jilly was now settling down into her
role as attendant niece.

Unfortunately the rot had set in elsewhere as well.
Throughout her struggles Jilly had been sustained by belief
that her work was of the utmost importance. Shakespeare
wrote for actors and actresses even if the latter were
portrayed by boys; he didn't write for scholars and disruptive
school children to read in their text-books. There would be no
new playwrights if there was no stage and amongst these there
might be another Shakespeare even if at the present it didn't
seem likely. Malcolm's remarks on the subject had shaken
her. Not that she gave credence to all that he said but the
words of a cynic always cast the first shadow of doubt. About
the market she had never had any illusions. It was horribly
crowded and although not unduly modest she admitted that
there were others in the profession more gifted and still
unable to obtain a foothold. She must finish her course,
taking care not to fall by the wayside, but once that was done
how useful, how very useful a little money might be. She

91

could cut a dash at more parties, make useful contacts, even attract an agent or a talent-spotter.

So, much to Donald's surprise, when he explained Malcolm's new project to her – which to his practical mind seemed pure fantasy – not only did she give it her blessing but he had a suspicion that she had heard it all before. Malcolm had got to her first. Donald had often played at being jealous, now he knew the real thing. Although agreeing that he should be the go-between, Malcolm had gone behind his back.

A factor in Jilly's compliance of which he was unaware was that she was now into Restoration Comedy in a big way. As the over-riding theme in this was the gross deception of the old rich for the benefit of the young and impoverished, she had begun to think of it as normal.

"In the beginning you were the one to hold back," he grumbled at her, "and now that he's come up with this simply crazy scheme you're all for it."

"Women's privilege. I can't see that it will do any harm anyway and it might be amusing. A bit of a giggle."

"How do you get the message over? Are you banking on a long distance call from outer space? Or will you whisper it through the entryphone?"

"We're thinking of giving a party."

"A party!"

From his childhood Donald had hated parties. He had to be taken to them by force and then he skulked in a corner whilst Jilly, in her element in frills, had shown off to the admiration of all. And she had given the game away by that plural.

"You've been meeting Malcolm on the sly," he said accusingly.

"He rang up. We had a chat on the blower. All it will take is a whisper, you're right about that. And I don't mind doing it. Malcolm's quite right. He can't speak more than one word on the telephone before I spot that it's him."

"In my opinion he's just trying to shift the blame if it's a cock-up."

"What blame? If Aunt catches on I should just laugh it off."

"Ha-ha. And also ho-ho. Did Malc think to tell you what a boob he made with our well-heeled aunt?"

"What was that?"

92

"He tried to sell her one of his paintings. Trouble with him is that he never does his homework. He thought that Uncle Hugh was some sort of dealer in foreign commodities. He soon got brushed off if you'll pardon the pun. Is his stuff any good, do you think?"

"Who? Malcolm's? I've never seen any. I don't think it can be after what he said at the Barbican. If he was a real artist he couldn't stop doing it."

"That settles it then. If he was so mad keen for money why did he go in for art?"

"He'd have done anything to get away from home. I guess they raised his expectations at school just as they did mine. On the strength of playing Puck in the *Dream*. If you're not good at anything else naturally you have to be tops at art. I shouldn't be surprised if he got his place at the college by that cunning old Rupert using Uncle Hugh's name."

"If so he didn't tell Malc. How long does that course last?"

"Three years if you don't drop out."

"So he's all right until then. What happens after?"

"If Uncle Rupert hasn't snuffed it he'll just have to live on his wits."

"That's just what I'm afraid of," said Donald gloomily.

"Well, he won't go into a religious order like Gus."

"Ah, Gus. Where does he fit in? Will you be asking him to your party?"

"Of course, when we've got a firm date. Then he will have to get permission from the Father Superior. We shan't let Gus in on the histrionics."

"He wouldn't stand for it."

"All he has to do is to ask for leave to attend."

"That shouldn't be difficult . . . in the circumstances."

"What circumstances?"

"Didn't Malcolm tell you that Aunt gave Gus a whacking great cheque for the monks?"

"So that's why he tried to sell her a painting," said Jilly, adding two to two as easily as Donald had missed the connection.

"No, he only told me about the voice. I know that he had that from Gus."

They were sitting facing each other at a small round table in

93

a coffee shop due to close down at any moment now as everything did in the City in the evening. He had asked Jilly to meet him here in order to warn her about Malcolm, and look what had happened.

"He's basing this whole hare-brained scheme on information he got secondhand."

"Gus never told a lie in his life."

"Yes, but. . . ."

"Don't you see, that's the beauty of it? Aunt would never tell us. She's far too cagey. And if she thinks we don't know she won't be on the look-out for tricks. I don't suppose that Gus should have passed it on and he wouldn't have done if he hadn't been over-excited about the cash for St Joe's."

"He's obsessed by the wretched Order. He'd do anything to keep it in England."

"No, he wouldn't. He'd back off from anything dubious."

"So should we, Jilly."

"There's nothing illegal in being kind to an aunt," she retorted defiantly.

"If you call deception kindness. . . ."

"Kindness is deception too, isn't it? Like taking her off to *Macbeth*."

"Is that what you're doing?"

"Do you suppose I enjoy theatre-going with someone antique enough to have seen Garrick in the title role?"

"Don't be a fool, Jilly."

"Well, Wolfit anyway."

"That's what you've done with your second cream cake. Come on, time to go. They're shutting up shop."

He rose from his chair clutching the check, but before he had reached the desk she caught at his sleeve. "Wait, whisper me something."

Obediently he put his mouth near her ear.

"Who's going to pay this bill?"

Up on her toes to gain the right height, she whispered back: "Why, you, you bloated plutocrat."

And then in her normal tones, "There, you see, you're a baritone but there isn't a scrap of difference. A whisper is a whisper and that's all there is to it."

But, piloting her aunt down the steps to the centre, Jilly was

94

silent. The old lady was more fragile than she had expected and the stairs awkward, too wide for one stride and too narrow for two. It would have astonished her to have discovered that Bertha felt guilty too. She thought that she might have given her young relation a false notion of her mobility. Really she moved around in a very small radius. When she wanted to go to the bank or anywhere outside the Barbican she either hired a car or took a taxi. She had never been a good walker and through lack of exercise her legs often behaved as if they did not exactly belong to her.

Once safely in the foyer she was glad to be planted on a seat whilst Jilly went off for a programme.

Bertha had often been to this theatre with Hugh. Going with Jilly was different. She felt rather like a child being taken to see its first pantomime. As soon as the doors opened her niece led her off to the stalls. Bertha was more than a little relieved. She was afraid that, as the tickets were complimentary, they might be destined for the heights. They were first in and there they sat in the middle of that vast auditorium all alone, Bertha full of a quiet satisfaction and wondering how on earth Jilly had managed it.

But Jilly was still strangely silent. Staring out at the dark, deserted stage on which four standards limply drooping were set at angles in front of simulated grey granite, she was held in the grip of a daunting psychic experience. Suddenly she felt as if the great open stage was shifting and drawing closer and closer, growing narrower as it came, and that the action beginning to enfold on it embodied herself and her aunt. She wanted to call out that it was make-believe like everything else done in the portrayal of drama, and anyway she had forgotten her lines. That it was utterly bogus to see any likeness to poor King Duncan in Aunt Bertha. Certainly they were both old and mild-mannered, but betrayal . . . how ridiculous. And it wasn't a dagger she was holding too tightly, only the handle of her stumpy umbrella.

"They're beginning to come in," said her aunt's voice, trying to penetrate her preoccupation. "You're miles away, Jilly."

"'If it were done when 'tis done, then 'twere well it were done quickly'," she gabbled at random, those words springing to mind.

"Always reminds me of 'Peter Piper picked a peck of pickled peppers'," said Bertha irreverently.

Jilly had rallied. She was quick to ad lib.

"I was thinking about what to do with my Potts."

"Your pots?" repeated Bertha, completely mystified.

"My horrid name, darling. What do you advise?"

"Marriage."

"You must be joking!"

"Well, I know your objections. What about adding a 'de' like Defoe. He hadn't any right to it either."

Jilly giggled. "De Potts!"

"No, I can see . . . I didn't think that it posed any real problem. I thought that you just chose a name that you fancied and that was the one they put on the programme."

"It's not quite as simple as that, but I know how to *do* it. It's the choosing . . . I mean it has to be once and forever . . . and all the names I come up with sound so horribly bogus."

"What could be more bogus than Marilyn Monroe? It didn't seem to interfere with her career."

Jilly raised her delicate eyebrows and widened her eyes in a very actressy gesture.

"Why not consult the telephone directory? They can't all be bogus though they may be phoney."

Bertha congratulated herself. She was growing brighter by the minute; it was getting away from the flat. But this sally had no effect on Jilly who complained: "The trouble is that it has to go with what's there."

"You mean Jilly? Why not go back to Jillian as it must have been in the first place."

"No, it really is Jilly. Ma insisted; she had a row with the priest. He maintained that there wasn't such a name."

How like sister Alice that was: mistaken but stubborn.

"I should scrap both of them. If you can get rid of the second surely you can get rid of the first?"

"That's just what you can't. No one will let you. My best friend re-christened herself 'Melanie' but everybody still calls her 'Maude'."

"Do they ask her to come into the garden?"

Jilly's brows wrinkled. She wasn't old enough to know what this meant.

By now the theatre was full and the play due to begin. The brass-bound doors at the sides were sliding to a close, the lights dimmed in the auditorium and brightened on the stage and Bertha settled down into her seat with a small sign of content. With the first entrance of Lady Macbeth she stole a look at her niece and there, to her surprise, was a different person. Jilly sat leaning a little forward drinking in the words, sometimes unconsciously mouthing them. She was up on the stage with the rest of them. Bertha no longer had any doubt about Jilly's vocation. There was the actress. But wasn't she, also, playing a role off the stage? And is this role for my benefit? Bertha asked herself with a small sense of shock. Most intelligent people present a face to suit their company . . . but does this girl really think that the way she projects herself is a suitable presentation for me? If so, I must really appear to her as a nitwit; a sobering thought.

Jilly was right. Bertha had seen many *Macbeths* and some with famous players. She could not remember their names though she could still remember what Hugh had said about it.

"A bowl of scotch broth souped up for King James."

The witches made that quite clear. Was it possible in any production now to make them convincing? she wondered, and decided that it wasn't. The scenery was scanty but the costumes were good. How glad she was they hadn't transposed it to the thirties. She remembered seeing the costumes in Ellen Terry's old home somewhere in Sussex and how sad and inadequate she had thought them. From that she passed to reflecting on the great mystery of memory. Why, for instance, search her mind as she might, she could never come up with the name of the girl who did her hair regularly? And if this was a defect in short-term memory common to the aged, why was the other kind so selective. Why should she recollect Hugh's rather fatuous remark about *Macbeth* when she couldn't remember any who had taken the title role? Perhaps because it was Hugh and because his disparagement was in line with her own feelings. She didn't think much of *Macbeth* and surely, if it hadn't been written by Shakespeare, everyone would have admitted that it was melodrama and full of false facts? A play more acceptable for its blood and thunder than for its psychology. How did a real murderer behave? Was she qualified to say when she didn't know any? Fortunately for her such matters were out of her province.

It was the interval. Jilly, now back on terra firma, said that they should stay in their seats unless her aunt wanted to go to the loo. Bertha said that was all right but now she was too hot. So Jilly helped her out of the sleeves of her fur jacket and draped it round her shoulders instead.

"Pretty pussy," she remarked, stroking the soft mink. "Just what I should like for my birthday."

But Bertha was too old a bird to be caught by such chaff; also, in view of her changed estimate of Jilly's character and behaviour, she had become wary.

She responded by saying: "As a matter of fact it's *my* birthday next week."

She was astonished by the reaction. Jilly's blue eyes widened; she expressed instant delight.

"Oh, darling, we must have a party in the flat, just the five of us. What date is it?"

"The fifteenth. But I don't think . . . I couldn't cope. . . ."

"But you don't have to do anything. What an idea! You're the party person. We provide the eats and the drinks. You just sit there and wait for it to happen. I'll contact the boys."

In the face of such enthusiasm it seemed churlish to produce objections even if she could have thought of any on the spur of the moment. It was easier to let it go, hoping that the others would dissuade her. Besides the audience was beginning to drift back. People stepping over her feet made further conversation impossible.

The second half of the performance was a worse trial to Bertha than she had anticipated. She began to have cramp, she started to fidget. The effort of concentration after long spells of silence in the flat had begun to tell on her. Speeches began to seem dull and interminable. Never had anyone wished more fervently for Birnam Wood to start coming to Dunsinane. At last it did and everything came to a grand finale with plenty of smoke and explosions. And then the cast were taking their curtain calls and she was able to stretch her legs which had become uncommonly stiff and which would have to see her back to the flat. Jilly took her to the Silk Street lift and there left her with a last cheerful wave and "see you on

Thursday". Thursday . . . her birthday! Now she was furious with herself for having mentioned it. She crawled past the bookshop, scene of that famous encounter with Mrs Jaffa, and then through the booking hall; it seemed like the end of a Marathon. Eventually she was safe home and sank upon the sofa without even the initiative to fetch herself a stiff drink. What a fool I am to think that I can do what I once did, she chided herself.

As soon as she had heard the Nine o'clock News, after a light supper of a poached egg on toast she went off to bed though not to sleep. She tossed and turned and finally fell into a light doze from which she woke hot and sweaty as she had felt in the theatre. She did not know it but she was about to suffer her second attack of nerves, the first symptom of which was that she felt the bed begin to move under her as if there was a man underneath making contact with the mattress. This was an illusion that she hadn't experienced since childhood and at her present age she recognised it as false. She did not know what caused it but the effect was unpleasant. There were two drawers under her bed filled with towels and if any man could get under that he would have had to have gone under a steam roller first. That did not prevent her from making sure. Then, emboldened but apprehensive, she opened one built-in cupboard door after another, moving the clothes on the coat arms but still discovering no intruder. She would have liked to search the entire flat but cowardice held her back.

She pulled on her housecoat and, first putting out the light, went to the window and lifting one edge of the curtain, peered out from behind it. No, no one on the balcony and she made certain that the window was shut; she usually kept it open a crack. Then she looked out again and through the net curtain under the velvet one met the blind stare of concrete. There was not the panorama that there was from the front although through a gap between buildings she could see the flower-beds of Exhibition Road. The scrutiny did not remove her fears because they were inside her. She blamed *Macbeth* for her fancies. She was beginning to think that there was more in that bloody old play than met the eye, or the ear, just as there was in her niece, Jilly. Was it like a ghost story in which one

99

had not the slightest shred of belief but which, if well-written, could bring out the goose pimples? Did that tale of deceit, treachery and murder still have enough power to penetrate the walls of the Barbican and frighten an old lady out of her wits when she knew that in reality her life was entirely remote from such happenings and thus there was no cause for alarm?

She looked for comfort towards Hugh's empty bed on the opposite side of the room but tonight, wherever he was, he had no comment for her. She stared at it until she imagined she saw movement in the shape under the masculine bedspread he had favoured. Pillows, of course; they had to be left somewhere.

Sleeping pills, that was the answer. As she had before forced herself to reach the television now she forced herself to go to the bathroom. There she found the tablets, scrabbled two out of their plastic nests and swallowed them down with a draught of bottled water. Then, sure of succour, she found her way to the bed, shed her robe and crept between the sheets. Mercifully, before long medication claimed her. Felled by the blunt end of its axe she slept . . . like the dead.

Chapter 12

The next morning Bertha woke with a hangover from her two tablets. It had happened before. One was too little, two were too much. She felt muzzy and languid. She made herself a large cup of instant coffee and, drinking it, began to come round. She recollected without any pleasure that it was Concetta's day to be with her. For the *tuttifare* had repented her recent departure. It was a grand gesture to leave her pay on the kitchen counter but soon regretted as it affected her budget. The work-load here was not half as demanding as it was in some other flats and she had a genuine regard for her lady even if it manifested itself in some curious ways. And Bertha could not do without her help, that also was true, so they existed in a state of truce.

What about this party? If party there was to be and the whole idea wasn't simply one of Jilly's wilder conceptions. Certainly her birthday was due but after a certain age one becomes scary of birthdays although Hugh always remembered to send flowers. But any hint of such an occasion must be kept secret from Concetta. If there was debris to be cleared up afterwards, that would be soon enough. She would be bound to disapprove and therefore could not be asked to bring provisions from the supermarket. But Jilly had said . . . but what exactly had Jilly said? Bertha did not want to remember her emotions of the night before; such things were better forgotten. They were "Hecate" inspired and vanished in daylight.

There was a knock at the door, followed by another. Oh damn, that would be Malcolm come to collect his wretched portfolio. Determined to send him off smartly, she could not abide these morning visitations, Bertha flung open the door, only to be confronted by Mrs Jaffa, looking at her nervously.

"Could I have a word?" she said.

"Better come in," replied Bertha ungraciously, thinking what an absurd way to put it. But it had an unpleasant association. People had "words" when something upset them. Mrs Jaffa must have a complaint to make.

"No, I would rather you came into mine," she now said and added as explanation, "I am expecting a call from my husband."

"Very well then. Let me just get my bag." She had no intention of being locked out and was already preparing the excuse to return to her own abode whilst following Mrs Jaffa into hers, where the door had been left ajar. She had never been in Mrs Jaffa's flat before and she could not help noting that it was curiously furnished as if with an assortment of those strange unrelated components to be found in consultants' waiting rooms all the way down Harley Street.

Mrs Jaffa was obviously in a state of the jitters. She was alarmed yet elated, like a child who has done wrong and enjoyed it but now awaits the reckoning. Bertha sat down uninvited; it was folly to expect the suggestion to come from her hostess.

"I am afraid that you are going to be very angry with me," began Mrs Jaffa.

Now what had the stupid woman been up to? Had her kleptomania been active again? Has she filched something from me which her husband had instructed her to return?

"You didn't put your rubbish out for collection last night."

Perfectly true, she hadn't. The boxes and papers and bottles, in fact anything which could not be swallowed by the Garchey, had to be stuffed into brown paper bags supplied by the management and put outside the door for early collection by the porter three times a week. It had been one of Hugh's self-imposed duties but she had been careful to keep up with it.

She knew that the porters were instructed to watch out for people living alone in case they were in trouble. No brown bag was the equivalent of an empty milk bottle. The previous evening she had been too tired to remember to do it but she had been quick to see that it was done in the morning before Lennie came by on his rounds. Now there was a pregnant pause in which she became increasingly apprehensive.

"We are always being asked to care for our not-so-young neighbours," began Mrs Jaffa, the soul of tact. "You will observe that I am a caring person."

Bertha stared up at this angel of mercy.

"I thought . . . I thought," stammered Mrs Jaffa, losing her nerve.

"Never mind what you thought," said Bertha grimly. "Just tell me what you did."

"I tried to phone you. There was no reply."

"I'd been to the theatre. I was not able to sleep. So I'd taken two sleeping tablets. Then what?" But she knew. She guessed.

"I . . . I 'phoned the housekeeper's office."

"Oh, yes."

"And they phoned the police."

"Well?"

"They came up."

"Who came up?"

"The man from the housekeeper's office. And . . . and the police."

"Then what happened?"

"They could see a light inside your door."

"I always leave it on. In case I wake up in the night."

"Well, they have a key."

"My God! you mean they tried to get in?"

"The police have to be there if there is an entry. You must know that, Mrs Harris."

"So they got in. They actually came into my flat?"

"No, they didn't. They couldn't because you'd put the chain across."

So something was saved; some shred of dignity. A habit had saved her. Her home was still inviolate. And as that chain would never have defeated any policeman really in earnest, that meant that the policemen had doubts. And who wouldn't have doubts about Mrs Jaffa? Donald had doubts.

"Was your husband there?"

"Yes, he was. Why do you ask?"

But she was genuinely perturbed and on her guard now. For despite his looks the Doctor was a force to be reckoned with. "Pop you inside a loony bin before you could say 'no, thank you'," Hugh had once joked.

"He had great concern," said his wife primly. "Things are not like they were when Mr Harris was alive. Many young men coming and going at all hours. And such scare the crows."

"Mind what you say about my relations! They are students and perfectly respectable," exclaimed Bertha who had never thought so before. "Students, excepting one and he is a bank employee." It sounded better than "clerk".

"Apart from that, my dear, you might have fallen. That could have happened to anybody. You might have been lying there helpless, unable to contact your neighbours."

"So, having decided that you'd raised a false alarm, what happened then? The gallant investigators went back to the station."

"No, they didn't, dear," proclaimed Mrs Jaffa with a sly air of triumph. "They came to the conclusion that you weren't in the front room so the police went through the fire door and had a look into your bedroom."

"You mean they *entered* it?"

"Oh no. There was a gap between the curtains. Just a small gap, more like a slit. They applied their eyes to it."

"What! When I was in bed policemen were out on my balcony snooping on me!"

"It's not snooping, dear. It's caring. And anyway there was the net in between."

"Then I can do without caring." Bertha felt anger rising in her. It started from the pit of her stomach and worked its way upwards. Her privacy had been invaded. So strong was the impact of this disclosure that she was sure that she had been awake in the night to see two eyes glaring in upon her. *Macbeth* indeed!

"Presumably they finally decided that I was still alive but asleep."

"They had to wait to see movement. You were lying so still, dear."

"And if I had been dead," said Bertha, "couldn't I have waited until morning?"

Rage, such as she had never known before mounted in her. Words began to pour forth.

"You are a wicked, wicked woman! You have poisoned your husband's mind against me. You want to make me look silly, to make people believe that I am not fit to live here alone. I shall be ashamed now to go to the housekeeper's office. I shall never dare seek help from the police. And all for nothing, because just that once I forgot to put out a bag. You must have heard me go out. You must have heard me come back. It wasn't even late. And I was with a young woman, not a young man. You are not sane, you steal things because you can't help it. But what do you want to steal now? My reputation as a responsible person . . . my name for good sense? Or do you want me out of my flat?"

Both women were trembling; one from passion, one from sheer fear.

"You have not heard the last of this," threatened Bertha, and grabbed up her bag and flung out of the door. It took her several seconds before she could find her key and several more before she could fit it into the lock.

She fumbled about in the cupboard until she got hold of a very small bottle of brandy, kept for an emergency. If this wasn't an emergency she didn't know what was.

Shuddering as each swallow went down she thought in despair: It is I who haven't heard the last of it.

When she had the brandy inside her and had calmed down a little, she began to go through the whole rigmarole as carefully as if she were examining a slide under the microscope. First she had to be clear about her neighbour's motive for the excuse of caring was really too thin. The Jaffas had never even sent a letter of condolence at the time of Hugh's death. As for the missing bag, living alone she might not have had enough rubbish to put out, and anyway surely she was entitled to one lapse of memory? Having set such an uncalled for train of events in action, the kindest thing would have been to have kept quiet about it, thought Bertha. She had to *tell* me, she had to *gloat*. Whatever did I do to her to provoke her ill-will? Nothing. Ah, but think again. Think back to the

Terrace Restaurant. That wasn't *my* fault. No, but you discovered a disreputable secret. She will never forgive you for that.

Did it matter? Of course it mattered. It opened her eyes to all sorts of alarming possibilities to which she had hitherto not given a thought. For instance, the flat. Although they had only rented it, she had taken it for granted that here she would remain until she died . . . or had a stroke . . . or broke a thigh . . . or. . . . The lease ended, one asked for a new one and the rent rose; otherwise there was no problem. If necessary she could buy it. That was the tendency nowadays and the policy of the management. But suppose the management was led to suspect that she was unreliable, a danger to other tenants? Capable of leaving on a hot-plate and setting fire to the block? If she lost the flat what would she do then? She who had lived here so long that she simply couldn't envisage settling anywhere else.

A new idea occurred to her. Did the Doctor want her flat for his own purposes . . . was the Harley Street lease about to run out? Did he plan to see patients here and nobble her as the first?

Right at the back of Bertha's mind lurked the worst suspicion of all. But it had to be brought forth and subjected to close scrutiny like the rest.

Had something gone wrong with her? Had the shock of Hugh's death put her off balance? What was the word Patsy had used: paranoia? The persecution complex. She was joking, of course. But Patsy was shrewd, and often her jokes had a hard centre.

Had her reaction to Mrs Jaffa's revelations been stupid? Wouldn't it have been far better to have laughed it off? She could have turned the whole episode into farce, instead of giving it further importance. How had the subject cropped up with Patsy . . . what were they discussing? It was Concetta, now she remembered. That peculiar new mistrust of Concetta of all people. Was there anyone else she had been misjudging lately? Yes, indeed . . . Jilly.

Immediately on waking (and how long ago that now seemed) she realised that going to *Macbeth* had been a mistake. She had enjoyed it but it had been too much for her. But this was not Jilly's fault. Throughout her niece had shown commendable kindness. She had procured the free tickets, come to fetch her, and if she had not brought her back, no doubt on a Saturday evening she had other plans in view. It is I who have to understand her and not the other way about; I have been young once, she has never been old. The reaction of any young girl to mink, unless she is against it ethically, is to want it. Well, in the future that mantle might descend on her. Her delight at the idea of a party, which Bertha shrank from as much as did Donald, was so spontaneous that it had to be true. Jilly might be silly but it was equally silly to imagine her steeped in guile. She must watch herself, Bertha decided miserably enough. No one likes to find themselves slipping. And if Mrs Jaffa held a grudge what a pity it was that Dr Jaffa couldn't be told that his wife could help herself to the top of St Paul's dome for all she cared.

At this point she could have made use of a little sympathetic advice. It was not something one took to a lawyer, one needed an old friend who could be frank. But, as she had told Patsy, the old friends were . . . dead. Let her not shrink from the word. A close relative would be equally frank and enjoy it but she was not prepared to ask Rupert, Alice, or even Fred, if they considered her to be unhinged. Certainly she felt alone and very shaken and frightened.

There was a knock at the door and she had struggled up and reached it before she decided that she could not, simply could not, face Mrs Jaffa again. Then there was a cascade of knocks and she remembered Concetta. Of course this was Concetta. She opened the door and there stood the *tuttifare* armed with the tools of her trade. If she hadn't looked so aggressive, her lady could have hugged her.

As for Concetta, one look was enough. "What is up now?" she demanded. "I will keel that nevvew."

Bertha hastened to save Malcolm from annihilation by remote control. "It is nothing to do with him. I have just had a row with my neighbour."

"Not Mrs Sprite?" It was Concetta's turn to look disturbed. Mrs Sprite was to her the acme of perfection, so smart, so lively, never forgetting to ask after her family which had long since been banished from their descendant's recollection.

107

"No, no, of course not. Mrs Jaffa."

"Oh, that *orange*. I spite out her pips!"

Robbed of her natural reserve, Bertha blurted out the whole miserable story, only omitting Mrs Jaffa's little idiosyncracy for decency's sake. No need for her caution as Concetta knew all about that already. Surprisingly she was as upset as Bertha by what had occurred. Not because of loyalty to her employer but because the intrusion was an affront to her own sense of propriety. To have strange men peering in on females in bed was not her idea of what was fitting. Hitherto her chief complaint against Mrs Jaffa was that her head appeared round the door every time she, Concetta, came out of the lift. A small irritation one might think, but small irritations to one of Concetta's constitution were not welcome. Now she had a real grievance. Mrs Jaffa had interfered in what was not her business. To note whether a garbage bag was out or not was Lennie's affair. As porter to this particular house, Lennie had the sole right to discover if one of his tenants was in distress or had died. Lennie was willing and conscientious if not too strong in the head. He had his own ways of rewarding or punishing those in his care. She would speak to Lennie.

First things first.

"You go along to the bedroom and get into your nightie," she advised Bertha, uncharacteristically gentle. "And pull the thick curtains. I will whip you up two eggs in brandy. Very good. Very pulling-together."

"Not eggs," implored Bertha, to whom even the sight of egg outside its shell would at this moment have proved disastrous. "And not brandy, I have had that already."

"What then?"

"Bread and milk," said Bertha in desperation. She had not tasted this since childhood, but it was the only thing to occur to her.

"Hot milk?"

"Oh, I suppose so. And a spoonful of sugar."

She supposed that it was being sent to bed like a child that had prompted the request. But she was glad to go. She felt bone-weary and longed for oblivion.

When she was in bed, Concetta appeared with a steaming bowl on a tray.

108

"First eat this and then sleep. I will go on with my work but not the 'oover today. Then I go out and close the door softly. Would you like me to ask Mrs Sprite to look in later?"

"No, I don't want . . . what about your money?"

"Next time, that will do."

She went out, leaving the door open so that she should be within call if her lady wanted her. But sometimes Concetta could be understanding. She understood that Bertha was not ready for Mrs Sprite yet; that she did not want anybody. Wounded pride can only heal itself and the best way to hasten the progress was to take refuge in sleep.

Chapter 13

The first thing that Bertha saw on her natal morning was the bowl of cold milk sop now covered by a scaly skin. It was an unwelcome reminder of what had gone before. She put on her dressing gown and carried it down the corridor and into the kitchen where she emptied it into the Garchey before making a pot of tea. Exhausted emotionally, she had slept the whole night through without the aid of any pill. Now she felt clear in the head but weak in the body as if she was at the start of a long convalescence. She did not want to listen to the news where one point of view was eternally being balanced by another. Instead she mulled over her own programme for the day.

She would have to write a short note of apology to Mrs Jaffa for behaving like a fishwife. That need not be done in a hurry as it was more to put herself right with herself than with Mrs Jaffa. Later she would take a taxi and go down to her bank in Smithfield where the busy bustle of the meat market was always of interest. It would be a sad loss when it went, she thought, though not likely to affect her. If what it dealt in was dead, it was itself lively and living, as opposed to the dull fronts of office buildings encroaching upon it. And she enjoyed the shops in Farringdon Street where as a tribute to her age she often received overweight or was undercharged. This was true compassion coming from the true Cockney, so spontaneous that it warmed the heart.

She had entirely forgotten that it was her birthday until she opened the letter box and found the four cards. Gus had found a print of his patron saint and St Joe clung to one corner of the chapel roof looking like a sleepy fly and no doubt wishing to be back on terra firma. "Hoping to be with you" was inscribed on the back. Donald's was white, chastely embossed in gold and saying that he would see her at seven o'clock. Jilly's had a harlequin with a home-made balloon issuing from his mouth stating "We bring the nosh". The fourth was signed "Your penitent Malcolm" and featured a bunch of primroses, very uncharacteristic of him.

Absurd children but she couldn't help feeling grateful for their remembrance, whatever motive was behind it. As for Malcolm he could demonstrate his penitence by taking his confounded portfolio away with him. If Concetta hadn't been preoccupied with other matters, her attention would surely have fastened upon that.

She dressed, rang up the wine merchant to replenish her small selection of drinks, with directions to deliver the order in the late afternoon. Then she set forth as she had planned. Her bank was an old-fashioned one; as yet it had not been refurbished with elevators, so if you wanted to discuss securities you went up in a lift to the second floor. At the moment all she wanted to do was to cash a cheque; the only progress attached to this was for the cashier to look at a computer to see if you had anything there. Often one saw white-coated workers from the Market paying in or drawing out, she was never sure which. These homely touches she and Hugh had cherished, they were a part of London fast vanishing, never to return. She did not reach Farringdon Street which suddenly seemed a great distance away but she walked back alongside Charterhouse Square, still hanging on to the last remnants of its individuality. She waited for others to join her as she fondly believed that there was safety in numbers, before crossing the street back to the Barbican and security.

In the afternoon she put her feet up and rested as she was unsure what a party for young people entailed. Would they want pop music; would they stay on until midnight? She was glad they were coming. Their antics were new to her and made her realise how different they were at close quarters from anything that she had envisaged.

Malcolm was the first to arrive, he came on the heels of the delivery boy from the wine-shop. He had made no attempt to

112

improve his appearance, that would have been foreign to his nature, but he was very subdued.

He put down the bag he was carrying before wishing her a happy birthday and kissing her on both cheeks.

"I am ashamed," he said, regarding her steadily. "Why didn't you tell me about Uncle Hugh?"

She didn't answer that question directly as she fancied that it would have taken too long to explain. Instead she used a question to reply.

"How did you find out?"

"From your reaction to my awful paintings. It was informed. So I started asking around at the College; not the students but the academic types and I soon had the answer."

He could just as easily have told her that he had it from Donald but he was never at a loss for a lie and often found that it was more readily believed than the truth.

"I was so afraid you might be deluding yourself."

"Oh, no, I knew that it was all frightful. The whole performance bores me to tears. But no one troubles as long as you're fairly regular in attendance, and I don't want to have to pay back my grant. When the time's up, we'll see."

"What shall we see?"

A nice big legacy from a rich relation. He nearly said it and might even have got away with it once. But this wasn't the evening for sheer impudence, there was too much at stake. And now they were nearly on the old footing, it would be silly to take risks.

"Oh, I might go for a soldier," he said lightly. "Aunt Bert, may I stash my little gift in your fridge? It's a bottle of fizz."

Did you steal it? Aunt Bert, like Malcolm, re-phrased the first words about to spring from her tongue and said: "Oh, Malcolm, you shouldn't."

"And you shouldn't either, you naughty woman. Didn't we say we were to be the providers?" He was referring to the bottles which she had not yet had the opportunity to put away.

"I don't see why you should spend your money on an old woman who has . . . who has some of her own."

"Oh, but that's simply to show how much we think of you," he replied, speaking the truth in this instance.

113

Further exchanges of mutual goodwill were at this point interrupted by the arrival of Jilly and Donald, both loaded with cartons and Jilly heartily singing "Happy birthday to you" in a nasal cockney.

Bertha stopped her in mid-song and hastily closed the door behind them. The last thing she wanted to do was to bring out Mrs Jaffa. Neither did she intend to tell them of the episode with her neighbour as it might start them thinking that she was losing her grip. In the light of recent events she might need them to testify to her sanity. Sometimes it was good to be safe in the heart of a family though she had never felt this when Hugh was alive. Apart from Gus, she did not think that they would have been so ready to seek out a poor widow mewed up in one room at the back of the street market. But Bertha was a realist. They were roughing it here in comparison with life in their middle-class homes; even Rupert lived in a largish house in a good neighbourhood. They may have been as glad to come to her flat as she was to have them. Patsy and Sam were today off on a flight to their sun-drenched island. She would miss their protective presence. It might be useful to have someone close at hand in an emergency. Donald? Perhaps even Donald might improve on acquaintance.

She was pleased and embarrassed by this lavish expenditure on her behalf by those who could least afford it. But her speech of thanks was interrupted by Jilly saying: "Don't fuss, darling. Now all we want is some dinner plates. We've brought you the nosh instead of a pressie."

"She means that we've brought you the food instead of a gift," translated Donald. As it had all come out of his pocket he wanted his aunt to know exactly what she was getting and what it stood for.

Jilly had already brought the plates from the cupboard and was arranging the contents of the cartons upon them.

"You can't have the champagne yet. It hasn't had time to chill," said Malcolm. "It should be in ice in a bucket."

"Perfectionist! We can have some sherry for starters."

"Is that OK with you, Aunt Bert?"

"Of course, Malcolm."

"Then I'll get down the glasses."

"I've just been reading a book by Virginia Woolf, where

114

somebody asks for a corkscrew to open the champagne," said Bertha. "Isn't that odd?"

Malcolm, to whom the name meant nothing but part of a title of a play he had never seen, soon dealt with that.

"They never had to open the bottles themselves, or else they never had any."

Jilly had been to a city caterers at Moorgate, she said, where she knew one of the girls. It was quite a spread. Little vols au vent, bite-sized sausage rolls, tiny sandwiches. . . .

"There's even an iced cake," she announced proudly.

"But, Jilly, it must have cost pounds."

"Oh, it's nothing, darling."

Donald winced. As provider of the feast he was now regarding it as a dud investment. Of all the escapades he had been persuaded into by Malcolm, this was the wildest. And if it went wrong, he doubted if Jilly would scrape out of it as easily as she imagined. Aunt might report it to the parents and then the balloon would go up.

How enchanting she looks tonight, thought Bertha, and it has nothing to do with her clothes for she was wearing a sort of dun-coloured unadorned shift. If she can be so keyed up for such a small occasion she must be very sophisticated at heart.

What a fool the girl is, thought Malcolm irritably, and handed her a frown along with her sherry. She acts as if she's in the wings waiting to go on stage. And Donald as glum as if his precious bank has gone bust. He must steer a course between the two of them. He gave Bertha a sherry and Donald a double dose in a larger glass before he poured out his own.

"We can't toast you yet, Aunt Bert," he explained, "we must wait for Gus to be here."

"Gus only drinks water," said Donald.

"Then he can have Perrier," said Jilly. "He can't be excommunicated for drinking a few bubbles."

The entry phone buzzed.

"There he is! Drink up your sherry!"

It was indeed Gus and in a suit instead of his habit.

"Why aren't you in your fancy dress costume?" enquired Jilly.

"It ponged a little," admitted Gus. "I'd been cleaning up after the hens. Father Superior thought this would be better.

He sent his kindest regards, Aunt, along with best birthday wishes."

"And well he might," muttered Malcolm under his breath.

So he did know, thought Bertha, who happened to catch it. He and Gus are in communication. She didn't mistrust Gus. Who could? But it explained why Malcolm had tried to sell her a painting; he was competing. She took her unfinished sherry and went into the living room where she and Gus settled on the sofa.

"Did you like your card?" he asked.

"Very much. The saint looked so bewildered, poor fellow. And I remembered you both when I walked through the Market this morning and stepped over a pig's tail."

"A live pig?"

"No, a dead one."

"Weren't you disgusted," asked Jilly joining them.

"Not exactly. I was relieved that modern farming methods had allowed him to keep his tail till the end."

They all laughed at this though it scarcely deserved it and suddenly the mood of the party was set, intimate and good-humoured. Malcolm stayed in the kitchen to deal with the champagne which he said they would have to drink from the old shallow glasses as Aunt Bert had no others. Gus told them the story about when his father, knowing how short the Order was of funds, sent them two fat lambs.

"Alive?"

"No, dead and skinned. The trouble was that they hadn't the foggiest idea what to do with them."

"And you cut them up?"

"No, I didn't. I didn't know how. I wheeled them round to the local butcher and gave him two joints for his pains."

"On a bike?"

"No, a barrow. One at a time. They were fearfully weighty."

"So then all was well?"

"So-so. I tried to cook some of it on a makeshift barbecue in the yard. But it ended up half raw and the smell and the smoke drifted all over the neighbourhood. So we stoked up the old kitchen range with billets of wood and cooked it in the oven, roast after roast."

"I hope the monks were properly appreciative."

"They were. I wasn't. I had far too much lamb to eat at the farm. Malcolm, do you remember that we always had lamb . . . or mutton?"

Malcolm came out with the champagne glasses on a tray and they all drank a toast to their aunt, though Gus drank his in water. Bertha in reply had to put her glass down to look for her handkerchief. The celebration was quite different from what she had expected. She and Gus remained where they were but the others sat round the table behind them from whence they passed round the plates and Bertha, who had not thought such a thing possible, was even tempted to eat.

Odd, there had been a time shift. These were not four young people perilously advancing towards adulthood by various paths; these were four children back in the past which they had shared in visiting each other's homes. Though Malcolm did not mention his, Bertha noticed. All the anecdotes related revolved round the farm or the town where the father of Jilly and Donald had his dental practice. Yet Malcolm was at the heart of every mad prank in which they had indulged; the prime mover. In that halcyon period when all was mischief and nothing a sin.

When anyone omitted a detail the others rushed in to supply it. How Malcolm had gone forth to do battle with the old ram, armed only with his uncle's umbrella, as black as the ram but by no means as powerful. How the umbrella had broken and the ram had chased his attacker who had run like the wind but been unable to escape a butt in the buttocks.

How Donald and Malcolm had rowed the unsuspecting maid of all work out on the mill pond until right in the middle she had panicked, stood up and upset the boat, spilling them all into deep water. As she could not swim and was anyway impeded by her clothing, they towed her by her serge skirt to the bank, where she came to spluttering to find Malcolm kneeling on her chest in an attempt to rid her lungs of water.

Even Gus burst out laughing at this, for children are cruel and apt to take delight in the physical discomforts of others. And Gus was high on Perrier water because he was with his cousins again for a short while and excused from listening to the reading of some dull religious work by the Novice-Master.

117

Jilly's first-night nerves went unremarked in the general hilarity and the glasses of wine which all except Gus had absorbed. Malcolm had taken care to re-fill his aunt's glass and she was happily half-listening to their tales of derring-do which she guessed had not been aired for years.

But, for the other half, she left them to their fun and was herself back with Hugh in the early days together. When love and sex were so intermingled that there was no separating the two things. How Hugh had often been late at the office and was reprimanded by the manager for being too virile. How they would leave London late at night and drive through the dark in his open-topped car with the sky above and the wind blowing her hair. Until, after various detours, they arrived in the early morning at some staid seaside resort to astound the natives by demanding a room and a bath into which they both plunged. After which they would descend decorously to partake of a breakfast nearly as substantial as the porters ate in the Market.

How they would sit hand in hand on one of the wide seats in some art gallery in front of a large painting while he expounded inch by inch on its composition for he was nearly as much in love with the old masters as he was with her.

The surrounding conversation gradually deteriorated into no more than a hum as she became muzzy with alcohol and tranced by remembering, when she was brought back to the present by Gus jumping up and exclaiming: "Look, I must be back by ten. I'll just do my share of the washing-up and then I'll be off."

Grasping the stems of two empty glasses and his own tumbler he disappeared into the kitchen to stand by the sink. She heard the tap running and meant to tell him to turn on the sink water heater but it proved to be too much effort. She heard chairs being pushed back but she did not hear Malcolm say "Now" or Jilly move round to her right side. What she heard quite plainly was Hugh's voice in her ear, low but perfectly audible: "Why don't you make them your heirs?"

She had been so close to Hugh in her recollections that the remark did not even surprise her. It was marvellous that they should still be in tune with each other. She did not speak for fear of spoiling this precious moment of reunion. She held her

118

head steady and closed her eyes. She must have drifted off for the next thing she knew was Gus kissing her and telling her what a wonderful time he had had. And then she was scrambling inside her handbag, looking for some money to give him to pay for his fare on the Tube.

"Don't bother, darling," Jilly was saying, "Donald will see to it."

And Gus was assuring Donald that he didn't need subbing as the Novice-Master had seen to that.

"I must . . . I must give you all something. I can't let you pay for it all."

"Just this once, darling," said Jilly. Her voice seemed to come from a long way away and was curiously deflated. "No, Malcolm, keep your paws out of that!"

What on earth did the child mean?

"Come and help with the tidying up," said Donald. "I'm not going to do it all. No, not you, Aunt. I'm speaking to Malcolm."

Various noises continued but she was too sleepy to care.

Finally she heard Jilly ask anxiously: "Shall I see you into bed, darling, before we go?"

"No, I shall be perfectly all right. I'll just sit here for a bit . . . perhaps have a little snooze, get my sea-legs. Thank you all. It's been a most beautiful party."

When she awoke they had all departed.

Chapter 14

Mr Lomax came out of the doors of a brand new building, granite-faced and blue glass, near Bun Hill Row, and breathed in deeply. Dust and petrol fumes – excellent! A great improvement on air conditioning. His firm, Lomax, Brand and Brand, now occupied a fine suite of offices on the fourth floor which impressed the clients, delighted the staff and only displeased Mr Lomax.

He longed to be back in the old Victorian quarters lately reduced to rubble. In his opinion law offices should not be light and with impressive views; they should be dark and dingy and comfortable and look out across the street to something similar. He would rather have had his old managing clerk and not the new legal representative. He mistrusted computers for being only as reliable as the persons who manipulated them. However, he was only the senior partner, due to retire next year, and who bothered about him? His one privilege was to be able to walk out without consulting anyone except his personal secretary, a woman of long service and mature age who fixed his appointments. He was walking down Chiswell Street towards the Barbican to see Mrs Harris who had requested his presence.

Chiswell Street was changing its face. It was a death trap with constant traffic, hoardings and scaffoldings. From above an emptied beer can landed a foot in front of him. It might have killed him. He looked above for someone to sue but saw no one, just the bare catwalk. But his narrow escape reminded him of the reason for going to see Mrs Harris. She wanted to change her Will. That did not surprise him at all.

Widows were addicted to making new Wills and never so badly as when they were recently bereaved. Any curly-headed young curate, or unexpected act of sympathy, would start them thinking about it. Perhaps it was just a cause; a hefty sum towards research into the disease which had carried off their husbands. Hugh Harris had died of old age. Well, perhaps Help the Aged?

Mr Lomax stumbled over a carelessly relaid paving stone and snorted his displeasure at both the one and the other. His considered opinion about helping the aged was to administer a nice kind dose of euthanasia at the right moment. He had not budged in his conviction only now he was not quite sure what was exactly the right moment. Now he had crossed the perilous junction and was in the shelter of the tunnel. He had a good many clients in the Barbican and although he had not been to the Harrises' flat before, he knew where to find it. Privately he thought of the Barbican as a very large toy. You gave a child a farmyard with animals, you gave the City of London the Barbican with people. The corporation moved it about, re-arranged it, altered its policies, and nothing mattered as long as it didn't lose too much money. Finally like the child they would grow tired of it and it would pass into other hands. A pity; it was the only real example of mixed community living, an inner city centre which had room for the arts.

He had made the last wills of Mr and Mrs Harris and had a respect for Hugh fostered over the years. He and Hugh had been on a friendly business footing and he was gratified that he had been called upon to assist Hugh's widow and, yes, perhaps to advise her. He was handling the probate and knew the amount of money involved. He announced himself on the entryphone and went up in the lift.

Bertha had coffee waiting for him and he sat down and enjoyed it along with Marie biscuits which she had judged suitable. He wanted to know how she was getting on and whether living by herself was bearable after so long in double harness.

She admitted that it was difficult but that everyone had been kind. Well, he knew that people were kind to widows, especially those who were not likely to be financially embarrassed.

122

He brought forth his briefcase.

"You know, Mrs Harris," he said after he had perused it, venturing on to what he knew was probably soft ground, "there is really no need for you to alter this Will. It clearly states what you and Mr Harris then believed to be a sensible decision. Like many of us he thought that money should remain in the family."

"I could never see why," said Bertha frankly. "He had no family of his own and he loathed mine. So much so that we never saw anything of them."

"He didn't loathe all the members of your family," pointed out Mr Lomax, "one of them he married and cared for until the day that he died, and left everything he possessed."

"Yes, and that reminds me, how are you coming along with settling the estate?"

"These things take a long time, dear lady, I'm afraid," said Mr Lomax hurriedly who hadn't come prepared on this point. "Should you need money, of course. . . ."

"No, I don't need money. We had a joint account as you know, on which I am able to draw. If I run short, I am sure that the bank will advance anything that I need. And I have credit cards."

"I'll look into it the minute I return and let you know the present state of affairs," said Mr Lomax. "Now, perhaps, if we could return to the matter of the Will?"

"Yes, of course. I don't want to will the money away from the family, Mr Lomax. I just wish to leave it to the younger generation, my nephews and niece."

Mr Lomax looked dubious. "Isn't that going to cause a certain amount of ill feeling between the seniors and the juniors? I take it that the parents of these young people will perhaps expect it to come to them rather than their offspring."

"I do not care a toss what they expect," said Bertha. "They have all provided themselves with sufficient incomes from their own exertions."

Her conscience troubled her a little about Fred. Did he really come within this category? But she consoled herself by thinking that when the longueurs of probate were over, she would send him a big cheque which would be more welcome to him than anything in the hereafter.

"You must excuse my curiosity," said Mr Lomax, proceeding cautiously, "but I never heard your late husband say anything about these young persons."

"Oh, but Hugh agrees . . . would agree absolutely with what I propose doing."

Mr Lomax smelled a rat. Had the silly woman been consulting a medium? There was no length to which widows would not go to seek advice other than that proffered by their own solicitor.

"Yet he appears to have had no personal knowledge of the proposed beneficiaries."

"I didn't even know myself that they were all living so near until his funeral."

"Oh, so they came to the funeral?"

"Yes, with the exception of one of them, Donald. He's a bank clerk in the City and couldn't get leave. I've seen him since, of course."

"They came with their parents?"

"Yes. Donald and Jilly come from the same family. Malcolm is my brother Rupert's son. And Gus . . . Augustus, is Fred's son. Fred is my younger brother. These are the legatees in the present Will, the one I wish to replace."

"Are any of these young people minors?"

"No. They are all over eighteen. There is no question of guardians or trustees or anything like that. I want them to have complete control of the money when it comes into their hands."

"You have told me that Donald works in a bank. What do the others do for a living, if I may be permitted to ask?"

"Malcolm is an art student in Chelsea."

"Ah!" Mr Lomax breathed out the word.

"Jilly is at the School of Drama here in the Barbican."

"Ah."

"And Gus . . . Augustus, is a novice in a Roman Catholic Order."

"Do you realise that his share would go to the Order and not to your nephew?"

"That is how he would wish it."

"Are you sure of that?"

"Perfectly certain."

"I ask because if he were tempted by the sudden acquisition of wealth to renounce his vows, if he has made any, I fancy that this might lead to a legal squabble which we should all wish to avoid."

"Gus will never change his mind as to his vocation."

A rum old lot, thought Mr Lomax, irresponsible to a man. He did not even exempt Donald who worked in a bank as there had been a mistake in his last bank statement. Those computers again!

"Mrs Harris, you say you did not know the whereabouts of these youngsters, but surely they knew yours? I am wondering why they never came to call on you when your husband was alive?"

"They would not have been welcome and I daresay their parents informed them of that. Hugh did not actually dislike the young but he didn't like close contact with them. He was a very private man. You must know that, Mr Lomax."

Yes, he did know it and he had known others like it. Admirable men hedged about with reserve, without friends and likewise without enemies; perhaps permitting only one intimacy, in this instance with his wife. It explained a great deal.

"They have been so kind to me since his death."

"So they should be," maintained Mr Lomax stoutly. In his experience the young were rarely kind to the old unless it was to their own ultimate benefit.

"If you want to reward them, wouldn't a codicil do? Perhaps a thousand to each? I believe that they themselves would regard that as generous."

He could see that she wasn't convinced.

"Why not think it over for a few days? It's rather a big step . . ."

"No, I've made up my mind. Mr Lomax, wasn't there ever a time in your youth when the bequest of a substantial sum would have made all the difference to you? I know there was in mine."

If Hugh hadn't rescued me, she thought, what should I have done then without a penny to my name? These have some training which I never had, but is life any easier?

125

Yes, admitted Lomax to himself, there was such a time. When he could have bought himself into a partnership . . . married . . . seen a bit of the world.

He capitulated. "Then I shall have to have the exact names and addresses." He took his notebook out of his briefcase and proceeded to take instructions. Bertha supplied him their home addresses, explaining that these were not likely to alter.

"And will you please stay on as executor?"

"I would happily, but I am retiring next year and I hope that this will not come into operation for a long time yet. I would suggest you leave it in the capable hands of Mr William Brand, my successor."

"Yes, of course, if he agrees. I didn't think about the retirement. Are you glad to be going?"

"In some ways. I shall no longer be a slave to commuting. On the other hand, I am afraid that my garden may devour me. I have an acre. Sometimes I envy you your window-boxes."

"At least they put gardening at a reasonable height."

"You have a point there."

"We . . . I shall miss you."

"And I shall miss the clients like you and the late Mr Harris whom it has always been a pleasure to serve. Now, I'll get this drafted and send it round for you to sign, with a duplicate copy for you to keep."

"I don't know quite where I shall find witnesses."

"Don't worry about that. I'll send two of my girls round with it in their lunchtime. I suggest that a small reimbursement for their services would reconcile them to the loss of their sandwiches."

"Will it take a long time? To get the Will made, I mean."

"Not as long as Probate," said Mr Lomax, grinning as he shut down his briefcase. He relented. "Not more than a few days. I'll telephone you when it's ready."

Having put up a fight and lost he was now completely relaxed. After all, it was better than leaving a sizeable sum to sustain a polly parrot or two neutered cats. Or even donating it to some large charity whose overheads would swallow it without even noticing.

He turned serious again. "Mrs Harris, there is one thing of

which I must warn you. Never tell one of these four what you have done."

"I wouldn't dream of it."

"And keep the copy under wraps."

She laughed. "You sound as if you thought they might be snoopers and lethally minded."

"The elderly are vulnerable," he said gravely.

Now, despite her previous reservations, wasn't this just the man to tell about her set-to with Mrs Jaffa? She was longing to confide in someone with an objective view; not prejudiced like Concetta, and certainly more intelligent. He listened carefully but was half-smiling when he pronounced judgement.

"You are quite right. It was an invasion of privacy. But in the circumstances, probably pardonable. I don't suppose that the policemen enjoyed it any more than you did. As a matter of fact I know the man in charge at Wood Street. A charming fellow, you have nothing to fear from him."

"But with nothing to justify it . . ."

"Well, if you were really in need of help you might have been thankful to see them."

"If I were dying I would rather do it alone."

"So would most animals. Not that I equate you with an animal, my dear Mrs Harris. But I believe that you shared some of your late husband's views on the subject of intrusion."

"I suppose I did. I don't like interference by neighbours."

"Well, there are always some people who in my day used to be called 'Meddlesome Matties'. Quite harmless, I'm sure, and with the best of intentions."

"I would prefer not to have them next-door."

"Does it make you unhappy?"

"I can never be happy without Hugh."

"That I can understand. Yours was a long partnership."

She made no reply, just standing there and biting her lip.

"But otherwise, are you content with the Barbican? Do you intend to continue to live here?"

"Oh, gracious me, yes. Which reminds me, would you be kind enough to look at my lease? I think it may be due for renewal."

"They'll tell you. But we will deal with it when the time comes. There's no problem."

"You wouldn't advise buying the flat?"

"Why put yourself to that trouble? Unless you fail to pay your rent you're as safe here as anywhere in the land."

"I don't know. I suppose this little altercation with my neighbour began to put all sorts of strange ideas into my head. I started to think how easy it would be to acquire a reputation for being . . . not with it. I mean, if there are two of you living together one can vouch for the other. But if there's only the one . . . I mean, when does being forgetful turn into being unpredictable? How long can one go on living alone without some busybody pointing a finger and saying you're not fit to do so? To oneself one appears to be perfectly reasonable. How is one to recognise when faculties begin to fail . . . when one is becoming confused?"

This was all delivered in a halting manner; it was hard going. Mr Lomax took the matter in hand.

"Your mind is as clear as mine, my dear lady, unless in this particular instance . . ." Here, jocular, he tapped his brief case.

"Then if so, might there be other intentions? No doubt you'll think this a nonsense but I wondered if my neighbours were interested in obtaining my flat."

Mr Lomax did prick up his ears at this. "Who are these neighbours of yours?"

Bertha told him, though she forbore from mentioning Mrs Jaffa's kleptomania. One step too far and her own veracity would be in question. So far all was well.

"Where did you say this shrink practises? Harley Street? Hmm."

Bertha thought it funny that Harley Street, once the synonym for respectability, now invited suspicion.

"I'll have a little look round . . . make a few discreet enquiries. If you have any trouble over the flat, get in touch with me at once. Immediately. Now, above all, don't worry."

"You are very good to me," said Bertha, seeing him to the door. "And thank you for coming."

"Not at all. It's a pleasure."

"I won't do this again, I promise you."

It was her turn to tap his briefcase.

"Why ever not?" He smiled benignly. "You keep changing your mind and I'll keep re-drafting the Will. That's how solicitors earn their living . . . or partly," he added.

Chapter 15

Blue sky, blue sea, yellow sand with a dressing of palm trees; if the holiday postcard ran true to form, Patsy and Sam were on their way home. On the back Patsy had scrawled, "Having a super time. Everything splendid except . . . lots of love from us both." Except what? Patsy was a scatter-brain. She might be disappointed in the cold table, perhaps it didn't live up to the brochure, or it might be the company; other people too much like Patsy and Sam. She would be told anyway when Patsy returned, if Patsy hadn't already forgotten what irked her. Their absence was a real loss. Not only did Patsy's flying visits mitigate the monotony of life but although Bertha rarely saw Sam, she felt that he was there as anchorman to be depended upon in a crisis.

Since the party, her young relations had forsaken her. She hadn't expected to see Gus as she knew that he needed a special dispensation to allow him out of his orbit but Malcolm hadn't taken his portfolio on the night as she had suggested. It remained to annoy Concetta when she hoovered the bedroom. Donald Bertha could do without, but Jilly she missed. Jilly had rung the day after to see if she was all right but didn't suggest any other excursions. Indeed she took pains to stress that she was very busy with loads of work, unspecified, and only spoke for about a minute and then rang off again. I didn't give them anything, thought Bertha regretfully, and they must have spent a lot on me. Then she remembered that she had rewarded them in a remarkably lavish manner though they didn't know about that.

She had no regrets. The evening had proved to be a tre-

131

mendous success; it had certainly made up her mind for her. She couldn't have sworn that Hugh had spoken to her; not now that the occasion had passed. But at the time it seemed so *real*. Could it be that she had to have his approval for what was her own decision? Perhaps she shouldn't think so much about Hugh. How would he have reacted if she had been the one to die first? Impossible to tell. They had never spoken of it. Would he have gone about it sensibly and methodically, settling for an expensive nursing home where his wealth could still command a certain degree of comfort and seclusion? Or would he find survival unsupportable and proceed to remove himself from the world, calmly and without fuss? He had absolutely no belief in a future existence. Whereas she . . . she had no belief either but perhaps she went on hoping. It was the difference between male and female. One thing he would never have done and as to that she was positive: he would never have sat about in the flat, a prey to morbid imaginings.

She looked about for an escape route and found it. Her window boxes, of which she had been reminded by Mr Lomax and which used to be her secret pride, were a disgrace, untended and unwatered. She put on a cardigan and went out on the balcony which was separated from its fellow flats by frosted glass, making each section private. She pulled out several frost-bitten plants, sifting the surplus soil from their roots with her bare fingers before putting the poor skeletons into a plastic bag. To be in the air did her good. Like Mr Lomax she preferred it just as it was, contaminated and unfiltered. Straightening up, for one had to bend to get at the earth in the window boxes, she observed the ruined skyline. City building was a lost art according to Hugh. But there was still the sky itself and plenty of it to be seen from where she stood. And if it was grey and not like the intense blue of Patsy's postcard that fitted in with her mood. Three ducks flew by in suburban formation.

Shaking herself from the dead weight of sorrow rather as she had shaken the plants she went in to wash her hands, scrub her nails and to 'phone for a hired car to take her to the nursery shop she favoured down near the market. She knew that she could never carry back what she might be tempted to buy. She loved best flowering plants whose blooms looked fragile and faded whilst still in their prime. She dressed the flower-boxes to adorn her room and not the exterior of the Barbican which was what was intended. She was against lobelias and geraniums and simply loathed petunias.

A man who had often driven them before arrived with the car and collected her from the underground garage. He did not mention her loss but the gaze of sympathy he gave her unsettled her right at the start. She was very conscious of Hugh's absence from the back seat. When she was put down at the shop the driver urged her politely to, "Take as long as you like, Madam." It all felt so terribly wrong. Hugh should have been there fuming at having to wait and she should have known what she wanted to buy without any hesitation. As it was, she dillied and dallied, distressed by the knowledge that there was no reason to hurry . . . never again would there be any reason to hurry.

At last she had made some sort of collection and paid for it and been transported home again. She was drained of energy and the various bags and containers continued to stand just inside the flat door where the driver, well tipped, had deposited them.

Tomorrow perhaps she would began to plant them out. Today she had to learn to live with the reality that what one thinks one does to please oneself is usually done to please some other person.

True to his promise, Mr Lomax proceeded with the new Will without any delay. Not that he considered it a sensible one to be signed as soon as possible. His legal antennae sensed danger in it. He believed his client to be a level-headed old lady – Hugh Harris would never have kept house with a fool – but when the emotions are disturbed one is subject to influence. What did she really know about these young relations come lately? He should have asked her if one of them had suggested it but that would have been to undermine the claim of their own parents and hardly seemed likely. Nevertheless, Mr Lomax in spite of his doubts drew up the Will with pleasure because, believe it or not, drawing Wills was his forte and even after all these years it was one of the few jobs that he really enjoyed. His Wills were concise and excellent, they never needed another solicitor to explain them. He had never had one upset.

The entryphone buzzed and a female voice announced that she came from Lomax, Brand and Brand. Two giggling but amiable girls emerged from the lift bringing the Will and the copy. Unlike Mr Lomax, although they came to the Barbican for concerts and the cinema and any free entertainment that offered, they had never visited a resident before. They were all respectful eyes. Whilst Mrs Harris read through the Will they gazed through the window and cooed over her new flower arrangement which in the end had turned out better than she expected.

Then they witnessed her signature. Their handwriting was immature and their performance slow, but this was no novelty to them so caused them no special anxiety. They gave Bertha the copy and she gave them the flat lease for Mr Lomax to scrutinise. She didn't expect him to pursue his enquiries into the standing of Dr Jaffa for she guessed that to be simply his way of allaying her suspicions, but the sight of the lease might at least jog his memory and she wanted to reassure herself about its future extension. The girls were delighted with their gratuity which was obviously more than they expected and told her shyly that as she had been so quick they were going down to eat their sandwiches on the Terrace before returning to the office.

"But we have this safe," said the one in charge, patting her briefcase. "And we shan't leave it under the table."

"Joyce, you haven't told Mrs Harris what Mr Lomax said," reminded the other.

The senior girl blushed. She thought that it sounded like cheek to a lady however ancient who plainly still had her marbles.

"Oh, it was just that Mr Lomax said would you please put the copy straightaway where nobody could get at it."

"Tell Mr Lomax that I shall certainly heed his advice."

She saw them into the lift, full of thanks and still giggling, then following instructions went along to her bedroom to place the copy along with the earlier one in the slim drawer inside the bureau. She turned the key but left it in the lock. She was afraid she might lose it.

When she had done that she came back into the front room and opened the window which she had shut to prevent Mrs Jaffa from hearing the girls' voices if she happened to be on her balcony. Though Mrs Jaffa never kept anything in her window boxes beyond the original soil which by now must be as hard as cement.

But sometimes she used it for the airing of clothes and when Bertha was doing her planting she was scared that the frosted glass door might open between them and another round of conversation begin. She had written the short note of apology since when all had been mercifully silent. Often she had wished that she might sit out on the Terrace – not at lunch time – and watch the somewhat murky water for its reputed soothing effect, but she was afraid that Mrs Jaffa might be doing the same thing. As we are creatures of habit, she knew when her neighbour was likely to be changing her books at the library so it was easy to avoid that encounter. She imagined that the Doctor did his romance reading in bed and she had an absurd vision of his elongated frame with his toes sticking out at one end of the sheet and his beard overlapping the other, whilst he revelled in the latest Mills and Boon. She wondered what he would make of Malcolm and then she fell into day-dreaming about what the children – for she thought of them as children – would do with their money when it came to them. Would Jilly take her bizarre taste in dress, and her cheque-book, into the world of high fashion and forget that she ever wanted to go on the stage? Or would she buy a little flat and have parties with canapés from a City caterer and there be beguiled by an unmarried man who wanted to, actually wanted to, marry? Or would the ready cash attract a resting actor, twice divorced, who would arouse her and fleece her with equal ardour. For, despite her posturing, Bertha judged Jilly to be capable of passion.

Would Donald stay on at the bank and say that it made no difference to him as some maintained who had an unexpected win on the pools? Or would he start playing the market and end up either rich or a beggar, according to luck? Who cared? unless it was Donald himself.

For Gus it would mean perhaps a short reprieve for his beloved Order.

135

As for Malcolm, it was idle to do any imagining about him. She nursed no illusions. She had seen for herself that he was tricky and deceitful; probably he was amoral. Of course, as an excuse one might plead that his father was a miser and that his mother had deserted him. And she could not deny her affection for him, faults and all, even on so short an acquaintance. Nor was she the only one. His three cousins who had known him for a lot longer obviously came under his spell . . . it was very marked when they were all together. So what was this charm, this chemistry, emanating from a boy who did all in his physical power to offset it? He both repelled and attracted and the combination seemed irresistible. Really, what happened after her death would not matter to her. She was perfectly content with her new Will. There would not be enough money divided between four to destroy them; only to offer opportunity.

As Malcolm had taken to making his forays into the Barbican in the mornings, he was doomed to meet Concetta on some occasion or other. This happened two days later. He buzzed on the entryphone and Bertha realised that he had come for his wretched portfolio. She hustled her hand maiden into the kitchen and hurriedly found her a job. Concetta was in no good mood either. She had just come from being reprimanded by one of her ladies for putting one of her numerous spray bottles straight down on a strawberry pink carpet where it had unfortunately left an ineradicable mark.

Hearing the lift arrive, Bertha hastened to let Malcolm in. She was afraid that he might start reciting some ridiculous nursery rhyme into the letter box.

"Hullo, Aunt Bert," he exclaimed cheerfully. His appearance was no worse than usual but naturally to Concetta it came as a shock. "Hullo there," he added for her benefit. Malcolm was nothing if not democratic.

Concetta came out of the kitchen to stare at him.

"So, this is the nevvew," she said. Even in these few words she packed a punch that was truly formidable. Her black-beetle eyes travelled slowly down from the top of his unkempt head to his bedroom-washed shirt, his creased and dirty jeans to his dreadful sneakers.

"Never before 'ave I see the nevvew." She then went into

136

an inspired mime of using an iron; only Jilly could have appreciated it.

"What the hell is she doing?" demanded Malcolm.

"She has the idea that your clothes could do with a press," said Bertha dryly.

"Oh, I thought she was asking us in dumb show whether we'd both like a nice cup of coffee."

Bertha did not take the hint. Malcolm screwed up his nose. "What is this place? A bleach factory?"

If he now thought that he had Concetta on the run he was mistaken.

"Shall I put him out with the trash?" she enquired, waving a brown paper bag at him.

"We call it rubbish. Trash is American."

As Concetta had just suffered from the lash of an American tongue, she thought that he must have the evil eye. He was now standing level with his aunt. He dismissed the little brush with her underling and said to her: "Is it okay if I go along to your bedroom, Aunt? It's back to the grindstone tomorrow so I have to collect my portfolio."

Before Bertha could answer, Concetta had stepped out between them. "Is not right for you to go into my lady's bedroom. I fetch. I know what you want. Is dirty cardboard."

"Don't be silly, Concetta. Of course he can go there. He wants his portfolio, and we shall both be glad to be rid of it."

Concetta continued to block the path. She looked squat and malignant; she was shorter than both of them.

"My gentleman would not have allowed," she muttered.

"What does she think I'm going to do?" Malcolm appealed to his aunt. "Steal your silver hair-brushes?"

"Concetta," said Bertha crossly, for no one likes to be seen as subservient to one in their employ, "do mind your own business. Go along, Malcolm, and get what you want. Let him pass, Concetta."

Malcolm, given permission pushed by and left them still arguing.

What price the old family retainer? he thought, grinning. He could still hear them at it, hammer and tongs, when he went into the bedroom and closed the door after him.

He went straight to the bureau and opened the shallow

137

drawer. It was there on the top, a new clean envelope; the one on the old Will had yellowed. His mouth went dry with excitement; that was quick work if you like. He dared not risk taking it out, he needed more time. One of his ideas came to him unsought and he acted upon it immediately. He opened one of the small drawers to the side of the long one. No dice; it contained old pocket diaries. The second proved lucky; Hugh's keys. Now he could come and go when he liked. He grabbed the portfolio and went straight back to the two women who had stopped speaking but still confronted each other.

"Well," he said in what he hoped was a placating manner, "that didn't take long, did it? It does look a bit shop-soiled I agree but that comes of carting it hither and thither. A nice bedroom like that really isn't the place for it. And your watch-dog can satisfy herself that I came out otherwise empty-handed."

Concetta snorted and went back into the kitchen.

"What do you say, Aunt Bert, to popping over to the wine bar with me and having a drink and a snack?"

"No, thank you. Not today." She sounded flustered as no doubt she was after the dispute with Concetta. Also Malcolm really looked too disreputable to take into the wine bar at lunch time.

"I'm due at the hairdresser's at two so I'll just make do with a biscuit and cheese here." Thinking that he might offer to join her she added: "Concetta will not be finished for an hour yet. Some other time perhaps."

"Well, be seeing you," he said, smiling to show that he felt no ill-will. "Ciao!" he yelled into the kitchen as he departed.

Concetta advanced holding a brown bag stuffed to the brim with paper and empty cartons, the stuff of household detritus. This she placed in a corner outside the door.

"Not forget," she explained. "No fuss," and she indicated the opposite flat door. Then she pointed dramatically first at the bag and then Bertha.

"Place for nevvew," she said. Bertha was not clear as to whether she meant inside the bag or outside the door.

"That nevvew I not forget until the day of my dying," she remarked, closing the door and not gently either.

She hastened to cross herself.

138

Chapter 16

For once Malcolm arrived first at the usual periodic rendez-vous in the Barbican foyer. He was full of nervous energy. Several times he jumped up from his seat on the banquette to see if his cousins were coming. At last, though they had not come from the same place, they arrived together.

"Why the hell are you so late?" he complained, grabbing Donald by the sleeve. "I'm dying of thirst!"

"Why couldn't you buy your own drink for once?" growled Donald, shaking him off. He was tired of being the sacrificial lamb.

"I was afraid of losing our pitch. Come on, the bar's been open for at least five minutes. Brace yourself, Jilly. I've got news."

One glance at him assured her of that. She sat frozen into stillness as she watched their backs diminishing in perspective as they walked away to the bar. Her muscles were tense like a cat on the hunt.

"This calls for something stronger than beer," said Malcolm as he leaned over the counter to summon the girl.

"Let it," said Donald, "I'm deaf in both ears. Three lagers please, Miss. Halves."

He carried two glasses, his cousin one. When they got back to their place Malcolm took a big swallow then put his glass down. He sat there charged with triumph, saying nothing.

"Look at him," said Jilly suddenly. "He thinks he's Peter Pan. Any moment now he'll start crowing."

"Dare me," he said. He already had one foot on the red leather seat. Jilly was quicker. With the flat of her long thin hand, so unlike her mother's plump one, she caught him on the shin bone just below the knee. He collapsed.

To punish them both he sat in silence rubbing the back of his leg. For quite a full minute. Then he could contain his secret no longer. It burst forth from him.

'She's made a new Will!"

Donald stared at him. "I don't believe you. You're having us on."

But Jilly believed him. She had seen that particular expression on his face on other occasions. It was the self-satisfied, arrogant look of positive accomplishment. She was too close to him both physically and spiritually to doubt it. He had made the simplest and maddest coup in history and without a drop of blood shed. Ah, but . . .

She said coolly: "I suppose she told you what she'd done."

"Don't be a fool, Jilly. She's not all that daft . . . I've seen it and read it. It's equal shares for the four of us. And that's all I'm prepared to say for the time being."

Donald was mulling it over. He bit at his thumb nail. "It's too quick," he mumbled. "She would have had to go to the lawyer the very next day."

"That's just what she did. I said it would speed things up. Congratulations, Jilly."

"Don't congratulate me. I've felt like a louse ever since."

"Well, you're going to be a rich louse by and by. And I shouldn't imagine that we'd have too long to wait."

"What do you mean by that?"

"Nothing lethal. You're far too theatrical, that's your trouble. Old ladies do die however much their heirs may object to it. They fall and break their thighbones, have strokes, succumb to a virus, surrender to hypothermia . . ."

"Not in that flat," interrupted Donald.

"You're both unspeakable," said his sister. "From now on count me out, understand? I've half a mind to go straight to Aunt and . . ."

"You can't, my sweet coz, you're far too involved. Who planned the party? Who whispered 'Open Sesame'?"

"He's right, Jilly."

"Even Donald has more sense. He knows that you're in this right up to your lily white neck."

"There's the parents, Jilly. Aunt would be bound to take it to them. They'd stop your allowance and then where would you be? You couldn't even stay on at the School."

"You can't blow hot and then cold."

"After all, what's done is done. Look at it this way. We took a calculated risk . . ."

"Who calculated it?" asked Malcolm, idly draining his glass.

"It doesn't matter who calculated it, we all took part in it and it paid off."

"Or will pay off in the future," amended Malcolm.

"Without a breath of suspicion. And no one a penny the worse for it."

"Several pennies the better."

"I meant Aunt. After all, it bolstered her own belief that she is still in touch with Uncle Hugh."

"Let's hope that he doesn't remember exactly what he said to her in the hereafter," said Malcolm. "What's wrong with you, Jilly? You're shivering."

"I don't wonder. However that money is left, I won't touch it."

"All the more for us, then."

"Now look here, go slow," implored Donald of his sister. "No need to fly through the roof. You might be very glad of your share. You don't have to make up your mind in a hurry. Aunt isn't going to die today or tomorrow."

"Maybe the next day," suggested Malcolm flippantly.

"She's my aunt as well as yours and I won't have her harmed."

"Who is going to harm her?" enquired Malcolm in silken tones. "You are very Grand Guignol this evening. And I must say that it comes strangely from you. You had to be hounded to see Aunt Bert in the first place. You hated the old; they gave you the shivers, same as you've got now. I hope that you aren't going to turn into a geriophile, if there is such a word. We've been very good friends in the past, Jilly, so I've been patient with you so far. But let me remind you, I'm not here to study your moods."

"And let me remind you, I'm not here to listen to merciless chit-chat. So I'll be off."

141

She got up unexpectedly, squeezed past Malcolm's knees and made for the door.

"What's got into her?" asked Donald bewildered.

"I'd say it's a bad case of conscience. Shall we stroll up to the bar for another pint, Donald?"

"I suppose we might on the strength of our prospects. How much do you suppose Aunt is worth at a rough guess?"

"I haven't the least idea. But then, I'm not really interested in money."

It was sometimes difficult to tell when Malcolm was joking.

Donald had, on occasion, envied the closeness between his sister and Malcolm. He enjoyed her temporary eclipse and the man to man feeling of strolling up to the bar although he knew that it meant another dip into his pay packet. He also knew that he must patch up the differences which had arisen between these two. The three of them had to stand together whatever happened. Three? No, four. He had forgotten Gus.

"Shall you tell Gus?" he wanted to know.

"No need. It might unsettle him. He'll learn in due course."

"Quite. In fact I wondered why you made a point of having him with us from the beginning."

"Because he inspires trust," said Malcolm. "I thought I'd made that clear. If you can run to it I'd like a gin and tonic."

"Don't take any notice of Jilly," said Donald as he felt for his wallet. "She'll fall in line when she's had a chance to think it over. She's very attached to you, you know."

That was the word for it, Malcolm thought. How queer that a blockhead like Donald should hit on it. He and Jilly had been like Siamese twins. But, however painful the operation, Siamese twins must sometimes be separated in order to live.

"Another thing," said Donald, "how do we go on from here? We can't very well stop visiting altogether. Aunt might feel deserted and start changing her Will again."

"A good point. As you say, we can't absent ourselves entirely but we don't want to overdo it. Undue influence, you know. I think that going again as a group is out. I suggest single visitations about once a week. How does that strike you?"

"Seems sensible."

"I don't know if Jilly will play ball."

"I'll mention it when I see her. I believe she's developing quite a yen for the old girl and that's what makes her so touchy. I don't think she'd take her out again though."

"Why not?"

"The stairs. It was quite a performance apparently. If you ask me Aunt has a heart."

"So do we all."

"Not a wonky one."

Malcolm was silent for a moment or two, then he said: "Have you ever met up with that old image who does Aunt Bert's chores?"

"Who? Oh, the Italian woman. Aunt mentioned her. No, I haven't."

"She's a real thug. Not at all the type you'd think suitable."

"Well, they're hard to come by round here. Too many offices."

"I butted in on the pair of them having a row. Wow! It opened my eyes, I can tell you. I got the impression that our dearly beloved relative is on a very short fuse."

"I shouldn't have thought . . ."

"It might not have been like this always. It might be due to the loss of her partner."

"I'll bear that in mind."

"Do that, Pozzo," Malcolm was down to a last small sliver of ice in his glass. It seemed to go straight to his tongue for he continued: "Everybody knows that you're the essence of tact."

There were times when even Donald knew that Malcolm had to be joking, and not too kindly at that.

As soon as Donald was alone, outside Malcolm's magnetic field as it were, all that lovely euphoria evaporated. Eating his cheese sandwich at the "Y" to compensate for the gin, he knew that he had to see Jilly at once. Of course she might not be available but he thought that she would be too upset to go out with the other girls – his false assumption as to how she entertained herself. As it happened when he rang he found that she had been washing her hair – to get Malcolm out of it, perhaps? – and was now busy with the dryer.

"When it's done, I want you to come out and meet me."

"What, again?" She sounded less than enthusiastic.

143

"It's important, it really is. I wouldn't ask it unless."

"Oh, well, then. . . . Where do you suggest?"

He couldn't afford any more drinks and he dare not make it the foyer for fear Malcolm was still hanging about. They could not go far as it was too late for that. In desperation he proposed the public seats in front of St Giles' Church. Grudgingly she agreed.

"Put on your cloak thing. It's bound to be cold. And if your hair's still damp wrap a towel round it like a turban."

Ever the careful brother, she thought. But she only remarked: "I shall know who to blame if I catch pneumonia."

By a paradox the public seats were as private as anyone could wish. All the sensible people had gone into the nearby pub. It was horribly draughty and the night air came through the seat slats as if it had found some new kind of whistle.

When Jilly came sweeping along in her overlong cloak, like some out-of-date tragedy queen, there was no one in occupation except Donald.

"Can't we go there?" she asked hopefully, nodding her head towards the cheer of the lighted windows.

"I'm skint," replied Donald, revealing his origins. "That devil Malcolm took me for two gin and tonics."

"So that's why you've turned against him."

"Don't be an ass. First of all I want your honest opinion. Is this some jape he's playing on us just to amuse himself at our expense?"

"What makes you think it might be?"

"Oh, I don't know. It all seemed to happen too pat. And at such speed. Aunt might have seen her law-man on the spur of the moment and she might have wanted it done fast. Solicitors are usually long-winded but I suppose he might have stretched a point to oblige a good client. But how could Malcolm get to see it practically before the ink was dry on the signatures?"

"He has his methods."

"I know what happened at the funeral. But then he had cover. I didn't cover for him; you didn't cover for him . . ."

"No, we only aided and abetted," she said bitterly.

"Then it isn't a hoax?"

"You'd like to think it was, wouldn't you?"

144

"I would and I wouldn't," he admitted, at conflict with himself. "Old people do die and the money would be a godsend."

"Or devilsend if it's connected with Malcolm."

"I'm not proud of the way it has been engineered if that pleases you. If you remember I was dragooned into being at that party when you . . ."

"I don't want to talk about that. You never liked parties anyway and I don't think you had any moral objection to what happened. You were afraid of being caught out."

"I was afraid for you."

"Baloney! Of course I must admit that Malcolm has been very clever. He's played us off one against the other. But then he *is* clever. I've always said that."

"You've always been besotted about him."

"What about you in the foyer? Fawning over him . . . giving him pats on the back."

"He can be pretty convincing when he likes. Is that why you made off in a taking?"

"If you want a straight answer I made off as you put it because I was scared witless."

"But why?"

"We're petty criminals just about capable of stealing out of Ma's purse but Malcolm's on the way to becoming the real thing."

"Still on about that. It would come to us in the long run."

"You may know you're going to be given a bouquet but you don't claim it until it's presented."

"The parents are not hard-up. Pa told me that Ma went and had her face lifted."

"So do lots of actresses."

"That's professional. What good could it do *her*? Do you know what it cost?"

"I have a good idea."

"Enough to keep you in luxury for a year."

Jilly hesitated a moment at that. Then she said stubbornly: "It's her money . . . not mine."

"You aren't going to peach on us, are you, Jilly?"

Now he sounded like the callow youth that he was and the very word took them back to their school-days.

"How can I? Malcolm made sure of that."

"And you'll still go and visit Aunt? I don't mean take her out."

"I might if I think I can face her."

"Good. I'm sure she'd appreciate it. And she's not really so bad on closer acquaintance. Obviously you thought we were being flip when we reeled off that list of unpleasant possibilities, but these things do happen to old persons."

"Or are made to happen."

The effect on her brother was as if, travelling at speed, someone had put a foot down hard on the brake.

"But that would be m—"

"Exactly."

"You don't honestly think . . ?"

"I *think*. You don't."

"But Malc wouldn't . . ."

"He can't wait."

"He wouldn't drag us into anything of that sort."

"What hasn't he dragged us into before now? He needs us to carry the can."

"Oh, hell, and I let on that she had a weak heart!"

"Don't be daft. Do you really suppose that Malcolm is going to jump out on her and say 'Boo'? He's a bit more subtle than that. I'm leaving you, Donald. I'm going back to my one-bar electric fire. I'm chilled to the bone."

Her flaxen hair floated out silver in the artificial light overhead.

"I told you to cover your head," he scolded.

"I'll tell you something," she said as they parted. "You said that it all happened too quickly. That he wouldn't have had time to study the Will. I'll bet you a spoonful of rum to a couple of aspirin that he has a key to that flat."

Hysterical nonsense, decided Donald, returning to his own base. Too much drama school. Well, at least he was reassured on one point. She wasn't going to rush off and tell all. He could imagine his father's wrath if informed. It was true that they didn't always see eye to eye but just now it was truce between them. He was earning his own living and keeping tabs on his sister. But Potts senior had a hard hand through use of the forceps and he wasn't slow to use it if roused. Sad to

146

relate, Donald was a coward. He had only once seen Uncle Rupert provoked and that was enough. Pa might be fiery and lash out with his fists but Uncle Rupert was vindictive and terrible and capable of anything. He didn't envy Malcolm if the truth ever got out.

He couldn't see any great change in Malcolm himself unless it was that he looked even more scruffy than usual. He had been on a high tonight, of course; not from drugs or drink but simply because things were going his way. That had led him to exasperate Jilly and thus put silly ideas into her head. He couldn't understand why she had fallen for Aunt. As a child she had howled lustily whenever invited to kiss a withered cheek. There were people who couldn't stand cats, who went mad at the sight of a bat, couldn't bear anything that flapped. The old affected Jilly like this. To Donald anyone over sixty-five didn't exist. Several had retired since he had been at the bank. They had a leaving party where they were presented with a cheque or its equivalent in goods. That was the finish as far as he was concerned. He could not deny that there were fabulously wealthy old men who governed financial empires, or politicians who clung to power, but he regarded these as figureheads; puppets manipulated by younger men who remained discreetly in the background.

It wasn't affection for his aunt that caused him to baulk at the prospect of Malcolm trying to hurry things up. Never in his life had he contemplated an action so taboo. Not only did he shrink from the actual deed, he could not even bring himself to name it. Visions of the Old Bailey swam before his eyes, himself in the dock. Not as the m—, not as the person most concerned, but as an accessory. Jilly had been right. At the party it was the notion of being found out that troubled him most. How could Malcolm by . . . by wanting to . . . to press on ahead endanger them all, when all he had to do was to be patient and wait? To do so would not only be reckless, but downright wicked. Was Malcolm downright wicked?

Another question occurred to him – one that had nagged at him before and had been only partially answered by his cousin. Why did Gus have to be in it? Donald was fond of Gus but he didn't see why the Order should benefit. And what had Gus actually *done* to earn an equal share of the distribution, if

147

it ever took place? Wasn't his own face equally honest? He was employed by a bank. But then, come to that, why did he and Jilly have to be in it? It was well-known that Malcolm, when he wished, could charm the birds off the trees. So why didn't he tackle the project alone and go on to scoop the pool?

If Gus was there to inspire trust, what were he and Jilly there for? Jilly had played a part certainly, a bit part one might say, but he had done nothing so far. Was his part still waiting to be played . . . in the third act? The night was cold but it was not the chill of the night which crept up Donald's spine. THE GUILTY CANNOT INHERIT. It might have been spelt out in neon on the dark sky. Suddenly came the dawn. Donald knew exactly what part Malcolm might have in mind for him to play.

Donald started to work himself up to a state which he had diagnosed in his sister as "hysterical nonsense". To demonstrate his comparative innocence it is fair to say that until Jilly's disclosure he had never envisaged his aunt as dying otherwise than naturally. The farthest he had got in any other direction was to wonder if it was permissible to wait before calling the ambulance if he found her in extremis. Now he would have her over to Bart's as fast as the siren could shriek through the tunnel.

He who had admired Malcolm's cleverness, now saw it as a threat. He knew that he couldn't match it. But what should he do? Should he warn Aunt to be on her guard against Malcolm? No, that would be fatal; it would arouse suspicion all round where none previously existed. She might even tell Malcolm; for he guessed correctly that she preferred Malcolm to him.

He couldn't keep watch on his cousin because he was tied up at the bank whilst Malcolm could cut classes at will. He could pop up in the Barbican whenever and wherever he liked.

Look at it from another angle. Wasn't the bank his best alibi? Unless at week-ends Malcolm would have to confine any operation to the evening hours when Donald would be on the spot. On the spot! Living the closest to a rich relative, Donald had once thought himself in a favourable position; now he wished he lived south of the river like Malcolm.

148

Thank God nobody could confuse the two of them!

His feet, apparently unaware of the afflictions of the mind, had brought him to his destination. He went up the steps and in. But his hands, better informed, were too shaky for him to play snooker. Anyway it was too late.

Off he went to his cubicled bed though not to sleep, even if under the duvet he had purloined from home he was comfortably warm. Too warm . . . he began to sweat. Guiltily he remembered that he had forgotten to tell anyone he had borrowed it.

Chapter 17

The Sprites were back from their holiday; Patsy the colour of a coconut husk and having put on again the weight she had been at such pains to lose. She came straightaway along the balcony to find out how Bertha had fared in her absence.

"Did you have a nice time? Ah, I see that you did," said Bertha, all smiles.

"Isn't it awful? I started off in a bikini, then went on to shorts, and when the zip began to protest, I had to settle for skirts."

"Was it too hot?"

"Not for me. Everything was just perfect."

"Except for what?" asked Bertha.

"Eh?"

"That's what you said on your postcard. Except for . . . and that's where you stopped."

"Except for wondering about poor old you."

A kind lie on the spur of the moment. Patsy had entirely forgotten what had displeased her.

"Let me look at you," she demanded. The examination was swift and so was the verdict.

"No, it won't do yet. You need feeding up. You must come in to lunch and look at the snaps."

Bertha did not know which to fear most, the lunch or the snaps.

"Not yet. Wait until you settle down."

"I haven't even unpacked. The flat's in a mess. Dust every-where. I swear I don't know where it gets in. Len says we were lucky that was the only thing that got in. They've had break-

151

ins. Over the other side, not here, so don't worry."

Len was their porter and burglaries, though infrequent, sometimes happened when people were absent.

"Len kept a watch when he was doing the watering. My boxes don't look bad but they're not as good as yours, Bertha. You've stolen a march on me."

Silly me, thought Patsy, when she's here on her own. She changed the subject.

"We've brought you a little present, a basket. Goodness knows what it's made of but it would have to be coconut fibre or palm leaves, they don't have anything else. But it was great for the duty-free bottles. When I've off-loaded them I'll bring it along. Well, I must return to my chores. The whole place needs hoovering."

"Shall I lend you Concetta? She'd love to come. You're her paragon."

"What's that? Thank you, but no. I'd rather have a naked islander. Did I say 'naked'? I meant native."

"The summit of excellence."

"Ah, out of one of those crosswords."

But Patsy loved to be liked, even if it was only by Concetta.

"How is old Conch? Still raging with jealousy?"

"I had a grand row with her. Both of us at the top of our form."

"What about?"

"I forget. Some nonsense about my bedroom. Oh, Patsy, I'm glad you're back. You restore my morale."

It was true. Twice she had let fly, once at Mrs Jaffa, once at Concetta, and it wasn't like her. Violence may be a necessary part of human nature but it isn't becoming in the elderly. The froth of Patsy's chatter was like a caress without emotion. Balm. She had to guard against emotion, it took too much out of her.

She has been lonely, thought Patsy, and out of that sprang a question.

"Are the youngsters still rallying around?"

"Yes. What do you think . . . they gave me a birthday party."

"For which you paid, no doubt?"

"You're wrong. I didn't contribute one penny. Lots of little

152

delicacies and even a bottle of bubbly. Champagne-type, you know."

"Great expectations!"

"I should prefer to believe that it was just open-heartedness."

"Bertha," said Patsy, now serious, "once you told me that you were leaving what you had to your brothers and sister. Don't, I pray you, change your mind about that."

"Oh no, of course I shan't." She often told Patsy small white lies but this she realised was a large black one. It was simply that she didn't want to provoke an argument.

"Well, I hope to meet these . . . paragons . . . one of these days."

"Yes," agreed Bertha, "one of these days. When you've caught up with your housekeeping."

"Sam has flown off to Germany so I've got a breathing space. I must love you and leave you."

Stay, Patsy, stay. But she was already at the window opening.

"How did they get in?" asked Bertha.

Back to the break-ins . . . why didn't I hold my tongue about that?

"Len thinks they had a key. Plenty of the cleaners have those . . . not that I should suspect Concetta of burglarious entry. It's boys, I expect."

"I meant into the flats?"

"Through the delivery cupboard as usual, Sam has ours sealed – and mind you keep your latch down."

"I always do."

"As I say, we've been spared so far. Whoever does it must be as thin as a lath. No one will ever be able to accuse me."

She patted her girth and was gone with a farewell wave.

Why did she immediately have to think of Malcolm? There were thousands of thin boys in London; thousands must visit the Barbican. When had she last seen a fat boy, in fact? Not since Billy Bunter and he was only a myth.

Since Hugh died, Patsy had begged her not to keep any large sums of money in the flat and Bertha had obediently complied. Though she did wonder how any sneak thief would know that she was so prudent. Perhaps she should stick a little notice on the door: "No money kept here". Since any burglary makes one seek reassurance that one's own belongings are safe, she at once went along to the bedroom to convince herself that the diamond brooch was still snug in the toe of her stocking. Of course it was; she took it out and admired it. Then she asked herself if it wouldn't be better somewhere else less unorthodox, but finally replaced it thinking that it would be the last place anyone would look. From this her thoughts went to Hugh's keys, which should have been returned to the office. They had been joint tenants, therefore they both had a key, whilst an emergency one was hanging up somewhere in the housekeeper's sanctum. Indeed Hugh had three on his ring, what the other two were for she had never bothered to check. They were to do with the tenancy of the flat but, as far as she knew, had never been used. She would keep those but the other one should go back. Why hadn't she done it before? Part laziness, part sentiment; Hugh had carried them in his pocket.

Well, now she would make amends. They were sympathetic in the office and no one would scold but it wasn't sensible to hang on to them in view of the break-ins.

She went straight to the small drawer where she knew they would be. They weren't there. There were four of these small drawers. She opened one after the other, hopefully believing that her memory had played her a trick. They were full of small useless objects which should have been discarded years ago, but no keys. Agitated, she racked her brain. Could she have put them elsewhere and forgotten? This was what old people did – Hugh had even been apt to do it himself.

Her mind flew back to the time when she and Concetta had stood wrangling in the passage and had left Malcolm alone in the bedroom. Would he have known where it was and taken it? Hadn't he once asked to borrow the key and been refused? Unbidden came the recollection that she herself had told him that it would unlock the door to any of the houses. Stupid Bertha! How could she have been so silly? Then she accused herself of suspecting him without a shadow of proof. Of course that key must still be in the bedroom somewhere. She spent the next ten minutes frenziedly searching without

154

result. One bedroom is not a very large area for concealment even if one keeps going back on one's tracks.

At last she gave up. The ring of keys was not here; that was the bare fact. Why must it be Malcolm? There was nobody else. Concetta had her own key, it was entrusted to her by the management. Of course Malcolm might have taken the key wilfully without being responsible for the break-ins. She had said that it was a special key – she had meant that it could not be duplicated by the ordinary locksmith rather than that it gave carte blanche to the residents to enter other houses, which it did. Not to other flats naturally. But those hatches designed originally to shield the refuse bags from public view, and contain the daily milk delivery, had always been a weak spot. They dated from when most people were honest and that was not as long ago as it seems. Was Malcolm honest? No, he was not. Small change was nothing perhaps but she had missed two ten pound notes from her bag. But there is a wide gulf between helping onself from a well-off relative's purse and breaking and entering. If he was responsible she must find out, and somehow make restitution. But until she was sure she had no right to prejudge him. In any case she had no intention of cutting him out of her Will. She blamed herself for not seeing his necessity. He might enjoy the risk but she didn't believe he would go robbing for fun. She must have a sensible talk with him, find out exactly how he was placed financially and, if Rupert was too mean to increase his allowance, make the boy a small allowance herself.

But he had temporarily absented himself. She did not know his address. Jilly would know it but Jilly was absenting herself too. She would not dream of applying to Donald, though he was the only one of whose domicile she was sure. No, she would wait for Jilly to ring up again and then she would press her to call round, even if only for a short time. Now that Patsy was back she wouldn't feel so isolated. Perhaps Jilly would pass muster with Patsy. Her prospective career might atone for her remarkable outfits. Besides, Jilly was exceptionally attractive. What Patsy would make of the others she shuddered to think and she had no intention of allowing them to meet.

Jilly consented reluctantly to appear after presenting a host

155

of excuses which didn't ring true. It would be misleading to say that Jilly was not herself as she had a number of selves available to suit the occasion. But here she was sitting beside Bertha on the sofa with a tray on her lap containing a plateful of prawns for which her aunt had bought a special dip, to the accompaniment of brown bread and butter. Jilly, though appreciative, gave the impression of being unable to concentrate. For the first time Bertha detected a trait reminiscent of her mother who used to behave in the same way on her potty. The recollection made her laugh.

"What amuses you, darling?"

Though Bertha didn't detail the circumstances she did admit that she saw signs of a family likeness.

"Why did you desert my mother when she was an infant?"

"I didn't desert her. Hugh took me away. I was too young to enjoy looking after a baby. I'm not sure that I should have ever been old enough for that particular duty. Come on, Jilly, drink up. That is a good hock you have in your glass."

Jilly took a thoughtful sip.

"What sort of a man was Uncle Hugh?"

"He was a man of rectitude." The words came from Bertha's lips quite spontaneously; once she had uttered them she thought how strange they were. It was an accurate description, but "rectitude" a word so old-fashioned and formal, entirely outside her usual vocabulary. To her surprise Jilly began to weep. Not theatrical weeping but childish sobs which made it imperative to take her wine glass from her and to remove the tray on to the table. Prawns and tears didn't mix. Bertha did not associate this grief with herself. What had got into her hard-boiled niece? A bad audition? A row with a young man?

"What is the matter, darling?"

The endearment uttered by her aunt shyly and full of solicitude, so different from its habitual use in the theatre, made Jilly cry all the harder. As Jilly volunteered no explanation of her distress, the only thing to do was to allow the storm to subside. When all had been reduced to an occasional sniffle, Bertha handed over her own clean handkerchief, much softer than those paper squares, even if less hygienic. She guided the slender fingers of Jilly's right hand round her

156

wineglass and replaced the tray in her lap. It was not until several prawns had vanished that she ventured to put what she thought was a casual question: "Could you let me have Malcolm's address?"

Jilly took the rest of a half-eaten prawn out of her mouth. "W-why do you want it?"

"I would like to have a little chat with him, that's all."

"I haven't got it. Nor has Donald. Or Gus. I expect it's some dreadful pad."

"How do you communicate with him then?"

"We wait for His Highness to ring up to fix a meeting."

"And he hasn't done that lately?"

"No, not lately."

"The last time he visited me here it was in the morning. How can he do that when he's at College?"

"Oh, he just skips a class, I suppose." Jilly, having said this, ate the rest of the prawn, signifying that absenting oneself from one's studies wasn't important.

"When he rings up next would you tell him that I'd like to see him? But not in the morning."

She had decided definitely on confronting Malcolm. She wanted things straightened out. She wasn't at all afraid of him. He had soon caved in when she had refused to buy any of his paintings. She thought that she knew how to handle her nephew.

"Don't see him," said Jilly, suddenly in earnest. "He's bad medicine for you, darling."

"If he's bad medicine for me, Jilly, why isn't he bad medicine for you?"

"Oh, but he is. It's just that I . . . that I . . ."

The tears showed signs of breaking out again so Bertha said hastily: "We're both fond of him. I suppose that's what it is."

"Mine's more than fondness. You can be fond of grilled sole, not that I ever see any."

"Would you like me to take you to Wheelers?"

"No . . . no. You can't understand. Malcolm has been a part of me for so long. I can't root him out without hurting myself. It's here." In an unrehearsed gesture she pressed her hand to her heart.

157

"It's legal, I know, but I don't think it's wise for first cousins to marry."

"I don't want to marry him. I don't even want to sleep with him. It goes far deeper than that."

In the face of such conviction Bertha had no advice to offer . . . or comfort. It was a situation outside her experience.

"It was all right before," continued Jilly. "He was just wild. A rebel, you know, like Shelley and James Dean. But he's changing. Now he's bad."

For a moment Bertha jumped to the conclusion that Jilly was privy to the Barbican burglaries.

"Do you know any particular way he is being bad here and now?" she asked.

Jilly looked petrified; there was no other word for it.

"No, no," she exclaimed, denying it vehemently. "There's nothing . . . nothing at all. Don't take any notice of me, darling. I'm hysterical. Donald is always getting on to me for being hysterical." As if to illustrate her point she began to laugh in an eerie manner. As suddenly as it had begun, this subsided. They both remained entrenched in an awkward silence until Jilly asked: "What do you want to discuss with him?"

She blew her nose on her aunt's handkerchief as a signal of a return to normality.

"Oh, this and that," answered Bertha evasively. If Jilly was ignorant of the exact nature of Malcolm's misdeeds, let her remain so. She certainly didn't propose to take her niece into her confidence at this stage of the game.

Like those who talk about the third alternative, Bertha felt that her dilemma had more than two horns. If Malcolm was responsible for these outrages she didn't picture him being caught. He would be a slick operator and he would be certain to watch and wait for the right opportunity. It is very difficult to expose one's own flesh and blood to the forces of law and order as many a woman has found. Besides, she had no proof. She had no proof that he had taken Hugh's key ring or, even if that were so, whether he had any intention of using it in a felonious manner. But she had a duty to her neighbours . . . and to Malcolm. He was on the slippery slope and must be stopped before he gathered momentum. Rupert being what

158

he was, she could not appeal to him for advice. Or Mr Lomax, with the new Will just made and Malcolm a beneficiary. She couldn't report the loss of the key to the office for, without telling them a lie about it, the trail would still lead straight to her bedroom. Malcolm must be stopped and it was her job to do it without outside help. She might have to use threats if nothing else worked. Since the other three didn't know where he lived, she doubted whether the College would either. She must try to find out more about what had been stolen. Malcolm would only take money, he didn't share Mrs Jaffa's lust for small objects. Sooner or later he would re-appear. If he was the perpetrator he would be haunting the Barbican and for practical reasons might need a bolt-hole and thus find his way to the flat.

Jilly had been automatically finishing her snack whilst debating, other persuasions having failed, whether she could make the supreme sacrifice.

She carried the tray into the kitchen and coming back made her offer.

"Darling, I don't like the idea of you being here alone, especially as there have been one or two cases of forced entry lately. How would it be if I moved in with you for the time being? I should be out during the day and there's an extra bed in your bedroom."

She was absolutely unprepared for Bertha's expression of horror.

"What! Share my bedroom with a young girl? It was as much as I could bear having to do it with Hugh!"

Chapter 18

Concetta was even later than usual. She did not apologise. Her face was flushed and a little swollen with self-importance as if she had been listening to gossip. She took off her jacket and donned her overall whilst Bertha watched her thoughtfully, wondering which was the best way to approach. Concetta had come from the lady she worked for on the other side over the green, where the burglaries had taken place. If she had any information it would be much more likely to be reliable than anything filtering through Patsy via Lennie. But Concetta could clam up; her boast was that she did not carry tales from one flat to another, and as generally Bertha approved of this attitude when she wanted to alter it in this specific instance she wasn't sure where to begin.

"How about a nice cup of coffee?" she asked hopefully. Concetta looked surprised but gratified. She was thirsty from hurrying. The bottle was in the cupboard and she had been told from the beginning that she could make herself a cup whenever she liked. Usually she did not bother but this was different. This was her lady offering to do it. She nodded her head. Bertha filled the kettle and plugged it in and Concetta got out the cups and saucers. My gentleman would never have mugs, she remembered and she respected him for it. Bertha put in the spoonfuls, Concetta added the boiling water. Bertha took the milk jug out of the fridge, Concetta produced the sugar basin and the spoons. All was harmony.

As they both waited for it to cool off, Bertha for the first time thought of her cleaning woman as a person. What a life! The everlasting round of manual labour every day except

161

Saturdays, Sundays and Bank Holidays; it was enough to embitter a saint. Concetta must be familiar with every design of flat in the Barbican from Type A to Type Z. But what contact did she ever have with its inmates? A scrawled list of duties varying with the movements of tenants which she had to ask Lennie to read, or a set routine to be followed until otherwise directed. Some occupiers she never saw at all and most of those she did see were only interested in getting a full return for her wages. No wonder that her English remained basic. How cruel Bertha felt she had been to deny this poor wretch a few snippets of ordinary, everyday conversation. It was nice to think that now she could kill two birds with one stone; make up for past reticence and find out what had really been happening.

"Why didn't you tell me about the break-ins?" she asked.

"Not here," said Concetta, firming her lips. Obviously she considered that one had no right to share in events which didn't take place under one's own rooftop.

"All the same, I like to be told."

"Not fit. Worry too much."

"Nonsense."

"All over now. Teef is caught."

Bertha's heart sank into her house shoes.

"Who was it?"

"They not 'ave yet. They 'ave 'is sneaker."

"Sneaker? Do you mean plimsoll?"

"What plismo? I not know, only sneaker. Same thing maybe."

"But all the young wear those things or something called 'trainers'. I don't call that much of a clue."

She drank some of her coffee. She felt that she needed it. Concetta blew on hers and drank too.

"Coffee have big smell," she explained. "Sneaker same thing. There are dogs to sniff out. Bombs, drugs, feet, anything they will find. They follow like the bleed hounds."

Bertha had an absurd vision of a poor pooch, its nose to the ground off to track Malcolm to his pad in South London.

"Whoever lost that shoe might live on the other side of London."

"No matter. They trace him. Also he was seen by the

162

daughter. Mrs Trounce have daughter, air hostess, very pretty, very smart. She is good at faces. Is train like dogs."

"What did he look like? Do you know?"

"He look like your nevvew, I tink." Concetta gave a snort which from her was a substitute for a laugh.

This was too near home for comfort. Whatever private doubts Bertha had about Malcolm she did not intend to share with her help.

"All students look like that."

"Maybe. But is a clue."

"My nevvew – nephew," she corrected herself, "has a rich father." That was true enough. "He does not need to rob others."

"I do not say *is* your nevvew."

"I should think not." She put down her empty cup upon its saucer before asking casually, she hoped, "How did it happen?"

Concetta shrugged. "Is easy. He watch the comings and goings."

So there it was again. Regular routine, in itself an admirable thing, too often the key to every crime in the calendar. Many women in the Barbican went out at set hours to work part-time, either because they needed the money or to keep their brains ticking over. By guess Mrs Trounce was one of the former.

By intense concentration Bertha extracted the facts from Concetta's account. It was like picking the plums out of a pudding. Mrs Trounce was, like Bertha, a widow. Her daughter had flown home from Hong Kong to arrive in the early morning. All that she wanted to do was to sleep off her jet-lag so her mother had a solitary snack and went out to a nearby office where she was engaged in clerical work from two to six.

Mrs Trounce's daughter slept on until three when she was awakened by a thud in the living room. In entering the intruder had knocked over a chair which stood in front of the hatch door. The intrepid girl, clad only in her nightie, rushed along to investigate.

At this point Concetta's dramatic instinct took over. The expression on her stodgy face became animated. With a lot of use of both arms and legs she took over the dual roles in this two-parter, being by turns the startled girl and the equally startled boy until in the end she looked down at her hand as if fully expecting to find it clutching the sneaker. As it was empty she utilised it to dive into her overall pocket for a handkerchief to mop the honest sweat from her brow.

Bertha was watching her as if mesmerised. She recovered and at once tried to imagine a possible sequence of events. The girl would not be likely to pursue the thief clad as she was.

"Did she 'phone the police?"

"First she sat on floor. Her bottom have bump. Then she get up and go to the toilet and put on the kimono she bring back from Hong Kong. Then she dial 999. Too late."

And thank God for that. If it was Malcolm he would have had an escape route mapped out. But one shoe! What did he do? Did he kick off the other and run in his stockinged feet? A dreadful thought struck her. He might have come to her for succour.

"So he got away. Did anyone else see him?"

"One is enough. She say he have long hair, thin face, thin body, is scruffy. I tell you before – like the nevvew, spit image."

Had Concetta voiced this opinion to others? No, Concetta was fiercely loyal; it was one of her virtues. In her own surly way she was teasing. If she had really thought it was Malcolm she would have held her tongue.

"We will leave my nephew out of it from now on."

"OK."

"So whoever it was got nothing from the Trounces?"

"He would be lucky. But t'ree, four hundred pounds he had already from the Goldsteins."

"But they have the penthouse!" The Goldsteins were wealthy friends of the Sprites. Bertha had heard of them often as they led colourful lives, full of incident.

"That monkey 'ave house key for sure." Concetta shrugged. "Delivery boys have house keys. I 'ave house key. Not me. Too squeeze."

Highly amused, Concetta snorted at the idea.

"Have any been reported missing?"

"How should I know? You get that Lennie to nail your box . . . make safe."

This slightly ominous suggestion only meant that Bertha should instruct the porter to screw up her hatch door, as Sam Sprite had done his, to lessen the risk of unauthorised entry.

"But not tip to talk," Concetta added severely, "he 'ave too big mouth as it is."

"I didn't hear from Lennie about the break-ins," said Bertha indignant. "I heard it from Mrs Sprite."

Concetta's countenance lightened. "She is back safely? No mugging? No engine fall off?"

"She is in very good health and beautifully brown. They had a splendid holiday."

"Ah. Now you will be happy. Is best neighbour to have, not like that orange." She glanced at the kitchen clock, seemed surprised and then announced virtuously, "I make up the time we have spend chatting."

"Don't dream of it," said Bertha hastily.

There are some prices too high to have to pay for information.

Patsy did not appear again. She might have been dodging Concetta or more likely battling with the aftermath of the holiday. But that evening Bertha did have an unexpected visitor . . . Donald. She was surprised by how glad she was to see him. Before Patsy's return it had been a dull week with a dull post; bills and envelopes falsely marked personal to delude her into thinking that they were dividend warrants. Donald at least did not pretend to be anything that he was not. There he stood, hair short back and sides, the inevitable mackintosh, and underneath, she did not doubt, the deplorable blue suit, looking every inch the bank clerk. But, after all, she had swallowed rather too large a dose of Jilly and Malcolm; if they were mild poison surely Donald was a suitable antidote. Of course when bank clerks became crooks they often operated on a grand scale but it was difficult to imagine Donald taking to crime in spite of her first impressions of him.

Donald had brought her a small box of chocolates and in return she gave him a small glass of sherry.

"How are you keeping, Aunt?" he enquired in his charmless way and she answered dryly: "Oh, I think I shall last over the week-end."

She had discovered something though; when they did not come she missed them. She was long past exploring the great interior of Widowland if it meant getting about, but they had brought exploration up to her door. And if exploration involved risks she must be prepared to take them as was done all the world over. She must handle Donald more sensibly. He couldn't help not being on the same wave-length and the trouble was that he did ask to be baited.

She looked at his solemn face with its owlish glasses and then at the clock and she thought that he must have come straight from the bank and had not yet eaten.

"I suggest that if you'd like it, I'll take you to The Cut Above. They start serving at six."

A Carvery had no attractions for her, she would have preferred an omelette. But she knew that Donald at home would have been nurtured on roast beef and Yorkshire pudding and she guessed that he missed them. Also she had noticed that he relaxed with alcohol and she thought that a bottle of red wine might induce a few revelations.

She could not be sure if his eyes brightened behind the glasses but his tone certainly did.

"That would be a real treat," he said. So much for the pull of macaroni cheese. Unlike his sister who, because of her glamour, had eaten at restaurants he never knew existed, no one had ever bought Donald a square meal.

"Then I'll 'phone up and reserve a table. It shouldn't be full as early as that but you never know."

Though Donald was secretly enthralled by the Barbican as a symbol of unlimited funding, he was its severest critic.

Now it was the small red tiles with which most of the walkways had been laid that he found fault with. There had been a heavy shower not long before and where sections of these tiles had got out of kilter through subsidence here and there, shallow pools of water had gathered and glimmered in the overhead light.

"Mind the puddles, Aunt," he advised. "They should have

166

known better than to have paved with these things."

"What would you suggest? Mosaic, perhaps? The yellow line would look rather striking in that."

He took her seriously. He shook his head.

"It would have taken far too long."

"But look how it would have lasted!"

"Anyway, I daresay it's not the tiles at fault so much as the plumbing."

"The Romans were good at that too. You should have been a plumber, Donald, highly profitable occupation."

She was still smarting from having to pay an exorbitant sum to stop a drip in her shower sprinkler.

"I wanted a profession," he said, sober as a judge if that still applies.

"Well, if barbers became surgeons what heights might plumbers not attain?"

"Heating specialists," he said. It was the nearest he had come to making a joke. But when he offered his arm as they skirted the bad spots, she refused it simply because she couldn't imagine herself attached to Donald's arm.

"I'm all right on the level," she explained almost apologetically. She had some plumbing to do herself, she thought. She wanted to find out how much he was involved in Malcolm's supposed activities, if at all.

By now they had reached the small open cloakroom serving the restaurant and Donald deposited his mackintosh with a girl who gave him an encouraging smile to which he did not respond. He did not even blush.

So he was immune to women, or anyway cloakroom assistants. At thirty he would probably marry a plainish girl with inheritance prospects.

They were given a window table. The maître d' remembered Hugh who had always been absurdly lavish. Bertha thought privately that this view was the best part of The Cut Above. The terrace, pseudo-continental, the ornamental water with its fountains, St Giles' and beyond, presiding benevolently over the scene, the dome of St Paul's.

Donald was still stiff. Malcolm would have carried it off with more aplomb though Donald had better schooling behind him. He was impressed by his surroundings which

167

were fairly hum-drum. She told him what wine to order and that pleased him; he was gaining confidence. He offered to fetch her main course and when he had brought back the one slice of roast lamb which she had chosen, he went off to superintend his own helping of beef. He returned with a plate piled high looking as if he had won the first prize for good conduct. The Cut Above was not expensive but it was expensive to Donald. He chewed away with evident enjoyment and in complete silence. Bertha left him in peace until his healthy appetite began to show signs of appeasement and then, the movement of his mouth reminding her of his father, the dentist – no, dental surgeon – she began on the time-honoured ritual of asking after the well-being of the old folks at home.

"They're fine," said Donald, wiping some gravy off his chin. He took a satisfying swallow of wine, after which he observed; "You know, they expect me to keep an eye on Jilly but I'm afraid that she still keeps on thinking of me as her younger brother."

"Well, that's what you are, aren't you?" remarked his aunt calmly.

"That's true. But I'm far more sensible. You see, I'm not in the least artistic."

Horrible word, thought Bertha, to whom it brought a mental picture of flower arrangements and craft objects.

"You think that art has a bad effect on people?"

"It makes them temperamental and moody," said Donald. "Jilly has always been that way inclined but she's worse now she's training to be an actress. Don't let on, but I'm a bit worried about her at the moment."

He sought consolation by forking a small piece of rare beef which had hitherto escaped his attention.

"Why is that, Donald?"

"Well, she has some rum ideas. She's like my mum in that respect."

"What sort of rum ideas does your mother have?" Bertha asked mystified. She wouldn't have said herself that Alice had ever had an idea in her head.

"Oh, she thinks Pa has affairs with his patients. As if one could fancy anyone after filling their teeth."

168

"But Jilly can't have ideas of that nature."

She beckoned to the waiter to fill up his glass. He was beginning to amuse her and that was better than wishing to control her investments. She decided that Donald had a mental age of sixteen.

"No, but she has a silly crush on Malcolm, which dates from our school days. Mind you, I think she's beginning to get over it. I think she's beginning to see him in his true light."

Bertha was really interested.

"What is his true light?"

This had Donald in a cleft stick. He wanted to warn her against Malcolm. Yet he knew that he mustn't overdo it in case she decided to change her new Will which by now he was convinced actually existed.

"Oh, I don't know. He's a bit of an enigma."

He was pleased with his own ingenuity. He thought that this solved the problem pretty neatly. It was sufficient to scare her off without committing himself too deeply. He was quite unprepared for her next question.

"Could you let me have his address?"

"You weren't thinking of going there, were you?"

"No. I just thought it might be handy to have it."

"Good. I don't think that the district is very salu . . . salu . . ." He stopped, at a loss for the end of the word. He went back to his own level. "I mean, I think it might be pretty grotty."

"Don't let that worry you. Just let me have it."

"I don't know where he lives. Malcolm plays his cards close to his chest. I only know that it's somewhere south of the river."

"Never mind. I'll ask him for it next time I see him."

A waiter came and took the empty plates away and asked what they would like as a sweet. Donald chose cabinet pudding, a thing his aunt had not heard of since she was a child. She only wanted coffee.

"You should finish the wine, Donald. I don't believe it will go with cabinet pudding."

"You haven't had your fair share."

"We won't fall out about that."

169

She had drunk only one glass. He was now dealing with the rest of the bottle.

If he didn't even know Malcolm's address they couldn't be very closely associated. Her next question confirmed this.

"Did you know we had been burgled at the flats?"

He spluttered the last of his wine.

"Not yours, I hope, Aunt?"

Jilly might have simulated such surprise and concern, but certainly not Donald.

"No."

"Or anywhere near?"

"No, it was on the other side of the green."

"That's all right then."

But it wasn't. The very fact that the break-ins were not in her house made Bertha more than ever sure that they were connected with Malcolm. He would be too clever to foul his own nest. Did Jilly know and was that what had upset her? Whatever pranks their cousin indulged in, she must never forget that these two came from a very conventional and respectable home where honesty was taken for granted.

Donald's pink and white complexion was flushed but he was now struggling gamely with his cabinet pudding and custard. If that were possible he had risen in his own self-esteem. He had put Aunt on her guard against Malcolm; he had explained away in advance anything silly that his sister might say and he thought that tonight's blow-out, for so he regarded it, was evidence that he stood high in his aunt's favour. Though a little unsteady on his feet and slightly dizzy he saw her home, took her up in the lift and left her at her own door.

His opinion of her had improved. As far as he was concerned she was entitled to die in her own bed.

Chapter 19

When Patsy dropped in the next morning, secure in the knowledge that it was not one of Concetta's days, Bertha tackled her about events.

"You didn't tell me that the Goldsteins had been burgled!"

Did she detect a whine in her own voice? Soon she would become like the woman she had known once whose continual plaint was "Nobody tells me anything!"

"Oh, that was just a joke."

"I don't call it much of a joke to lose hundreds of pounds."

"Bless you, they'll never notice it. He's into diamonds in Hatton Gardens . . . amongst other things. No, the joke was that he'd had a special safe installed, new locks fitted to all the doors – and clean forgot to do anything about the hatch. Sam will never let him live it down."

"I should have thought that there would be an alarm."

"Oh, there was; some super electronic device. Mamie kept setting it off so they had it taken away. They they went off to Paris as gay as the birds. But I forgot, I mustn't use that word."

"Where was all this money then?"

"Under tissue paper in a drawer. Didn't you know that tissue paper is always regarded as burglar proof by females? Mamie had stashed it there in case she'd had a spending spree and came back penniless."

"I wonder that whoever it was didn't go after her diamonds. She must have them."

"Oh yes, she has; as big as pigeon's eggs. There's those birds again but no pigeons are gay. Luckily they were in the safe. No sneak thief goes after safes; they're out of their range."

"Concetta tells me that he's as good as caught."

"So they like to believe. But he must be a slippery customer if he escaped the Trounce girl. She's as smart as paint."

"I didn't even know that Concetta worked for the Trounces."

"She doesn't, pet. They're as poor as church mice. I can't think why I'm so stuck with the natural world this morning. It's seeing it all the time on TV, I suppose."

"Then how did she know about what happened to them?"

"Her 'lady' is next door. But I thought Conch never gossiped."

"She doesn't usually. She has to let go now and again like the rest of us."

"Are you all right, Bert? You look a bit washed-out to me."

"I'm fine. That's what everybody says nowadays when they aren't feeling so good. I don't know. I feel a tiny bit sorry for myself, I suppose."

"You aren't worrying about these break-ins, I hope?"

"No, of course not. Why should I?"

"Well, being here alone. Lennie tells me he's going to see to your hatch. And you know if you are in trouble, you only have to bang on the wall."

"Yes, I know. I'm sure he won't come here."

"I don't think he'll go anywhere. He'll have had a good scare."

This was Bertha's belief as well. "I'm sure you're right."

Patsy gave her a quick glance. "And I'm sure you're still starving yourself."

"Rubbish. I went to The Cut Above last night. What could be more sustaining than that?"

"Nowhere. If you like that sort of thing."

"My nephew took me. The one who works in a bank."

In reversing their roles Bertha thought that she would also ease Patsy's mind. She was correct. Patsy sighed and said; "Why do I never get to see these paragons? The only one who ever sets eyes on them is old Jaffa."

"Does she complain?"

"Like anything. But she'd complain of the Archbishop Gabriel."

"You mean the Archangel."

"So I do."

"Oh, Patsy, you do make me feel better. I admire you almost as much as Concetta does."

"I'm flattered. Now I must love you and leave you. Sam is coming in for a bite. He says he's sick of living it up on expense accounts. Especially his. He's got a disbelieving Inspector of Taxes."

"What are you giving him?" enquired Bertha, interested in spite of herself.

"Bread and cheese. I don't want him to make a habit of it."

In the afternoon Bertha rested on her bed and felt all the better. As she had eaten no lunch, it was too much trouble, she devoured a bar of something she had bought at Crispin's and re-read *Alice in Wonderland*, a desire sparked off by Donald's remarks on his mother. Whilst idly trying to separate the flesh and blood child from the literary creation, she dozed off for half an hour and woke feeling refreshed and clear-headed.

She still had no address for the enigmatic Malcolm but this did not matter as he turned up that very evening in person. He did not announce himself on the entryphone but only said, "May I come up, Aunt Bert?" As Jilly had maintained to Donald, his voice was immediately recognisable. Anyway, whoever else called her Aunt Bert? Her spirit lifted. With all his faults she still liked him the best of the bunch except for Gus perhaps and Gus belonged to God.

"Yes, but don't start any nonsense on the landing," she warned. She did not wish to attract Mrs Jaffa's attention.

When she opened the flat door to him she found herself speechless. This was not the real Malcolm but a facsimile of Donald. There was the mackintosh, near Burberry, the white-collared shirt, blue-trousered legs and, for her gaze was drawn to his feet, the black loafers. Only the hair was not the same for though he had been shorn in the identical manner, he was still dark where Donald was fair.

He stepped in with his own half-crooked smile, willing her approval.

173

"Well," he said, "what are you thinking?"

"I was thinking about hair," she said.

"The difference it makes?"

"No, though it does. I am thinking that it must have cost you a lot to abandon your own style."

"Oh, it did. Nearly broke me."

"I don't mean that," she said, closing the door with him safely inside. "I don't know why it is but people will do practically anything to preserve the right to dress their hair as they please, however ridiculous it may appear to others."

"I feel like Samson. And it's damned draughty. You don't approve of the transformation? I only did it for you."

Of course she knew this was false. What he had done was to defeat the memory of Mrs Trounce's daughter. He dared not come back to the Barbican in his old guise.

"Take off that absurd mac," she commanded irritably.

"I must admit that I feel devilishly cumbered with it."

He took it off and left it on the hall chair.

"Aren't you going to sit down? I'm a gent now and can't sit down until you do."

She sat on the sofa and he took the wing chair so that they were facing each other.

"Does Donald know what you have done?"

"Not unless he can see through a telephone."

"Did he tell you that I wanted to see you?"

"Yes. I was flattered."

"You need not be. I wanted to have a straight talk with you."

"When you take that tone I'm sure that you want to give me a scolding."

"I want Hugh's keys back . . . at once."

He put up a wonderful show of bewildered astonishment.

"Uncle Hugh's keys? Why on earth should you think that I have them?"

"For two reasons at least. You must remember that you asked to borrow them once and that I refused you."

"But I've never wanted to come here in your absence. Why should I with the main attraction away?"

"You said at the time that it was because you wanted to collect your portfolio when I was at the hairdresser's."

174

"Now I do have a vague recollection. Your memory is better than mine, Aunt Bert, it's no good pretending that you're losing it."

"I often forget the days of the week, because all days are alike to me now. I forget names of those who mean little to me. But if I put my mind to it I can recall anything I consider important. Hand over the keys, Malcolm."

"Do you want me to turn out my pockets? I have lots of pockets now in my new suit."

"Yes, your new suit. That too, requires explanation."

"Let's say I got tired of presenting myself as the poor relation. You have neighbours. Residents of the Barbican prefer visitors to look respectable."

"Residents of the Barbican prefer not to be burgled."

"What's that about burglaries? First I've heard of it. I hope nothing has happened to you?"

"No, it hasn't. Or to anybody in this house. That only confirms my suspicions."

"Do you mean you are openly accusing me of burglary? Really, Aunt Bert, this goes beyond a joke. It is insulting. If you weren't my own aunt and under stress I should be very angry with you."

Under his protestations ran a thin vein of mockery.

"You being my own nephew and hard-up doesn't prevent me from being very angry with you."

"Oh, come, Aunt Bert, if there have been any break-ins here that isn't exactly a novelty. No safety measures are one hundred percent infallible. Who has caught it this time?"

"You should know."

"With all the wide boys footloose in the neighbourhood why in heaven's name should you pitch on me?"

"Because Hugh's set of keys is no longer there in the drawer."

"Oh, is that all? You admit yourself that your memory is patchy. May I suggest that you've moved them yourself to some other place and have since forgotten what you did? It will come back if you don't fuss about it."

It could have happened like that but she did not believe it. She shook her head.

"We're all human, Aunt Bert. Would you like me to help you look around a bit?"

175

Oh yes, and relieve me of my diamond brooch, she thought.

"No thank you."

"Still suspicious, eh? If I didn't find it comic I should be thoroughly indignant. I don't claim to be a saint but I know how to keep my hands off other people's property."

"Do you?"

"It must be obvious that I'm often short of cash but I don't like being told I'm dishonest."

Should she continue to accuse him? Would it be wise? He was too plausible; altogether too clever for her. She didn't wish to antagonise him further, not because she was afraid of him but because she didn't want to lose him entirely.

She sighed. "When I was a child and picked an apple off a tree in somebody else's orchard I was sure that I stole and my parents would have agreed with me. Even a peach that came over our side of the wall. But now taking what doesn't belong to you seems almost acceptable, so long as one isn't caught. I may be old-fashioned in my views but don't ever mistake me for a doddering old fool. I *know* when you don't give me my change and take notes from my purse."

"Now that really is going too far. I must admit that on one occasion I may have forgotten who paid and slipped the change into my pocket unthinking. But to take notes from your purse would be a mean trick. You must have a pretty poor estimate of my character if you think I'm capable of that."

He looked genuinely upset. Stupidly, she drew back.

"Perhaps I miscounted. Anyhow, Malcolm, I do realise that you need more than you get. I know that your father keeps you short of cash and that a student grant doesn't keep pace with inflation whatever they say. I was going to suggest that as your aunt I should like to make you a little additional allowance."

"I wouldn't dream of it. I suppose I should thank you but don't you see it would destroy our relationship? When you don't get silly ideas into your head you are quite my favourite aunt."

"Just as, if you behave well, you are my favourite nephew."

"Then let's leave it like that."

176

"All the same, I think that there is something wrong or why are Donald and Jilly so uneasy?"

"What are they saying?"

"Nothing of moment. It's their general attitude."

"Then I'll tell you what's the matter if you promise to keep it confidential."

"Of course. I don't voice my doubts of you to them – or to anyone else."

"The fact is that Jilly has a *tendresse* for me. It was all right for her to be all over me when we were both kids, but now we're adults it's time that it stopped. Both Donald and I think it's unhealthy. I'm not saying a word against Jilly. She's a sweet thing and talented too. We don't want to hurt her but she has to get rid of this fixation. That's why I'm not seeing so much of them. We're trying to wean her. When the right guy comes along this will soon die the death."

Like most of Malcolm's impromptus, it was half true and half false. The *tendresse* was true but Malcolm was the last person to allow it to worry him. He would use it for his own benefit until it wore out or he himself cut the knot.

"And you are sensible not to confide in them your belief that I am the new Raffles of the Barbican. They would love that but they would also think that you were out of your tiny mind."

"You are preposterous and I don't know why I let you get away with it."

"We are kindred spirits and kindred spirits can say anything to each other."

"Then as one kindred spirit to another, where did you get the money to pay for your new outfit?"

Did he hesitate for a moment? He said: "I had it from the old man, if you must know. He must have had a narrow escape with his car or saw someone resembling my mother across the street. Who can tell what motivates a miser? Others have birthdays besides you, Aunt Bert."

She couldn't remember the date of his birthday though she could remember sending a silver christening mug to mark the occasion. And he could be certain that she would never write to his father to check up on it. They did not communicate except on matters of family urgency such as Hugh's funeral.

177

"I must take your word for it. But do tell me what on earth possessed you, if you wanted to change your image, to model yourself on your cousin Donald?"

"I thought that then you'd take me to the Cut Above."

They began to laugh simultaneously.

"So your nose was out of joint, was it? Well, name the day."

"What's wrong with here and now? I'm famished."

"Then I'd better ring for a table."

"I'll do that if you give me the number."

"I must change my dress. I wasn't expecting to go out on two evenings running. They'll have food for scandal when I arrive with another young man. You'll find the number in that alphabetical thing on the table."

"OK. You run along to the bedroom and I promise not to steal the silver teaspoons when you've gone."

She didn't think that he could get up to much mischief in the kitchen or the living room, but as a precaution she took her bag with her and closed the communicating door between that and the rest of the flat. She would let him see that she was taking no chances.

When she re-opened it he was standing by the flat door and already had his hand on the knob. The offending mack was draped over his arm.

"As you won't be coming back you can leave that in the cloakroom as we go by."

"Oh yes, Donald told me the drill." He gave the crooked smile. "You have to admit that my gear fits better than his although I don't mind betting that it all came from the same place."

Chapter 20

No sooner was she back from her outing than the telephone rang. It was Jilly wanting to show her over the School of Music and Drama. It had been a wonderful evening; the same food but not the same company. Malcolm had been at his most entertaining with a glint in his eye which Bertha hoped did not presage more mischief. Now she was over-stimulated and tetchy. She tried to put Jilly off.

"I don't think . . . all those stairs . . . another time perhaps."

"But, darling, I've got it all laid on. You can come along the flat to the library and then take the lift down to level five and I'll meet you there. You did ask, you know."

How many things one asks for and doesn't want when they materialise!

"I had thought of taking a cab to the West End to buy a few things."

"You can do that too. I was going to suggest one o'clock. It's better to come in the lunch hour and then we shan't risk barging in on anything important."

"Oh, well . . ." she agreed grudgingly.

Now they are starting to compete with each other for my favour, she thought. What a bore! I wish I could tell them they'll all have the same however much they set out to please. But she remembered the solicitor's warning.

"Get a good night's rest and be fit for tomorrow," Jilly had advised. "And mind you put on a pair of comfortable shoes."

Bertha, who had not really wanted to go to the West End, now felt that she had to in order to satisfy her conscience. She

179

started off early, remembering to put out the laundry for the man to collect around noon. As she stood waiting for the lift she thought that the only thing that she and Mrs Jaffa had in common were their coir mats, both in need of renewing.

She must have been nearly the first customer; the shoppers had not yet arrived from the outer suburbs. This used to be her favourite store, but no longer since it had begun to change its image for something younger and smarter. The elderly assistants with their plaint of "Can I help you, Madam?" had been pensioned off. The stock reply: "I'm only looking" now was a dismal truth. There was no one to help and one had to hunt for what one wanted. This was all the more aggravating as the items that Bertha wanted were fast becoming very rare; stockings with seams, corselets with suspenders, tailored knickers.

She bought a pair of gloves which she no longer wore and six embroidered handkerchiefs from the Far East which she would have to wash herself if she didn't want the laundry to rip them to shreds. Then she went up the escalator to find a cup of coffee which she decided was richly deserved.

From there she went on to the designer room where the good dresses were all chained down. This put her off. And anyway, she came to the conclusion that they were really suited to someone who lived in a tower block.

She remembered that she needed a refill for her compact and went down the escalator again to wend her way through an array of cosmetics until she found the right stand only to be beaten at the post because the attractively made-up young woman in charge couldn't find the right shade. Disenchanted she rode the escalator once more for more coffee and this time an open sandwich which made a nice change from cuts from the joint. As she consumed it slowly her thoughts once more turned to her neighbour . . . why did she have that woman so much on her mind? An ordinary shop lifter stole for profit; Mrs Jaffa stole to compensate for a psychic injury she had suffered in the past. Malcolm's behaviour appeared to be a combination of both.

In a way she was pleased by his refusal of financial help; it showed a desire to be independent. In a way she was perturbed because if he couldn't accept what she offered who could

180

predict his next move? She grew tired of her sandwich. Why did prawns nowadays taste of nothing at all? She made her last descent by escalator and went through the porch and on to the street. There she stood on the pavement waiting a long time for a taxi which didn't sail past her. Finally one arrived and the driver, having set down his fares, consented to take her back to the Barbican. She thought how much she now preferred the East End to the West.

The cab deposited her in Silk Street by the lifts. Jilly immediately came out from behind the glass doors where she had been patiently waiting.

"Clever old you. You found another way to get here. Did you do any good?"

Bertha feebly wagged the thin plastic bag at her in answer.

"Fine. I never visit those shops except when the sales are on."

"And I never visit them when the sales are on, so we're not likely to meet."

"Why are you hobbling?"

"I like to walk like that," said Bertha sourly.

"We'll go round by the back. There's a conference on at the Centre."

"What a pity! I envy you your stretch by the lake which is marked off as private. It always looks so beautifully peaceful."

"You can go back that way. The bods will have gone back inside by then."

"Who are they?"

"I don't know. I couldn't get up close enough to see. Something dreary I've no doubt. Cheer up, we're nearly there."

"Surely that's the back of The Cut Above?"

Bertha was astonished to see it from a different angle.

"I heard you took Donald there."

"Don't say you want to go as well!" groaned Bertha.

"Not my scene, darling. But Donald adored it. It's just his glass of claret. I'm glad you're getting on better."

"Are we?"

"He says so. He's not so bad, really. He's dependable. I suppose that I'm used to him because he's my brother. This is the door we go in by."

In close-up the school was not a little forbidding. With its bluish bricks built out like ramparts and cement loopholes it looked more like an under-nourished fort than an Academy.

Inside, Bertha found it disappointing, perhaps owing to her fraught morning. It was, in her opinion, far too much like a school; or too much like the rest of the Barbican. Seated down both sides of a long hall was a fair sample of its students, chewing glumly away at their luncheon snacks provided by a canteen housed in the basement. Unlike the majority of students these seemed wholesome and clean, if shabbily dressed. She observed that Jilly, too, wore a cotton dress and a cardigan instead of her usual flamboyant attire. But they didn't seem the stuff stars are made of and she wondered which ones, if any, would reach the dizy heights to which they aspired. The glances which followed their progress showed Jilly as well-established; Bertha didn't make the mistake of thinking them due to her aunt.

The theatre was being re-decorated but they were allowed into the music hall where a massive display of instrument cases heaped on the floor indicated that a rehearsal would soon be in progress. As this was not Jilly's province it was dismissed with a few words. Yet Bertha could see that she doted on every square inch of this horrible building. It was hallowed to her because of what it stood for; it was the place where she was being taught how to make full use of her natural ability. In it she was being prepared for achieving the one thing she thought of real importance in life – her conquest of the stage. How young she was under that thin layer of sophistication!

Afterwards Bertha recognised that she must have been shown over rooms besides those devoted to practice. But then it seemed as if practice room succeeded to practice room, an infinite series of practice rooms. At last she was released from what must have been the most monumentally dull conducted tour in the world and that is saying a lot. They came down a lift and out by the entrance hall, where Jilly abandoned her in a hurry as she suddenly remembered that she had a date with a visiting teacher. This Bertha would have enjoyed being present at but unfortunately it was never allowed.

Still hobbling, Bertha walked as fast as she could, which

was not saying much, along the pleasant water front which she had praised to Jilly. Dearly she would have liked to cast herself down on one of their garden seats which looked more comfortable than the cast iron ones on the terrace proper. But she knew that if she once sat down she would be unable to get up again. Once past the barrier she saw the backs of the last of the delegates disappearing into the maw of the Barbican foyer. She saw from the posters that it was some sort of a Trade Congress. Good. It might have been doves and peace. Bertha had the idea that only Trade would bring Peace. It had done so in the past and would do so again. As she dragged herself up the last flight of stairs leading to her flat with the aid of the handrail, she knew that it was Peace that she wanted for herself. Peace with a capital P.

Completely exhausted, she hung up her coat in the bedroom cupboard, put on her bedroom slippers and went along to the living room prepared to make tea. But just as she was about to plug in the kettle, there was Patsy at the window, tapping to be let in.

"Knock, knock, who's there?" Her thoughts reverted involuntarily to *Macbeth*.

She loved Patsy but there were times . . . Grudgingly she went to the window to pull back the lever. It would have been impossible to deny entry to Patsy in her present mood anyway.

"Oh, Bertha, I'm so glad you're back safely! There's been a disaster and poor Lennie is in it up to the eyeballs!"

"What's happened to him?"

"It's not what has happened so much as what is going to happen. The Orange has taken a bad tumble and says it's his fault."

"Well, it isn't mine, thank goodness. I was out."

"I know. That's why he decided to wash the tiles on the landing and down the passage. He has to get it in when he can, poor lamb. He saw you go out and Jaffa doesn't usually come out with her washing until twelve. So he thought it would have plenty of time to dry out before it came back into use again. Would you believe it? That woman came out early with her laundry box and slipped on the mat. She has one of those rope things like yours."

183

"No wonder I was thinking about her."

"Were you really? Down she went and couldn't get up again. That was her story. And no one came until the chap called for the laundry. There she lay like a stranded fish. He fetched Lennie and neither dared move her in case she'd broken a bone. So then they sent a nurse over from the Centre to assess the damage and it appears she was only bruised so between the three of them they man-handled her into bed and 'phoned up the Doctor."

"So for once he had to come home for his lunch?"

"No, he didn't, the unfeeling scoundrel. His secretary said he had an important patient at two and couldn't possibly get back until half-past. She asked if someone would stay with his wife until then. The nurse couldn't so Lennie came for poor Muggins. I had to go in with a can of soup. Slimmer's soup, but she lapped it up anyhow. My dear, what furnishing! He must have bought new stuff for the consulting room and dragged all the auction room debris back to his lair."

Bertha looked at the clock. "Is he back yet?"

"Yes, I've just been let off the hook."

"Perhaps I should offer . . ."

"You stay right away. I only wanted to warn you. I wouldn't tangle with that man for all the tea in China. Besides she has a down on you. I don't know why."

"Well, I do. But it wasn't my fault."

"Never mind. It's Lennie who's for it this time. For leaving wet under the mat. I heard him telling her that he took the mats and your laundry box and put them all at the top of the stairs before he started in with his mop. Those tiles don't dry off at once and they may be a bit slippery when they're wet especially if she pushed off with her foot as if she was skating. Holding the box she couldn't save herself. Luckily, there's not much damage done but there could have been, I suppose."

"She should have seen that the tiles were still damp."

"Well, the Doctor is hell-bent on blaming someone. I left him getting ready to go down to the housekeeper's office to chase up poor Lennie."

"Thank goodness I wasn't here!"

Now she could look back with less jaundiced eyes at the School of Music and Drama.

"It's rough on Lennie but I did feel a teeny bit sorry for the Orange. She did have a fright and she looked such a waif amongst all those dreadful consulting room cast-offs."

"I used to feel sorry for her too. But lately I've taken to dodging her."

"Keep it up. Keep it up. I only came in to warn you. Let them sort it out. You haven't done anything."

"Perhaps that's why I feel guilty."

"Such goings on. We should be in a soap opera. Or a soup opera. You look as if you could do with a little bit of shut-eye, if you don't mind me saying so."

"All I want is a nice cup of tea," exclaimed the exasperated Bertha.

"I could do with one too. Come along, sweetie. Plug in the kettle."

Chapter 21

After the nap recommended by Patsy, Bertha began to feel human again and in better command of the situation. Her neighbour had suffered a fall. That, fortunately, was nothing to do with her. Except that, of course, in spite of what Patsy advised, she must later offer condolences and ask what she could do to help. And send flowers? Grapes? A murder mystery?

She switched on the six o'clock news which was bad as usual and after that settled down on the sofa to continue reading *Alice in Wonderland*. So relaxed was she that when her front door bell rang she didn't immediately think that it was a burglar or even Malcolm but supposed that it was someone collecting for something. This was the time they usually chose as the one most likely to find anyone at home.

She opened it without even bothering to put on the chain and there on the threshold stood Dr Jaffa, all six foot and over of him. She was so surprised that she didn't at once ask him in; not that he requested permission to enter. With one broad palm he pushed the door wider open and walked past her with an authoritative air, leaving her to close it. When that was done she turned to find him already seated in the wing chair and signalling her to sit in the small tub opposite. She sat there like a rabbit transfixed by a stoat.

Le Fanu's Uncle Silas . . . that was the resemblance. He had never seen her at close quarters before, she supposed, and now he gave her a thorough examination from head to bedroom slippers, returning to make a special study of her face. Pity the poor lunatics, she thought, but even so she was

187

totally unprepared for the first words which issued from his lips.

"Mrs Harris, I must insist that you stop persecuting my wife".

This broke the spell and released a torrent of protest.

"Really, if anything it's the other way round."

"You may like to think so. The reversal of roles is a classic example of the mind at bay."

"This is ludicrous! Complete nonsense. Whatever makes you imagine . . ."

"Ever since you discovered her poor little secret you have made capital out of it."

"I didn't discover it. That absurd object popped out of her bag and I helped her retrieve it. I can assure you that I've never mentioned the occurrence to a single soul. In fact, I did my best to forget it."

"Before that you used to exchange courtesies like good neighbours. Now you send her to Coventry."

They are both foreign, she thought wildly. Whatever English person would dream of using such archaic phrases?

"Certainly I used to wish her good morning when we met on the landing. Now I seldom see her."

"You avoid her."

It was true. She sat uncomfortably silent.

"You came into our flat and berated her after she had shown her concern for you and reported the incident when you failed to put out your refuse bag for collection."

"Oh, but that was an invasion of privacy. It upset me very much at the time. Later I realised that she meant well and I wrote to apologise."

"You hurt her feelings. She is extremely sensitive."

"Perhaps I am over-sensitive too. Since my husband died . . ."

"Ah yes, a mitigating circumstance as they say in the Courts. But it doesn't excuse a malicious attempt to cause her actual bodily harm."

Bertha was greatly alarmed. What outrageous accusation would this gorilla announce next? And she did not doubt that he could make things unpleasant for her if he liked.

"But I didn't. I was very sorry to hear of her fall. I was going

188

to enquire after her if you had only waited. I had nothing to do with it. I wasn't even in the building when it occurred. I can bring witnesses . . . I was told that you put the blame on Lennie for washing the tiles."

"That is right. I had Lennie on the mat," he said with a ponderous attempt at humour. "He insists that he uses no detergent in the water, only a small quantity of disinfectant. He admits that he washes right up to the door, but before doing this he removes the mats. When he has finished he replaces them. Naturally his other duties do not permit him to stay until the tiles dry off. He may not have expected my wife to come out so soon."

"Well, that explains it, doesn't it? Those tiles become slightly slippery with water, even without a detergent."

"My poor wife was convinced that you had a hand in it. So, to please her – she is quite bruised, you understand – when Lennie had gone I took in the mat and examined it carefully, both above and below."

"I should imagine that it was probably still damp."

"Underneath the mat I detected a strong smell of lemon in addition to the disinfectant. I then used the tips of my fingers on it. Mrs Harris, that mat had been deliberately daubed with washing-up liquid. It was not damp, it was dry. I moistened it. It became at first tacky, then slippery. Need I say more?"

"Dr Jaffa, this is really too silly!"

"It is not silly, Mrs Harris, it is serious. I did not tell my wife but I scraped off a small sample for analysis. But there is no doubt in my mind at all. Washing-up liquid."

"I can't argue with you. I can only repeat that I had nothing to do with it whatever."

She found that she was trembling. He observed it.

"Come, Mrs Harris," he said in a tolerant voice. "I shan't eat you. We all do things under stress that we should not do otherwise. My wife is only bruised, but she might have broken her thigh. She might even have hit her head on the skirting and fractured her skull."

He did not seem unduly distressed by this possible outcome. He scratched his nose. After a short pause he went on: "There are other indications that all is not well with you."

"Oh?"

"Since your husband's death, a man for whom I had the utmost respect, my wife tells me that you have been visited frequently by three young men and a girl."

"A niece and three nephews."

"They did not come here when Mr Harris was alive."

"They were my relatives, not his."

As she said this she realised that as an explanation it was not altogether convincing. But why did she need to convince the doctor? It was her own business, not his.

"I have only caught sight of one of them myself. I was not favourably impressed."

"I don't suppose you would be."

"My wife said that you claimed that one of the other young men was a theological student, but that he wore a dirty blanket with a rope round it."

"Your wife is a Roman Catholic. I should have thought that she would have recognised a member of a religious order when she saw one."

"I am only repeating what my wife says. She is of the opinion that the young woman is a prostitute."

Her aunt found her cheeks burning.

"Anyway, they are not the sort of visitors we are accustomed to see in the Barbican. I suggest to you, Mrs Harris, without seeking to give offence, that these young people were originally picked up by you to relieve your loneliness and that they are now making the best of their opportunities."

"Dr Jaffa, you are insulting!"

"Not so. It is simply that I wish to protect you. And believe me, dear lady, there is good reason for my behaviour."

"Then tell me that reason!"

"It is my opinion that, subsequent to your husband's death, you have been temporarily thrown off balance. My medical opinion, understand. I do not speak lightly."

"Do you mean to infer that I am off my head?"

"No, no. I do not say that my wife is mad because she has this compulsion to pocket small objects. Unfortunately, I cannot cure her. Her condition is too deep-rooted. But you need only complete rest and relief from anxiety to return you to sanity."

"But I'm not insane!"

"You could not be certified, that is manifestly true. But I do not like the sound of these voices."

"What voices?"

"My wife told me that you confessed you heard voices."

How had she come to confide in that crazy woman? As far as she remembered, it was a natural response to offset Mrs Jaffa's embarrassment in being revealed as a kleptomaniac. Who would ever have thought that it would rebound in this way? Instinct warned her to be careful as she attempted to explain.

"I hear only one voice and that is my husband's. It sounds real but I know that it isn't. It's a trick of memory. After so long a marriage, and being so close, our thoughts were often identical."

The doctor considered this carefully. Then he demanded, as if springing a trap: "Does this voice ever instruct you to do anything?"

Being a stickler for truth she hesitated the barest moment, with the recollection of the birthday party.

Immediately he pounced. "Ah!"

"It certainly didn't instruct me to put washing-up liquid under your wife's mat."

His teeth gleamed at her. He had excellent teeth.

"Mrs Harris, shall we forget that unhappy incident for the time being? I have a suggestion to make to you. Out at Epping I run an excellent nursing home, with a well-qualified matron and trained staff. Do not look so startled. It is not a loony bin. It caters for those who are having small problems through the loss of a loved one, involvement in an accident, being mugged . . . trauma, in fact. They come as voluntary patients and submit themselves to my treatment for an agreed period, say three months. They return home as different persons."

The audacity of the man . . . the sheer cheek! One could almost admire him for it.

"It is like a holiday in a perfectly appointed hotel."

"And how much does this . . . holiday cost?"

"It is not inexpensive but not beyond your means, my dear lady."

If he had been less intimidating her reply would have been

191

different. As it was she said lamely: "I could not possibly leave here for three months."

"But, Mrs Harris, you must know that some of the tenants are away for a year at a time. Your flat would remain undisturbed until you came back to it. Of course you might decide that the life there suited you as a refuge from the irksome responsibilities of present day living. Alas, as the years pass we do not become any younger. There comes a time . . ."

There did indeed come a time to put a stop to this monstrous salesmanship. Or was it blackmail?

She braced herself to get rid of him.

"No," she said as she rose from her chair. "No, Dr Jaffa, I do not wish to take advantage of your kind offer. I am not quite alone in the world as you seem to imagine. I have two brothers and a sister, the parents of those young people who come to visit me. They would shelter me in my old age if that become necessary." And what a lie that was! crossed her mind. "I have the assurance of my solicitor who visited me recently that there is no deterioration in my faculties and that I am perfectly capable of conducting my own affairs without outside interference. I hope that your wife will make a swift recovery from her domestic mishap, and now I have letters to write so perhaps you will excuse me?"

Reluctantly he came to his feet.

"Two acres of delightfully landscaped grounds," he murmured. "Gourmet food such as one does not get at The Cut Above."

"I am not interested."

"Think it over," he urged, half way to the door. "After all, we are only across the passage."

And how I wish that were further, she thought.

At the coffee table he paused and picked up the book she had been reading. His beetle brows rose as he put it down.

"*Alice in Wonderland*! That is a child's book, is it not?"

"It was written for children. It is not a child's book," she said firmly. Let him make what he likes of that, she thought as she closed the door on him.

At his departure her wits sharpened. She had a clear picture of Malcolm standing there waiting for her to come out of her bedroom. She went into the kitchen and inspected the bottle of washing-up liquid. It was nearly empty. On its front it had the word LEMON inscribed in conspicuous lettering.

At least it doesn't say DRINK ME, she thought.

Although it was still far too early she went off to bed.

Chapter 22

All through the night Bertha's anger seemed to have burgeoned and spread until by the morning it was in full flower. Whilst she was sleeping the unconscious, the id, or whatever one liked to call it, had been busy at its secret work, collecting and collating the evidence until it was ready to produce its computerised result when required.

In a way she was there before it, because she knew what had happened before she took to her bed. Lennie had innocently switched the two look-alike mats; what had befallen Mrs Jaffa had been intended for her.

Insufferable Malcolm – hadn't he yet out-grown the age of practical jokes? For at first she had seen this as merely a schoolboy prank, worthy of the lower fourth, depending for its success on unknown factors. For although he might have foretold that the tiles would be washed sooner or later, not even Lennie could have told him when.

It had been one of his famous ideas which had come to him as he stood between the kitchen and the door waiting for her to get changed. And it had landed her in a thoroughly disagreeable half-hour. She did not really believe that the doctor would fulfil his threat to have his sample analysed as he was not the sort to invite ridicule. But it had given him the whip hand in a conversation from which she still smarted.

Ungrateful Malcolm, for what had she ever done to deserve this of him? The id had the answer to hand. She had interfered in his nefarious activities, she had accused him of stealing Hugh's keys, she had offended his pride by offering him financial support.

On second thoughts, was it a joke? What had the doctor said? It was only a tumble but it might have been a broken hip . . . or a cracked skull. Didn't he care if he immobilised her? Or killed her? Practical jokes sometimes had fatal results which were never intended. They could be the product of immature minds . . . they were often cruel.

This jelled with his youthful escapades, his slap-dash paintings, even the crude attempts at pornography.

If it was an act of revenge that put it in another category. Neither of these possibilities meshed with the behaviour of the charming young adult, brimming with wit and consideration who had accompanied her to The Cut Above and given her a memorable evening.

If her relations with the doctor next door had been different she could have asked him to sort out Malcolm for her. For though he might be half rogue, he was also a trained psychiatrist. And if he was knowledgeable about trauma, he could have told her how much of Malcolm's split personality was due to his unfortunate family history. With a father obsessed by money and a mother who had deserted him rather than live under the shadow of this obsession, what chance did he have of normality?

And to hark back further, what had made Rupert a born miser for his condition was certainly as manic as Mrs Jaffa's? Oh, it was idle to seek for first causes. To pursue that would be to find herself back with Adam. And it was equally idle to think of enlisting the doctor's help when he had her down as a suitable candidate for Epping. Even if it had been explained to her what was wrong with her nephew it didn't solve the problem of what to do about him. She shrank from another session with Malcolm. Instinct warned her that it might be too dangerous. Anyway, she still didn't know where he was to be found.

She couldn't take her trouble to Patsy. She had so far kept Patsy in the dark as regards her relations and she couldn't now tear down that curtain between fantasy and reality. Besides it was beyond her friend's range. It might not be beyond Sam's, but she knew what he would advise. Insist on, perhaps. That she should turn the whole business over to the police. She couldn't do it. She might be brought into contact with the very

196

men who had gazed in upon her from the balcony. Perhaps this was only an excuse. The bare fact of the matter was that she could not bring herself to hand Malcolm over to the forces of law and order. Yet wasn't it exactly this particular human frailty, the inability to inform on one's nearest and dearest, that kept so many criminals at large in the community? Malcolm was dear to her; now she was forced to admit it. There was an empathy between the two of them which didn't exist with the others.

In the midst of her anxious reflections the 'phone rang. She came to with a start. When she answered it she was, for the moment, completely at a loss. The call had one advantage. It had nothing whatever, she thought, to do with her present preoccupation. It was an aged, aged voice, asking her if it would be convenient for the Father Superior of St Joseph's to visit her that afternoon? Caught on the hop, her immediate reaction was, Oh, bother, he is coming to ask me for money for that was the worst of charitable donations, they always invited more. However, because this quavering falsetto at once brought to her mind a vision of one of those old monks of whom Gus had spoken who felt the cold, who subsisted on gruel or something similar, she did not like to be too severe. He was obviously acting as an intermediary, a kind of ecclesiastical secretary. And how did one refuse a request from a Father Superior? She had the usual unbeliever's respect for one placed high in the religious hierarchy. She found herself asking what time was suggested. Any time to suit her. Four o'clock? Yes, that would be fine. And now he will expect tea, she thought, cross with herself. With a repeated thank you, the instrument was put down at the other end.

Had this poor old body taken her number from the directory or had he got it from Gus? Biscuits, she decided, it will have to be biscuits.

Concetta came and was persuaded to clean the silver teapot which from disuse had become golden. Concetta greatly disliked cleaning silver and would advance all manner of arguments to avoid it but, on this occasion, Bertha stood firm and after a preliminary show of spreading out newspapers, donning rubber gloves, etc, her handmaid got on with the job. Once started she went on to clean the milk jug, the sugar basin and even a pair of tongs to strengthen her sense of grievance. Luckily she was mute. She must have heard of Mrs Jaffa's downfall from Lennie but she did not mention it; perhaps she thought that she had been too loose-tongued about the robberies.

At two o'clock she departed leaving a long space between then and four. Bertha began to feel nervous, she scarcely knew why. Certainly she had never entertained a Father Superior before though she had once had a set-to with a forceful Mother Prioress over the exact definition of a State of Grace. Perhaps this was what coloured the forthcoming meeting. She arranged the tea tray with cups and saucers; though she put away the tongs and finally substituted a bowl of granulated sugar for the basin along with a spoon. Then, fearing that the biscuits might prove inadequate she cut a plateful of very thin bread and butter, an art which she thought she had lost through neglect. She poured milk into the silver jug. She wondered if he should have China tea or Indian, and settled on Indian. These preparations completed there was still ample opportunity to roam round the room, pulling out the spines of books in the open bookcases, arranging suitable titles which might catch his eye, plumping up cushions. Plump? Yes, he would be like Friar Tuck. Was he the one to be consulted about Malcolm? To reassure her, gently patting her arm? Had Gus instructed him in the use of the entryphone? She went along to the bathroom to rinse her hands after contact with the books and as she dried them on a towel, the instrument buzzed at her. After a hasty glance at her face in the mirror she hurried down the passage to give him admittance.

As soon as she opened the door to him, her fears vanished. Except for his Roman collar, there was no other indication of his standing. He wore a blue raincoat which looked as if it had once been purchased from an RAF surplus store. It hung, faded and limp, above grey flannel trousers from which emerged old-fashioned laced shoes polished to such extreme brilliance that it emphasised the creases running across the width of the foot. On a scraggy neck was positioned a face so thin that its bones hinted at the skull beneath the parched skin. So much for Friar Tuck! But the eyes were remarkable;

very light in colour, they seemed to be luminous. They were not the eyes of a fanatic blind to everything outside one purpose, but very sagacious. As she helped him out of his raincoat, they appraised her. Not like the Doctor, seeking for signs of abnormality but weighing her up as a woman. But strangely enough he was as nervous as she had been; it showed in his hands.

"Tell me what I am to call you," she begged impulsively. "I haven't the least idea of how one addresses a Father Superior in private conversation."

"Just call me Father Jerome. And I know you are Mrs Harris, of course."

"Would you like to sit down while I make some tea?"

"I'd rather look around if you don't mind. I've never been to the Barbican before."

"Do. Why don't you go out on the balcony for a better view? The window is unlatched. It slides when you push it."

She went into the kitchen to bring the kettle back to the boil and warm the pot before putting in the tea leaves. She added a strainer to the contents of the tray. When she carried it in to put it down on the coffee table he was still on the balcony examining her flowers in the window boxes.

As he came into the room again, closing the window behind him, she asked: "Well, what do you think of it?"

"It is much more homely and familiar than I imagined. Small children playing on the grass; that huge expanse of sky. And your flowers."

"Some people find it unfriendly."

"Possibly they are unfriendly people."

"How do you like your tea, Father?"

"Just as it comes. It was a wonderful concept for an inner city. All sorts and conditions of men living together with the Arts at the centre. The planners forgot only one thing."

"Oh?"

"The very poor."

"In August the Centre is open to every city child . . . and its parents."

"The crumbs from the rich man's table, wouldn't you say?"

"Perhaps. Would you like a biscuit . . . or bread and butter?"

"Bread and butter, please. So exquisitely thin. I had almost forgotten that it could be cut like that."

"So had I, to be truthful. Milk? Sugar?"

"A little milk, please. I don't take sugar."

She had meant to talk to him about France to put him at ease but there was no need.

He sat quietly drinking her tea from the delicate china and nibbling at the wafer thin slice held between finger and thumb. He ate the whole plateful. When he had finished, without any self-consciousness, he licked a small suspicion of butter off the top of one tapering finger with the tip of his tongue. Still he sat silent as if the taste had brought back to him the taste of the past, just as it did to Proust.

At last he said: "Mrs Harris, I have come to repay a debt of gratitude."

He put away his plate and declined another cup of tea. He became more serious as if bent on business.

"I want to talk to you about Gregory."

"Gregory?" She was quite at a loss. The only Gregory she knew was a nasty grey powder associated with her extreme youth.

"Oh, that is his name in the Order. Of course he has another one by which you would recognise him at once."

"Do you mean Gus? Augustus. We call him Gus."

"It had slipped my memory. How silly of me. We might just as well have changed the ending to 'ine' and left it at that. Augustus is rather too reminiscent of the Unholy Roman Empire."

He gave a shy smile at his own little joke.

"What has he done?"

"It is a sin of omission. Now, if I may have your complete attention, I will be as brief as I can be."

"I can't believe that Gus . . . Gregory . . ."

"We will call him Gus for this purpose then you won't be confused. Now Gus is not the usual novice. If he weren't so easy to live with I should say that he might make a saint."

"That's exactly why . . . I'm sorry, Father. Please carry on."

"He has this extraordinary sense of rapport. He goes everywhere in the district and everywhere he is welcome. It isn't sympathy exactly; it's as if he became one with those who seek his help with their problems. I can't come nearer to it than that, I'm afraid."

"Is that good or bad?"

"It is an excellent prospect. For, later on, as he gains experience, he will also have an answer to queries which plague them. And if he does not have the answer, he will be able to teach them to live with and accept the unalterable which is a part of Divine teaching."

He paused. "Do you know, I think I will change my mind and ask for another cup of that fragrant tea. We are now coming to the difficult part."

"I'm afraid it has gone cold."

"Never mind. Oh, thank you, thank you." He drank it all off at once.

"You see," he said, " it is the custom of the novices to make regular confessions to Father Ignatius. He is a wise old bird greatly versed in all the small sins and knows how to deal with them faithfully. Our boys are kept so close that they have little chance to commit anything but the most venial of offences. If they came to me they might be tempted to embroider and that it is wise to prevent. However, when Gregory – Gus – asked if I personally would hear his confession I was sure that the lapse must be genuine and probably beyond the scope of Ignatius. Obviously I could not deny him. I thought that he might have got into deep water in the neighbourhood. He moves about more freely than the others and not always as a pair." Again he paused. He regarded her thoughtfully.

"Why come to me, Father Jerome? Even I am well aware that confessions are sacred."

"Yes, of course. That is why I cannot tell you directly what he confided in me. But I can send him to you and advise him to make a clean breast of it, which is what I have done. I consider the matter sufficiently serious."

"It is very mysterious . . . and a little alarming."

"I don't want to frighten you but to be alarmed is to take precautions."

"I cannot associate anything dubious with Gus."

"Exactly. That is the reason for my apprehensions. I may

be mistaken. I hope that I am. He needed to come to me. You know, when I was a novice and found myself in a quandary I used to think, I will take that to the Father Superior; let him decide. Now I am the Father Superior and it is not so easy."

"All the same, you make the decisions."

"Yes, it is my duty. I see implications which I should not have seen as a novice." He rose. "You have been patient in listening to me and I hope that you will be equally patient with Greg . . . Gus. May I send him round tomorrow at about the same time?"

"If you think it is necessary."

"Mrs Harris, I have known you for only a few hours. I was indebted to you as a benefactress. Now I think of you as a generous, kindly woman in need of protection. If you will forgive the presumption, would you permit me to make a suggestion?"

"Of course, Father."

"At our House in France there is a guest house run by the nuns. It is very comfortable and I am told that the sisters are excellent cooks well up to French standard. They grow their own produce. I can ensure that there will be a vacancy for you. Would you consider leaving here almost at once for a few months of perfect rest and security?"

She began to laugh and saw his surprise.

"I'm sorry, Father, but you are the second person to offer me asylum in the last two days."

"Oh well, I see that you are well cared for," he observed rather stiffly.

"No, really. I am deeply grateful and your proposition sounds much more rewarding than his. May I think it over?"

"Certainly. And thank you for my excellent tea. I shall remember both it and you."

She assisted him into his shabby old blue mac and went with him to the door.

"Bless you, my daughter," he said, with these two words putting her in her proper place and distancing himself from any closer relationship.

As the lift opened its door for him he said quickly: "Should you consider a change in your Will, give a thought to St Joseph's."

It closed on him and he was gone from her life.

Chapter 23

In order to catch Donald before he set off for work Jilly rang him early on the following day to tell him that she would not be at their usual rendezvous as she had an invitation to a party in Chelsea. Not best pleased at being torn from his cornflakes, he responded grumpily.

"You can come if you like."

If she had not been well aware of his aversion to parties she would not have risked asking him. It was not the sort of gathering of which Donald would have approved. Indeed, she was doubtful about it herself and would not have accepted if she hadn't been assured that at least one television director would be present.

He now replied pithily in the negative.

"Oh, well. You can't complain, you've been going it yourself. Two nights running at The Cut Above with Aunt."

"One."

"Don't try to deceive me, my boy. I have my spies. The girl in the cloaks is a buddy of mine. She recognised Aunt. She said the first time you acted stiff and proud but the second time she gave you the eye and you responded."

"Rubbish!"

"Well, she is on the whole. She's goofy about anything in trousers. But she wouldn't make a mistake about a thing like that. She hung up your mackintosh."

"It wasn't me."

"Quite the city gent you looked, she said."

"Look, Jilly, this is quite ridiculous."

"If you want to keep me in the dark about the progress you're making with Aunt, that's OK with me."

"Jilly, I swear I wasn't there. If Aunt appeared with someone who bore a superficial resemblance to me it means that she's in tow with another fellow. I shall have to look into this."

"How?"

"I shall ask her straight out."

"I wish you luck. Have you seen anything of Malcolm lately?"

"No, I haven't. Now I must go. I haven't finished my breakfast."

Good as his word, he rang Bertha from a call box in his lunch hour. She heard the pips and wondered who it might be. Concetta never used a telephone as they didn't convey mime.

"Donald here," he said.

"Oh!"

"I just wanted to thank you for my meal out," he went on. "Very enjoyable."

She was surprised but gratified that he still obeyed the conventional courtesies.

"It was nice to have you."

"Look, Aunt, I don't wish to be nosey but I've been told that you took another young man there the night after. Now, of course we can't interfere with your private life but naturally we're concerned with your welfare. Is this someone you know well?"

There was a pause. The next candidate for the use of the box scowled at Donald from outside. Bertha began to laugh.

"Oh, that was Malcolm!"

"But surely, I mean . . . I didn't think that Malcolm looked respectable enough to take to a place like that."

"Didn't you know? He's turned over a new leaf sartorially."

"But his hair . . ."

"He's had it cut, short back and sides."

"I can't believe it."

"You wait until you see him. He's patterned himself on you, Donald."

His reply was spontaneous. "Of all the damned cheek!"

She laughed again. "Even to the mackintosh." In the midst of her tribulations his consternation really amused her.

"You should be pleased. Don't they say that imitation is the sincerest form of flattery?"

"Not in this case," he retorted sharply and slammed down the receiver.

How delighted Malcolm would be with his reaction, she thought. Self-preservation may have counselled the change in his appearance but he certainly knew how to get under the skin of his cousin.

For the moment her anxiety about Malcolm was replaced by her curiosity about Gus. It was beyond her to imagine what the sin of omission could have been. The Father Superior was a strange man, likeable but strange. She thought he was sufficiently unworldly to have magnified the transgression. But it was Gus who had sought his opinion in the first place and Gus had a leavening of commonsense, imparted by his own father and the years on the farm. Why did the Father have to present himself as an intermediary? Surely Gus could be trusted to follow his instructions? A sin of omission; she was sure that she had several in her own past. She knew she had one in the making; it was unlikely that she would visit the suffering Mrs Jaffa. She felt a pang of sympathy for the boys of St Joseph's who yearned for a worthwhile sin to confess. A storm in a teacup, that's what it was. But Gus could have his in a mug and the bread and butter she would cut for him would be much thicker than yesterday's.

She looked forward to a tête-à-tête but when he arrived she saw at once that something was badly awry.

Although he wore his tweed suit, a penitential garment would obviously have suited him better; his air was totally dejected. She sat him down and made tea which he drank thirstily. He took a slice of bread and butter but after one bite put it down. "I can't eat. I'm sorry, Aunt."

"Better get it over, then, if that will make you feel better."

His chin sunk on to the knot of his tie. "I'm ashamed," he said, "so very ashamed."

"It can't be as bad as all that."

"I don't know where to begin. It has been nagging at me

205

ever since it happened. It was at the party, you know. Your birthday party."

"But I thought that was such a success. I know I enjoyed it and you all seemed so happy and carefree together."

"Yes, that's what makes it worse. It was right at the end when we were getting ready to go. I went into the kitchen to wash up a few things and the others were still in the living room larking about. You were sitting on the sofa, half asleep, and Jilly leant over and whispered in your ear. I heard what she said and I let it go by. I should have rebuked them (rebuked, what a word! it smacked of his confessor) and later on I should have told you what they had done."

Like Alice she felt herself, after progressing through a long tunnel, suddenly falling down a deep well; so deep that she wondered if she would ever reach the bottom. Down, down, down . . . It was quite painless and her progress was slow. On the way down she passed their four faces, apparently bodiless, regarding her from small cupboards in the wall. Malcolm, smiling crookedly, Donald solemn, Jilly vivacious, and last of all Gus, doleful with his sin of omission. Finally she reached ground level and picked herself up, dazed but knowing that she would have to ask questions to find out where she had landed.

Her voice, when she started to use it, sounded hoarse and strange. Like Alice, she wasn't at all sure that it was making good sense.

"I was sure it was Hugh."

"Yes. That was why it was such a shabby trick."

"But they didn't know anything about that. You were the only one I told in the family."

"*I* told Malcolm. It was just after you had given me the cheque for the electricity bill. I was over the moon about it. He rang up and I told him what you had done. Then I went on and repeated what you had said about Uncle Hugh. I can't think why I did it. We were only chatting and I believe he asked me how I thought you were. Later on I realised that I had probably abused a confidence but, of course, I didn't go further and consider where it might lead."

"So it was all false. None of you ever felt the slightest affection for me as a person. All any of you cared about was what I had in my account at the bank."

206

"No, that's not true. Don't forget that in the beginning you were a complete stranger to us. We had no idea what you were like, As we got to know you better we thought that you were great."

"A great fool. So the famous party was just a sham. Staged to give Jilly her debut."

"It didn't start there. It must have begun soon after the funeral. Malcolm knew how the money was left; he said his father told him. He had this idea that if we were sufficiently nice to you, you might change your Will, as you weren't all that keen on our parents. I thought it all airy-fairy. You know Malcolm."

"I'm beginning to know him."

"He was badly treated. He . . ."

"Spare me your excuses. The four of you met and discussed this . . . this project?"

"I never met the others anywhere but here. All I knew was what Malcolm passed on to me by telephone. I'm not allowed to ring out but Malcolm sometimes rang me and the Novice-Master turned a blind eye. He was my cousin. He might have had family news for me."

"The only family news he had was how to cheat your own parents!"

"It must look like that. But Uncle Rupert . . . and Jilly and Donald's parents are very well-off. As for my own father, you might think that he needed it but he didn't. He had all he ever wanted at home and the land won't support any more sheep. My mother would have been only too pleased to see her share go direct to the church."

"The devil can always find reasons."

"I knew it was wrong. But I couldn't help thinking how wonderful it would be if the Order inherited sufficient funds to enable it to stay in England."

"To inherit money, the possessor of it must first die."

"Aunt, I swear I never wished for your death a day before God willed it. We all have to die in the end."

"And you thought that I had had a long run for my money."

His ruddiness turned dusky but he did not deny it.

"It's true. Hugh and I had a long run together." She fell silent and then asked: "Do you think that as a result of what was done at the party I did change my Will?"

207

"Yes. I knew what you felt for Uncle Hugh."

"What about the others?"

"I don't know. I hadn't been told what they meant to do at the party because Malcolm at least knew I would never agree to it. They didn't even know that I heard what was going on. After all, I was tucked away in the kitchen. You may not remember but I left immediately after."

"The funny thing is that they need not have bothered. As time went by after Hugh's death I began to realise that what I thought I heard was only a replica of my innermost thoughts. I should have made you my heirs anyway. Though not as quickly," she added with a wry smile.

"Then what happened wasn't really so unforgivable?" he asked eagerly.

"Yes, it was. It was low-down . . . despicable."

He sighed. "Father said it was a betrayal of trust. An act of treachery."

"Strong words."

"You see, I knew in my heart. I couldn't sleep. I couldn't concentrate on my prayers. In the end I had to unload it on him."

"Why didn't you just come to me? You could have asked for permission."

"I couldn't make up my mind. It was done, I couldn't undo it. I wanted the money for St Joe's. I told myself you hadn't been harmed. That it might be worse if you were disillusioned about your belief in hearing Uncle Hugh's voice. Reasons, again."

"Do you know the real reason I stopped thinking it was Hugh's voice? I never heard it when I needed it most."

"And do you know the biggest of reasons why I didn't come out with all this earlier? It was the party. It brought it all back; the marvellous times we had together as children. You must have seen how close we were to each other. I couldn't bring myself to peach on them. That was what we should have called it then. To tell tales; in our eyes it was the worst crime of all."

Suddenly he covered his own eyes with one large, workmanlike hand. He had begun to weep and the most touching part was that he did nothing to stem his tears. They rained

208

down his cheeks soundless. He did not sob and make a fuss like Jilly had done but it was for the same cause, the same person.

"I didn't take enough care of him," he said. "All over the village people used to say to me, 'Mind you take care of your cousin, Gus.' I didn't take enough care of him."

She let him be; in the meantime she had plenty to sort out for herself.

The Father Superior had been far from pulling his punches. Begone her estimate of him as unworldly, he was the most shrewd of observers. He had said there were implications. He must have turned poor Gus inside out to get to the bottom of this unsavoury mess. He had not met Malcolm but he met his like. Otherwise why would he have offered her sanctuary at his Parent House on the outskirts of Paris? She was tempted to accept but she couldn't bear to leave the flat and her memories of Hugh. Besides, what would she do amongst those dedicated, black-robed ladies whose objectives, apart from their zeal for cooking, were foreign to her?

And he was again right. Her faith in Gus had stopped her from suspecting duplicity elsewhere. So he, innocently guilty, had helped things along. Clever Malcolm! She was sure that Gus was ignorant of his cousin's deeper designs. He wept for what was past, not for what was to come. Where was his extraordinary empathy now? He could grieve with Malcolm for his childhood misery; understand the defences that had to be put up to cope with it . . . the cynicism, the rebellion against authority, the wild behaviour . . . even his famous ideas. But he could not identify with homicidal tendencies; he could not follow Malcolm into the maze of madness.

Should she change her will again as the Reverend Father had suggested? Mr Lomax would be only too happy to oblige. But would that save her? She doubted it at this stage. And she still preferred the second generation to the first; Jilly and Donald to Alice and her dentist. Even Malcolm to Rupert.

St Joe's would do well enough with the fourth share. The whole might nullify the object of the exercise by drawing attention from France. She did not think that the peculiar gifts of her nephew Gus would survive in a French climate.

His grief had subsided. He wiped the last tears away with his coat sleeve.

She asked him, "Have you seen or heard anything of your cousins since the party?"

"No. I am forbidden to see or communicate with them ever again. It is my penance. Anyway, I couldn't face them. They'd think I'd betrayed them just as much as they betrayed you."

Tears threatened to return so she said briskly: "Eat up your bread and butter, there's a good chap. Or my exertions will have been wasted."

He started on it, obedient if not enthusiastic.

She could not think of anything he might know that she did not.

Recalling Mr Lomax's admonitions she chid herself now for being so careless. Of course Malcolm had seen the new Will, probably almost as soon as it came home. Now that he had the key what was to prevent him from making investigative visits whenever he thought fit? Although she did not go far, she went to Crispin's every morning to collect her paper, just as Hugh had done, and she was subject to routine as much as anyone else in the Barbican. He might not have learned of Mrs Jaffa's . . . accident but he would know that *she* was still on her feet, unharmed. And if he thought that Mrs Jaffa kept an eye on the lift, he could just as well have used the stairs.

"Would you like something on it? Jam? Honey?"

"No, thank you," Gus said politely. He was still having trouble getting it down.

She smiled. "I have forgiven you, you know. Not that it matters. You have had absolution."

"Your forgiveness counts, too, if you would believe it. One of the reasons why I didn't come until instructed was because I didn't want to forfeit your good opinion of me. I liked having an aunt in the Barbican."

"Well, you still have, *pro tem*."

"I shan't be able to visit you here any more." He brightened. "You could come and see me."

"Not I. I should be too afraid of being converted."

"I think that Father Superior has you in his sights. This is very good bread and butter."

"So he thought. He could pray for my soul," she suggested.

"Oh, that only happens when you have departed. I hope you'll be with us for a long time yet."

It cheered her up to hear him say it.

"Perhaps. And, Gus – may I advise you to confess to Father Ignatius in future. From what I hear of him he won't let you exaggerate your sins."

At that he spluttered, swallowed and burst into a genuine laugh, the first of that visit.

She thought, He is saved. And she did not refer to his ultimate destination but to his sojourn here on earth.

Chapter 24

Again it was breakfast time and again Jilly rang Donald.

"Donald, it's Malcolm in the mackintosh!"

"I know," he snarled back at her. "Aunt told me."

"Well, I didn't. But yesterday morning about eleven I sneaked out for a breath of fresh air and strayed near the barrier and there was this fellow sitting at one of the tables drinking coffee with his back to me and I swear I thought it was you, Donald."

At this point she stopped to take breath and Donald said sourly: "It wasn't."

"No, the hair was the wrong colour. But it was the set of the shoulders; I suppose it's just a family thing. You know how it is when you are staring at someone. It gets to them and they turn. Well, he turned and we both saw each other. He got up and started to walk away fast so I called out 'Hi!' and he speeded up and began to run. I made for the barrier and went after him. But of course he had the lead and off he veered down the steps, unlocked the door of the caged walk and went across to the other side of the lake. All I saw was his back. I don't know where he went after that."

"You said he had a key. I don't see why you're so surprised."

"Well, I haven't got one so I couldn't follow him. But, Donald, I had to tell you. What does it mean?"

"It means that he's going into action and wants to confuse the issue. He's got me pegged out as a fall guy."

"But that's crazy!"

"He *is* crazy. But now that I'm wise to him I'll take good

care that I don't fall into his trap. I don't want a noose round my neck."

"Donald, they don't have nooses any more."

"A life sentence then, if you like that better."

"You'll have to go round to the flat as soon as you get home from the bank. To see if Aunt is all right."

"I'm not going anywhere near that flat."

"Someone must go."

"It won't be me. I'm going to stick close to people I know and who know me from now on. And if you've any sense you'll do the same."

"I can't believe all this is happening. And it would be just now. Donald, they're casting and I've been practically promised a part in a television play. A real play, not a sit-com."

"I've been chosen to go on a course at the end of the month and I can't wait to get out of London."

"Donald . . ."

"I can't stay to hear any more. I can't afford to be late now there's a chance of promotion."

Bertha rang Patsy to ask if she would mind collecting her paper from Crispin's which was an arrangement they had agreed to if Bertha didn't feel up to it.

Patsy came in by the window with news obviously waiting to burst from her lips. When she saw Bertha's face she deferred it to enquire anxiously: "Are you all right?"

"I'm fine," responded Bertha automatically.

"All I can say is you don't look it. And if you were fine why didn't you go down for your *Times*?"

"I don't like to leave the flat unattended."

Patsy's eyes widened. Was poor old Bertha going a bit ga-ga? she wondered. Sometimes . . .

But all she said was, "That's good. Because, what do you think, Sam has agreed to go with the Goldsteins to Paris for a long week-end."

"This week-end?"

"As ever was."

Bertha's heart sank. She said the first thing to come into her mind. "He'll miss the fireworks."

Some large company was promoting a show to make a special occasion and Sam, that astute businessman, had a school-boy's passion for fireworks.

"There will be plenty of fireworks in Paris," commented his wife dryly, "if of a different kind. Oh, Bertha, isn't it super? What shall I take to wear?"

"You always look nice in anything," said Bertha, supplying the conventional answer.

"Ah, but this is the Goldsteins. Now, shall I go all out to trump Mamie? Or is it better to go as the humble stable companion, just there to keep the other horses good-tempered?"

"I wish you weren't going."

"I knew something was wrong. What's up, pet?"

"Nothing, Patsy, nothing."

"We could cancel."

"Don't be absurd."

"Couldn't you get the young people to come in and keep you company?"

She hesitated. But she simply couldn't unload on her volatile neighbour her doubts and her fears.

"Of course I could."

"That will make us feel better."

"Where are you staying?"

"It's a spanking new hotel and he's on the Board of Directors. It will be red carpet treatment in at the door and right up the stairs. Oh, Bertha, I really am a teeny bit excited. I'll leave you the telephone number and then you can get in touch if it's necessary. And when I get back we'll have a special slimmer's lunch and I'll tell you all about it."

"I shall look forward to that," said Bertha as steadily as she could manage.

In spite of supporting evidence and constant examples in the daily press it was very hard for an ordinary person like Bertha to accept that a near relative was intent on her death. Liquidate, rub out, take for a ride, as they used to say; there are several euphemisms for murder, but they all have the same result. It was scarcely credible. They had all deceived her; Malcolm had gone further, robbed her of Hugh's keys and attempted to incapacitate her but still . . .

215

murder. There were times when she was inclined to believe that it was all in the mind . . . her mind. Paranoia, the persecution complex, that scourge of the old and solitary.

It was in one of these phases that she decided that whatever the outcome, she must see Malcolm in person. She must make him aware of the risk to himself; if anything went wrong he might be put away for years. Went wrong! Did she want it to go right? She would ask him to come round while Patsy was still next door. In an emergency she could bang on the wall.

But where was he to be found? Suddenly she had an inspiration, why hadn't she thought of it sooner? The School, of course. She still remembered the stamped impression on his wretched portfolio. Before she went off the idea, indeed before she had planned what to say, she looked for the number in the London Directory and called it. A snippy female voice from their switchboard informed her that she had connected with the right place.

"This is Mrs Harris speaking from the Barbican. May I speak to the Principal, please?"

"You mean the Director."

"I mean the Director."

"Sorry. He's at a meeting."

Bertha had heard this one before.

"Then may I speak to his secretary?"

She had advanced. A voice like silk, or at least polyester.

"I'm afraid that he is on the 'phone at the moment. Can I do anything for you?"

At least he was probably in the same room.

"I'm afraid it's a personal matter." She could be afraid too. In fact that was just what she was if they only knew. "I'll hold on. Would you please tell him that it is the widow of the late Hugh Harris, the art expert, who is speaking."

Never before had she used Hugh's name in order to gain a hearing. And she couldn't be at all sure that this man would remember Hugh, he had been so long retired. It depended entirely on age. In this she was fortunate. When the Director came on, not only did he remember Hugh, he had once attended one of his lectures.

"As a student myself, Mrs Harris. A very long time ago. Now what can I do to help you?"

She explained the position. She had lost the address of her nephew who was one of *his* students. She knew that it was slightly irregular to ask for it like this but she really needed it badly. The matter was urgent. He asked for the name and it seemed strange to her that it was her own maiden name too.

"Now, Mrs Harris," he said amicably, "we have a great number of students here and I regret to say that I don't know them all. I suggest that I have a word with our Membership Secretary who holds all the records. It might take her a little time to trace your nephew so I suggest that you hang up and she will ring you back with the information. If you will let me have your number? I presume you are still living in London."

"At the Barbican."

"Ah."

She gave him the number and he jotted it down.

"Thank you so much. I am very grateful to you."

"Not at all. It is my pleasure. Sad loss, your husband. If he were still in business there wouldn't be so many faked old masters undetected." He gave an academic laugh and rang off. It was all rather involved but so far so good. She sat down to read yesterday's paper while she was waiting. She hadn't gone past page three when the Membership Secretary came on the line. Now the voice was brisk, very no-nonsense.

"Mrs Harris?"

"Speaking."

"Sorry, I don't have the information you require. I looked through the current records without success. Then I went back to last year and I found that your nephew dropped out halfway through the spring term. He had been with us six months. I have a few notes about it. Some we try to persuade back but apparently it was found that he lacked sufficient aptitude to make this worth while. He should have repaid his grant but applications to the address we had been given came back marked 'Gone Away'. Are you still there, Mrs Harris?"

"Oh yes, yes. I'm sorry to have put you to so much trouble. It comes as rather a shock."

"Not to worry, Mrs Harris. It happens all the time. These young people find their own level in the end. If you do come across your nephew eventually you might remind him that he still has one of our portfolios."

She went back to her seat on the sofa. So there it was, the plain explanation. And too obvious to be seen, like Poe's purloined letter and Chesterton's postman. What had he been doing since then? Sooner than admit failure to his father he had stayed on in London, on the dole she supposed. Yet at one time Rupert must have had his address or he wouldn't have been able to summon him to the funeral. It would be easy to write "Gone Away. Return to Sender" on an unwelcome envelope, especially to one with Malcolm's ingenuity. Since that time he must have been constantly on the move, she decided. She had never credited herself with much imagination but it served well enough to keep pace with Malcolm on his downhill course. Behind with his rent; kicked out by his landlord – or did he prefer to do a moonlight flit with his few belongings? From one squalid lodging to the next, each one a grade below the one he had left. Presenting himself as the typical student with this excuse for his appearance. Sharing begrimed bathrooms, or perhaps with no bathroom at all, it must have taken all his wits to keep reasonably clean. Until by now he might not be so far off that cardboard box on the Embankment about which he had joked in the wine bar.

In contrast she had a picture of her brother Rupert with his house full of disused rooms whilst he sat under a neon strip in his out-of-date kitchen doing his household accounts and ruminating on what might be saved by future economies. For what purpose? For no purpose at all.

If Malcolm had to kill somebody why didn't he start with his father? He had good cause. But here her opinion matched with Jilly's. What he felt for his father was love-hate. Denied the return of the one, he fed on the latter. And that was about all he did feed on, poor boy, she thought. No wonder he was always hungry. No wonder he helped himself to notes from her purse, and forgot to give her back her change. Rupert wasn't the only one from whom he had concealed his split with the School. She was positive that his cousins were not aware of it. He, who had been their leader in childhood and still believed that he could make them dance to his tune, would never have risked losing face by that admission. He would have done anything to keep them from learning it. Anything? Yes, anything. Even murder.

Young people find their own level . . . but what level was Malcolm's? Once he had severed his connection with art, did Malcolm try for a job, however humble? She doubted it. Work was not his forte. And would anyone employ him, looking as he did and insolent into the bargain? She could easily see him pilfering a few tins from the shelves of a supermarket; it was impossible to see him checking out customers from one of their tills.

Although all this must have been distressing to Malcolm, it had its comic element too, black comedy in which his own personality took part. But when did that personality first begin to split – when did one of his famous ideas begin to turn inward and, like a maggot, start to worm its dark way towards the core of his brain? She felt a sudden chill. She knew exactly when it happened. It had happened on the day of the funeral, here in this very flat. When he saw, contrasted against his miserable existence, the solid comfort which a state of affluence could ensure. It was possible that the unaccustomed presence of his father had contributed to it. Such was her aversion to Rupert that she was prepared to believe that his obsession was contagious. Anyway she was sure that from this moment Malcolm became convinced that he had to have money to obtain for himself the sort of life that she enjoyed. She liked to fancy that he had not immediately arrived at the conclusion that hers was forfeit if he was ever to begin on his.

The plundering of the Goldsteins, high risk if he had only known it, was simply an interlude suggested by his possession of Hugh's key. Its success went to his head, and encouraged by the easy acquisition of funds he had gone on to tackle the Trounces where he blew any chance of permanence in his new career. He had put every policeman and security man on the alert.

At this point he had bought the mackintosh and its accompaniments. Not being privy to his or Donald's thoughts she didn't know why he had chosen to disguise himself in this particular manner but she doubted if it was to ingratiate himself with her. He was too sure of her anyway. Yet he had refused her offer of an allowance. Now why was that? Pride, that was the answer . . . the devil's attribute. How it must have galled him to have to stand in the dole queue!

219

She and Malcolm were on a collision track; headed for disaster.

Patsy slipped in for a moment to make her farewell. They were on their way to the airport. She wore her best fur coat and had blued her eyelids, indicating that there was to be competition with Mamie. She had also used a new lipstick which left its bow on Bertha's cheek. But, though this brought them into close contact, she was too full of her own affairs to mark her friend's condition. However she did say, "I've asked Lennie to keep a special eye on you, sweetie. And if the worst comes to the worst, there's always Conch."

Had she forgotten that Lennie was always off on a Saturday and thatConcetta hadn't been since the Thursday, an alteration in her time-table to oblige another one of her ladies? How else had Bertha known about the fireworks? She had asked her if she was going and Concetta had stated simply, "Is free." It was sufficient answer.

"But you stay on your balcony," she had added sternly. "See just as well . . . better. Not good for you outside. Too crowd."

Much later on in the evening, the entryphone buzzed. It was Jilly.

"Darling, let me in. I have something to say."

"Go away," said Bertha. "I never want to see you again in my life."

Jilly was left standing on the podium, looking up at the steel and glass structure which enclosed the lift and the staircase, the only means of access to her aunt on the fourth floor.

Although life was beginning to open up for her – unless her newly-met director had a sudden change of mind, she was headed towards the television screen and a permanent Equity card – somehow she felt as if she had lost something of value.

Chapter 25

Next morning Bertha awoke with the instant recognition that something important was due to happen that day. Then she remembered what it was.

It was more than a hunch. She had a positive conviction that Malcolm was ready to go into action on this very day. How often she had watched on the television screen one of the big cats stalking its prey whilst a herd of ungainly beasts (moose, would they be?) browsed uneasily by. Was there amongst them a certain animal instinctively knowing that it had been singled out for extinction; joined by a psychic cord going from predator to victim? If so she could sympathise for this was exactly as she felt now. She believed that the waiting period had been stretched to its uttermost; for various reasons Malcolm could not restrain himself any longer. And with the fireworks festival timed for this evening came just the sort of opportunity he would choose. All attention would be focussed elsewhere. Besides she was sufficiently attuned to him now to realise that the actual setting would appeal to his warped sense of humour. He would send her off with the same verve he would have experienced in dispatching a rocket.

How much did the others know about this – Jilly and Donald, fellow conspirators, one-third willing and two-thirds reluctant? Gus she entirely absolved from the final act of a sordid little drama. But Jilly's behaviour reeked of guilt. She didn't need to be told, she guessed. And if Jilly – Donald? But of course Malcolm wouldn't have spelled it out in so many words. He would never have dared to confide in them to such an extent and anyway was by nature secretive. Obviously they were ignorant of his possession of a key. Or were they? They certainly did not connect him with the burglaries.

Bertha decided that their part in the proceeding was finished. They had been used for cover; it was Jilly who had done the whispering at the party. Remembering this act of treachery, Bertha boiled. Strangely enough, it seemed worse to her than an attempt to murder.

But yet, think again, was it finished? Were they to be drawn in again at the end? To be incriminated perhaps? Did that stupid impersonation of Donald have some ulterior motive at the back of it? It so, didn't it serve them right? But murder? Was this really happening to her? Lying in bed on her back, she watched the morning sun sketch sharp outlines of light and shadow on the avocado wall. Yes, Malcolm's intentions were as clear-cut as that, there was no room for doubt. And really, did she much mind? Her best days were over; from now on they could only further decline.

She gave a rueful smile for her own benefit. If this was to be her last day on earth, better make the most of it. She put on her housecoat and went along to the kitchen to make herself a strong cup of tea. Then she had a most enjoyable soak in hot water softened and scented by her favourite bath essence. She did not go to the window to see what horse-chestnuts had done for her because there wasn't one. The bathroom was tiled from floor to ceiling with only a circulatory vent which was what acted as a convenor of voices. Voices? Well, she heard no voices today. Not even Hugh's.

Dressed in a blouse and skirt and cardigan, those garments in which she felt most at ease, she sat down to a bowl of cornflakes. Whatever had happened to them? They tasted delicious. And a slice of toast and marmalade . . . superb! She could now believe implicitly in that improbable sentence, "The condemned man ate a hearty breakfast."

Indeed she began to have a curious sensation of exaltation; rather like, she supposed, that of a martyr preparing for the stake. Or was it simply an enhanced perception such as one has when first in love?

Going along the podium towards Crispin's to buy her morning paper and looking over the parapet certainly the grass looked uncommonly green. Crispin's itself attained a new significance. From an under-sized supermarket it took on the status of Harrods offering recherché delicacies. She bought a packet of smoked salmon, a brown loaf, a lemon, and a bottle of Chablis to go with it.

The Asian at the desk smiled at her, an exercise he did not often permit himself.

"A party?" he hazarded.

"A very small party." She smiled back at him. "One person only."

On her way back she was thinking what long hours he worked and how fortunate her life had been compared to his, condemned to live in an alien country where only Christmas Day, which was probably a commemoration of a religion not his own, was a holiday. She went up in the lift, said a cheerful "Good morning" to Mrs Jaffa who was apparently mobile again, and retreated into her own flat. She would even have been prepared to exchange the time of day with Dr Jaffa, had he been present.

She made herself a pot of real coffee – wonderful aroma! – and sat down to read *The Times*. Could the state of the world really be as bad as it was portrayed here? She should consider herself lucky to be on her way out of it. But here she turned serious. She dwelt on the past, the long happy period she had been permitted to spend with her husband, Hugh. The places they had visited, the marvels they had seen, mostly in the great continent of Europe. There had been the bleak interruption of two wars but again they had been fortunate; Hugh was too young to be drawn into the first, too old for the second. They had removed to the West Country where the impact was at its slightest; Hugh had acted as temporary Curator of a small museum from which the man whose post he held had gone into active service and been killed. Killed!

Hugh had earned his good fortune; he had contributed to the public good in the way he knew best. But whatever had she done personally to merit this primrose path through life? Nothing . . . nothing at all.

It had occurred to her that she might relieve Malcolm of his self imposed task.

As Gus had remarked, everyone has to die sometime. But

223

Hugh would have been against that. Hugh, who had no belief in hereafter held that each moment of living was valuable. If fate intervened that was another thing. How glad she would have been for his verdict on Malcolm; he, whose whole life was devoted to the delivering of judgement. But that was on works of art, not on humans. Malcolm was amusing and colourful; as colourful as the blues and reds in the work of old masters. Was that a virtue? He was devious and a thief. Also he was capable of a cruelty she could only imagine. If he wasn't bad he was mad and that is a distinction that has puzzled wiser heads than hers throughout the ages.

He did not look mad. Even in his old clothes, if placed beside Doctor Jaffa, any independent observer would have elected the doctor. And in the mackintosh and blue suit he might have passed for any deserving clerk or office worker.

But surely to attempt to kill for money which would have been his after a reasonably short period of waiting, was insanity?

Surely to refuse an offer of a decent allowance and then to follow that up by putting washing-up liquid under her door-mat spoke of a disturbed mind rather than immaturity? The only other explanation was that he felt that he had to compensate for past failures; he had to patch up his pride.

Jilly loved him, Gus loved him; she too . . . But he was a failure for all that and they knew it. Even his plan, his plot, was amateurish and bungling and if it hadn't been for her own foolish co-operation could never have succeeded. He was an opportunist. She left drawers unlocked or with the key in them and he opened them. If his vigil at the Trounces had been longer, he would not have been surprised by Mrs Trounce's daughter. He couldn't wait, that was his trouble. He couldn't wait.

Yet she went back to the long ordeal of his sufferings and grieved for him. No one of his composition should have been subjected to such a test.

She put care aside and opened her packet of salmon and, after it had thawed out, ate half of it with brown bread and butter. She also drank half the bottle of Chablis. She thought of starving children elsewhere, and Malcolm adrift in his wits, but still she enjoyed the small feast. That was because she was

224

old, she decided; it is well-known that the old have no deeper emotions.

After that she snoozed a little on the sofa, and waked shocked to find that she had lost half an hour out of her day. She washed her face and hands and then went out on to the balcony to tend her flowers. The day had started with a fine drizzle but had now dried out to leave the air exceptionally clear. Across the lake, in front of St Giles', preparations were in full swing for the presentation of the fireworks. Men in dungarees scurried about like ants; it was queer to see work going ahead on a Saturday. It was still too damp on the grass below for sunning oneself though there were more residents about than usual at the week-end. Sometimes they chose this occasion to give dinner parties. As Concetta said, the fireworks were free.

She removed dead heads from the flowers in her window box and stirred up the soil with a fork; it was mostly peat.

She looked over at the view of the flats opposite where Mrs Trounce probably was and the Goldsteins certainly were not, and gave a sigh at the thought that it would look very much the same the next day. Whereas she . . . She thought of Mr Lomax and his large garden and how he might still find enough time before his retirement to administer her Will. Staring up at the vast expanse of sky washed clean by the rain the words of an old prophecy returned to her. "In my Father's House are many mansions." She wondered if it was blasphemous to imagine up there somewhere in space another Barbican ready to receive residents of all sorts.

She came in, closing the window and pushing up the lever. She thought that she might switch on the television and catch the last part of Grandstand but it seemed too trivial on what might be one's last afternoon to watch men kicking a ball or racehorses at the behest of their jockeys striving to outpace each other. She fiddled with the knobs of the radio and by pure chance happened on a foreign station starting the third movement of Beethoven's String Quartet Opus 126. She had not been to the Concert Hall since Hugh's death. She had funked it because music was his great love next to painting. Now, to this most emotional music of all, she listened with head bent, hand on her forehead. After it had finished she sat silent for a long while.

At last she pulled herself together and made more tea.

She looked at the clock which Hugh used to wind every week with such care. Tomorrow it must be wound by her. Wound by her? It was now ten minutes past five. The fireworks were not due to begin until nine. Time which had been going too fast for her liking now began to crawl. She took up her paper. She knew that it would be useless to try to do the crossword. She turned to the leader, the letters. The leader seemed pretentious and the letters seemed stupid. She went back to *Alice in Wonderland* but it no longer amused her. What had been witty turned out to be acid, what had been funny turned out to be cruel. She had been right. It was not a child's book. At the very bottom of the well was poor Dodgson himself.

At six she went to turn on the news then suddenly recollected that as it was Saturday it would have come on at five. She switched off again.

She went into the bedroom and re-read her short Will. She wondered if Malcolm would ever inherit his share.

She got out her diamond brooch from its nest in the toe of her stocking. She pinned it on her blouse and admired it. It was beautiful but it did nothing to raise her spirits.

At last it was seven, time for Newsview. That absorbed three-quarters of an hour telling her nothing she did not know before but embellishing it with captions.

Another cup of coffee took her on to eight. As eight o'clock struck she had a bright idea. She would put the door on the chain. She did not think it would stop Malcolm but at least it would give notice of his arrival.

The screws had been removed from one side. A residue of paint held the brass plate in place but the screws had gone.

The effect on her was as if someone had let off a fire-cracker close by her heel . . . a squib. Pursued by it she rushed into the bedroom. She pulled aside the veiling curtain from the window. If there had been but one square-shouldered male on the concourse below she would have opened that window and let out a shriek: "Save me . . . save me!"

On that entire vast expanse of tiles there was not a soul to be seen. In the wine bar there was nobody.

She supposed that the security men were saving up their energies for the evening performance.

She went back to the sitting room, averting her eyes from the useless chain which hung there looking as solid as ever.

Throughout the day she had been acting out a macabre charade in which she only half-believed. She had been feeling her way into a part in a way of which Jilly would have approved. But this was for real. Malcolm must have slipped into the flat when she was at Crispin's. That meant he was in the neighbourhood now . . . any moment . . . but, no, he would wait for the fireworks.

To every creature under the sun right up to the end is given an instinct for self-preservation that has nothing to do with higher reaches of the intellect. So now Bertha's whole being was centred on summoning up someone to come to her succour. She had sent away Jilly but Jilly had once told her that Donald was dependable. She had his number, it was only a question of finding it. Her hands were trembling. She had to hold on a long time while he was brought to the phone; it seemed like eternity.

"Oh, Donald," she said, "I was wondering whether you could come round to the flat."

"When was that, Aunt?"

"Now. To be exact, this very moment."

"I'm sorry, Aunt. I'd love to but it's too short notice. I'm afraid I've got a prior engagement."

But Bertha knew better. Now she was sure that he was privy as to what was to happen, no matter how he had come by the information. But she must press him if he was to be her salvation.

"Can't you get out of it? I badly need your advice. On some important money matters," she added as bait. If that didn't fetch him, nothing would.

"I would like to help but I can't possibly. The fact is I've got an obligation to these chappies I'm meeting. I'm afraid you won't be able to contact Jilly either. She hates fireworks and she's gone off somewhere up West."

"Never mind. I shall have to . . . never mind." She rang off. He might have been bent on constructing a good alibi, but he had not fooled his aunt. He was as convinced of Malcolm's

227

intention as she was; he was mortally afraid of being manipulated into the position of suspect and so he had chickened out.

There was a possibility in the mackintosh masquerade which spelled danger to him.

So, write off Donald, that responsible citizen. Swiftly she passed in review anyone who might have been able to help her in her extremity. Lennie, the man in the box in the garage, the housekeeper in his office . . . But, alas, it was Saturday. Lennie was off duty, the man in the box one of a series of substitutes brought in for the week-end, and the housekeeper's office would be closed as tight as a drum.

Concetta had a telephone number to ring but she was found to be out, probably at her local waiting for the fireworks to begin. That only left the Jaffas and she would rather die than petition them.

Rather die! Wasn't that exactly what Malcolm proposed?

By what means? That was the terrifying part. Who knew what form of quittance Malcolm had in store for her. He was far too familiar a figure for her to fear his appearance, even if manic. It was the cold steel she feared; the pair of tights round the neck; the bludgeon descending on top of the head. Or a sharp knife. She saw blood spurting, crimsoning avocado walls, pooling on top of the off-white carpet. It was now growing dusk but she did not pull the curtains. Let her draw comfort from the bright lights of the party givers, now changing into suitable clothes for the evening. She remembered the evening soon after Hugh's death when she had imagined she saw those curtains moving and billowing in towards her. That was an illusion, brought on by starving herself perhaps. No, not starving herself; she couldn't eat – not at all the same thing.

Well, this was no illusion. As she felt the relentless approach of death in some unknown guise, but probably messy and squalid, her thoughts began to refuse to focus, crowding and jostling each other in her poor head. The flat was as warm as ever but she was clammy with fear. She forced herself back into a simulation of calmness. The door continued to fascinate her. She fancied she saw it open without sound, yielding to Hugh's key. Nothing happened so she gathered strength to walk past it into the bedroom again. She held the curtain away again from the window and saw that the space below was no longer deserted. An ever increasing stream of people was making its way to the Terrace and points of vantage. The sight of this band of pleasure-seekers, talking and laughing and intent on their own enjoyment made her feel totally isolated.

Oh, why had she been so stupid as to allow herself to be brought to this pass when sensible behaviour would have prevented it? After the funeral she should have gone straightaway on a world cruise or an extended coach tour; anything, anything, from which she would have returned a new, brash woman ready to slap down any relative who came within reach.

At the first explosion, the first rocket to go winging its flight up, her nerve broke completely. She couldn't stay in the flat an instant longer. She grabbed an old coat off its peg in the corridor, huddled herself into it, and clutching her handbag, she began to gather up her night things and to throw them feverishly into an over-night bag which she brought from the cupboard. Fingers trembling, she zipped it up. Then, pausing only momentarily in the corridor to stuff her toothbrush and a tube of toothpaste down amongst her money, she went out of that useless door. There was a bad moment on the landing waiting for the lift to answer its call. She thought that if Mrs Jaffa suddenly appeared she would be met with a scream. At last it arrived, to her eyes opening in slow motion as if, like herself, its mechanism was caught in a nightmare. Thank God it was empty; she descended alone.

With a frenzied glance from left to right, she let herself out of what now seemed a cage, hastening to join the throng making its way to the steps. Never before had she been thankful to be caught up in a crowd. In its security she was borne along to the top of the stairs. A flow of adrenalin took her down them intact.

Where she would usually have clutched on to the handrail, she went down regardless, somehow navigating the edge of each riser, still grasping her baggage. She reached the bottom with her one free hand planted on the unprotesting back of the man in front of her. She was nudged by her neighbours into the middle of the terrace where the surge ended.

The tempo of the fireworks was increasing with every moment. Flares had been lit on the other side of the water; already a blue haze hid the operators from the spectators. High-flying rockets were starting to compete, each striving to throw its cascade of coloured stars further than the last one. Bang succeeded bang. And the sky at the level of the exploding bursts bore banners of murky pastel colours which hung for brief moments before they melted into each other and dispersed in bluish smoke. Above that the night was made of ultramarine and in it the genuine stars seemed a long way off, piercing with pinholes of brightness, celestial sparklers, while away to the right, moving in its full circle of majesty, was that false firework, the moon.

Like everyone else, Bertha stood with face uplifted, absorbed in the sight. If she did not share Sam's intense passion, she thoroughly enjoyed fireworks. They did not seem to her to be a waste of money but rather a grand gesture, like burning banknotes. Safe? Well, safer than nuclear fission, safer than a ground to air missile. Safer than runaway aunts and demented nephews.

Brought back to herself and her own predicament, beginning to wonder how long her legs would hold her up, she turned her back on the show and started to struggle towards the doors of the foyer, pegged back for the benefit of the crowd. It was like trying to leave a tube train in the rush hour. Elbow and shove; at last she was there. She sank down exhausted on the nearest banquette. She was relieved to find that she still held both bags; she had a grip round their straps which had become almost rigid. From behind her knees, right down her calves to her ankles, her muscles quivered. She waited impatiently for their protest to die down whilst she peered nervously about her. In the first flush of the excitement outside the whole huge area of the foyer was deserted. Only in the far distance the dwarfed figures of bar-tenders awaited the eventual onslaught.

She was terrified lest, in the midst of this solitude, the slight, menacing presence of Malcolm might suddenly materialise before her. But wherever he was it was not here. Whatever happened she was not going back to the flat – not she.

As soon as she was able she made her way slowly to the Silk

Street entrance, having no precise objective except to get away as far as possible from the source of danger.

And there, directly opposite in the narrow street as if by a miracle, stood a solitary taxi with its driver at the wheel. As she crossed the road towards him, he came out of his cab possibly with the idea of taking a squint at what went on; but when he saw an obvious fare coming towards him he waited for her to come up. He was one of the old school with a face criss-crossed with furrows yet still bearing the signs of an underlying good nature. He had met with plenty of her sort and she had met with plenty of his; they appreciated each other.

Though robbed of a small pleasure, "Where to, lady?" he asked amiably.

"Could you find me a bed in a good hotel?"

He looked at her steadily, a little dubious.

"I have a flat here," she said quickly, "but I want to avoid a relative who is coming to visit."

"Don't we all?" he inquired, grinning and apparently satisfied. "What would suit you best? Somewhere quiet?"

"It doesn't matter. It's just for tonight. I'm thinking of taking a long holiday starting from tomorrow."

"Where would you be thinking of going? I don't want to be nosey but only to be able to put you down where it's going to be most convenient for you."

"I don't know exactly. I haven't made up my mind. It has to be a nice long way away."

His bristly eyebrows rose.

"What about Edinburgh? They say that's the place to be nowadays."

She considered for a moment. "I think that would do very well!"

"Then as it's getting lateish why don't we try the Station Hotel? They're more likely to have a room there and you'll be right on the spot for a start."

"That sounds very sensible."

As he helped her he was thinking: If the old dear is not exactly one hundred per cent when she wakes up in the morning she won't be too far from home.

But leaning back in the cab, Bertha's mind was now as clear

as a bell. Strange to say she had been shocked out of a long period of shock. She was already beginning to form plans.

When she paid him off at the Station Hotel, he said: "Now take your time, Madam. I'll wait here until I know that you're settled."

"Thank you. You have been very kind."

"No singles, I'm afraid," said the young woman at the desk. "But I can let you have a double if you don't mind paying the difference."

"That will be quite all right," said Bertha. And to the night porter who stood ready to take her overnight bag she remarked, "Would you first please give this to the taxi driver who is still outside?" And she gave him a five pound note. Always tip for a service but never over-tip. That had been Hugh's creed.

As she sat, half reclined, propped up by pillows in a bed not much less comfortable than her own, Bertha took stock of the room. Although it had been refurbished in hotel style she was glad to see that it had retained some of its old-fashioned flavour. She would look for something like it in Edinburgh; big, comfortable and impersonal. But before she set forth to the capital of Scotland, there were things to be done. She noted them in her diary. Write to Patsy; tell her that her advice was being followed. Her neighbour was starting on an extended holiday, address to follow, and would she please put matters right with Conch? With much love. She thought that she owed this to Patsy. And then a brief letter to the House-keeper's Office asking them to keep tabs on her flat while she was away. Later she would brief Mr Lomax and either he or one of his young ladies would collect the post and see to her business affairs. He and her accountant could manage between them and not the devil himself would be able to wrest her new address from Mr Lomax if that was what she decreed.

Was this the same woman who had dithered and dissembled and hadn't dared to say "Boo" to Concetta? In her present mood she could have met Malcolm at the door, relieved him of any lethal weapon and twisted his ear before sending him off with a flea in it.

Her thoughts returned to Hugh, lovingly but not sadly. All

that had happened was that he had reached his journey's end a little ahead of her. Arrivals and departures were as much a part of life as they were the business of a great station, and it was only those who were turned off the train before they reached their destination who justified grief.

As for money, she was glad that it was in plentiful supply. She would spend freely whatever was necessary to make life pleasant and agreeable. She meant to enjoy what was left to her. She would donate frugally to causes but whenever she saw a person in need she would try to help out. She would let her Will stand and what was left the children (for so she now thought of them) should have. She would have no need of it then. And suddenly and quite unexpectedly she heard Hugh's voice. It was the exact intonation; half amused and half serious: "Blood is thicker than water, but heaven preserve us from our relations."

But now she recognised it for what it was – her own thought. Not the top one but the one secreted beneath which was the true one and which she had desperately desired to hear ratified as it always had been throughout a long marriage.

And Malcolm?

"Too late for Malcolm. He was the rift between mother and father. He never really existed in his own right."

The fireworks over and nothing left but their untidy remains, the crowd swiftly dispersed. Making her solitary way home by the path at the back of the School, when she had nearly reached the corner of the building, Concetta came upon Malcolm. He was leaning over the railing by the water, gazing upwards at his aunt's flat.

She recognised him at once even with his shortened hair and though he was wearing a turtle-necked sweater and dark trousers. Concetta had a good eye for her enemies.

She hailed him. "Hullo, No-good."

He ignored the epithet as if he had more important things on his mind. Turning his head towards her, he regarded her through slit eyes.

"Where is my aunt?"

"In her flat where she should be, of course."

He did not contradict her though he knew otherwise. He had been all through the flat looking for her.

"There are no lights on."

"She was on her balcony seeing the fireworks. Now fireworks over she go in to bed. What else?"

"Why aren't the curtains drawn then?"

"She old . . . she forget. You leave my lady alone. She nice lady; too nice for nevvew like you."

"You mind your own business."

"She is my business while I work for her."

"Why don't you get off her back then, you bitch?"

Impatient he turned away from her, muttering, "Dirty Wop . . . scum of Naples."

She had often been called a bitch and a Wop. Such usages did not disturb her. But at the word "Naples", a city which she had never seen, she erupted into a sudden belated fervour of patriotism.

She leant over and with brawny arms lifted his legs from the ankles and tipped him into the lake.

She did not intend to drown him. She just thought that he would be all the better for a ducking. And because she also thought that he might not be altogether the best person to be alone with when he emerged dripping, she ran as fast as she could round the corner, along the paving stones, through an underground garage on the way back to her one room flatlet.

Although this was the deepest part of the ornamental water it had never before drowned anyone. But, because he was quite unprepared for it, Malcolm went straight to the bottom and hit his head on the concrete. This knocked him unconscious and gave the water time to get into his lungs. Nor did he come to the surface immediately, weighted as he was with a lead-filled cosh tucked away under his turtle-necked sweater. He had been standing under an overhead spotlight but whether it had been dimmed for the fireworks, or if it simply needed a new bulb, the glow it gave was insufficient to attract attention to his sudden disappearance, even if any resident had nothing else to do but to keep watch on sportive charwomen. He was down there all night with his head in the weeds, his only company being the inquisitive red carp who took a nibble at him now and then to discover what he was made of.

234

In the early morning a security man spotted him lying there half submerged and, with the assistance of his fellows, had him up and away before he could give offence to anyone.

He carried no identification; no one claimed to have lost him. Only Jilly and Donald wondered where he had gone and if his non-appearance was somehow linked with the continued absence of Aunt Bertha.

But Jilly had her small part in the television play and Donald had been offered promotion. They were both too busy to bother and even forgot their hopes of becoming their aunt's beneficiaries. Much later on Mr Lomax was to search for him with a persistence that went unrewarded though his cousins insisted that he must be alive somewhere.

There must have been a Coroner's Inquest but Concetta wasn't at it and it never appeared in the papers. As to where the poor remains ended up – that information could probably have only been obtained from the porters and was of insufficient interest to stay in their memories.

The Barbican was at its most discreet in its disposal of bodies.

You have been reading a novel published by Piatkus Books. We hope you have enjoyed it and that you would like to read more of our titles. Please ask for them in your local library or bookshop.

If you would like to be put on our mailing list to receive details of new publications, please send a large stamped addressed envelope (UK only) to:

Piatkus Books, 5 Windmill Street
London W1P 1HF

PIATKUS

The sign of a good book